ANGELA HUTH has written twelve novels, four collections of short stories, and has put together various anthologies, including one of eulogies. She has also written plays for radio, television and the stage. After thirty years in Oxford she and her husband, the historian James Howard-Johnston, now live in Warwickshire. She has two daughters and, to date, five grandsons.

ISBN: 978 1 902421 26 1

Colouring In

ANGELA HUTH

LONG BARN BOOKS

For
Gina Hall

Chapter One

ISABEL

I was forty last week and I didn't mind. Everyone warned me it would be a terrible day, traumatising. But it wasn't. I said I didn't want any fuss, and there was none. Some jokey cards. A few pastoral scenes from those who know my love of the country. Sylvie had taken great trouble in painting a bunch of bright tulips – the black parrots, done with a wobbly hand, made their petals authentically frilly. She also gave me a pair of purple kid gloves which she confessed, even before I'd unwrapped them, that Dan had paid for 'mostly.' Dan produced a first edition of *Jude the Obscure* and took me out to dinner. He was all for going somewhere with a star or two. But I chose our local Italian, where I'm never disappointed.

So the fortieth birthday was no more than a brief interruption in our normal life. Carlotta, still at the superior age of thirty-six, rang to warn me that from now on I should pay some attention to my appearance and well-being. Daily vitamins were a help, she said, and suggested various expensive potions that could be rubbed into the skin at night. I agreed, but took no notice. I only take Carlotta's advice on more serious matters. When she tries to be helpful in a practical way she assumes an earnestness that doesn't become her. I listen politely, but ignore all she says. She couldn't resist adding that from now on I should also be aware that my powers of attraction would diminish visibly. I said I couldn't care less: so long as Dan didn't find me wanting, I was happy. We both laughed, but could not read each other's laughter. It was one of those short, off-key conversations with a great friend that leave a silt of unease once the telephone is put down. It stays with you for a few moments, faintly unsettling, before it's put aside.

So now it's back to routine life, thank God. The birthday forgotten, the daily hum resumed. Once the front door has banged – Dan and Sylvie gone – I climb the three storeys to the attic room which I turned into my studio five or six years ago. By the time I'm half way up the stairs – the balding edges of the carpet widen a little every week, I notice, but they've done well for fifteen years – I can hear the hoover in the hall. Gwen arrives at 8.30 every morning through the back door. She's never late, and her routine never changes. Hall, sitting-room, dining-room, kitchen – either a 'thorough' or a 'flick over' depending on the day. The upstairs floors, we agreed when we devised this routine, need never receive the same attention as the downstairs.

Gwen came to us nine years ago. Her reliability, good humour and apparent love of domestic work proved to be understated in the formal reference from her previous employer. She has the energy of someone half her age. I'm not sure precisely what that is, but she must be over sixty. My respect for her, and devotion to her, are boundless. But I don't want to talk to her – or to anyone – before I have made a start every morning. I like to arrive in my studio unencumbered by greetings and small talk, and feel I'm well into a pool of solitary silence before I sit down and begin.

I explained all this to Gwen when she first came. She understood absolutely, said she liked to start quietly, too. She couldn't abide talk when she was polishing, she assured me: it disturbed the concentration. So our understanding on the matter of how we like to begin our working days is one of so many things we agree upon, and is part of the great fortune of Gwen in our lives.

There's no telephone in the studio: I've no wish for any calls. I do have a mobile, a very complicated affair which Sylvie has explained to me a thousand times but I still haven't quite understood, so I find it easier not to turn it on unless I'm in the car. Thus I'm unobtainable until lunchtime: a state I relish greatly.

This morning when I went down to the kitchen for coffee with Gwen at ten-thirty (we allow ourselves ten minutes) she said the telephone had rung at least five times. As persistence always seems to me to threaten importance, I felt a frisson of irritation. I did not want this fine morning to be broken by some vital news outside my work. But I assured Gwen I'd ring before going back upstairs. 'You carry on', I said.

By this I meant you go ahead with your resumé of news in the *Daily Mail*. She likes to read me a few snippets from her own copy every day, and is very good at picking out the bits bound to entertain, and leaves out the provocative views that she knows would annoy me (Gwen is very right wing but she doesn't like to argue about politics). This daily reading service, which came about unplanned last year, provides me with an insight into tabloid thinking which, Gwen feels, is necessary to one like me who lives mostly in a narrow world of her own (she's never been so impolite as to call it narrow, but I believe that's what she thinks). In fact the routine continues for her own enjoyment rather than my interest.

I've never quite been able to bring myself to suggest the habit should be broken, but one day I will.

Before going back upstairs I reluctantly listened to the answering machine. Four of the five messages were from Dan. Could I ring him as soon as possible? He'd just been speaking to Bert Bailey, back from New York, and had invited him to supper tonight. Would that be OK? Nothing complicated. No need to make a great effort.

Bert Bailey? Nothing complicated?

I racked my brain. Both about supper – thinking of delicious uncomplicated suppers is not my forte – and this Bailey man. Then it came to me: *Gilbert* Bailey. Of course. Dan's oldest friend, not seen for years. It would be good to see him again, though I wish there'd been a bit more notice. Sea bass, I thought, and ginger cheesecake. Quick and easy. I rang Dan to agree, hoping I sounded eager. He then suggested it might be a good idea to ask another woman. Carlotta, why not? They'd known each other as children. I contained a sigh. That would mean more telephoning. If I didn't ring Carlotta *now*, she'd be in one of her eternal meetings. But I agreed again. The small thought that perhaps Gilbert would have preferred to be with just the two of us, after so long, would have taken more precious moments of discussion with Dan. I rang Carlotta – as always having to dash, but yes, delighted to come – and saw Gwen open the fridge. She shot me a look of sympathy which meant there wasn't much by way of help within it. I stomped back upstairs. By now the morning was a broken thing, crumbled to bits. I knew that whatever I accomplished between now and lunchtime would not be much good: the spell, that earlier had been strong, had vanished. *Practicalities, arrangements,* are lethal to the concentration. It was one of those days on which I wished I was alone in the Shetland Isles close to sea, rocks, churning skies – nothing, and no one, to disturb.

DAN

The telephone was ringing as I got into the office – ten minutes late, usual bloody traffic. I snatched it up, before Lesley had a chance. She was still fiddling with her watch. One day I'm going to buy her a new one that doesn't take up so much of her time. It was Bert. Bert! I couldn't believe it. Didn't recognise his voice for a moment. Then he said '*Gilbert*. Your old friend – remember?' I apologised. *Bert*, hell. Friends since school – best friends, declared formally somewhere on the banks of the Thames. Oxford together, saw each other a good deal before Isabel and I were married. Travelled together all over the place before we settled down to earning a living. But he'd chosen the army, was so often posted abroad. We lost touch, though of course I read about his heroism in the Gulf War and sent congratulations. Then he left soldiering, a distinguished colonel, and went to work for an oil company in New York. Now it seems he's returned home to retire. Retire? He's the same age as me. I chided him. He changed it to 'semi-retire'. 'And to find a wife, perhaps, at last', he said. There'd been no time in the army, and he hadn't fancied any American girls. Wonder if he'll succeed. My impression is he's a bit clumsy where women are concerned. Anyhow, I asked him to supper tonight and he's coming. When I suggested to Isabel it might be more entertaining for Bert if we asked some girl, too, said she'd ask Carlotta – though no hope there. I rather wish this first re-union could have been just Bert and me, get through all the stuff that won't interest Isabel much. But never mind: we'll have lunch together next week.

Looking forward to seeing Bert in the evening put a brighter colour on the day. There wasn't much to do, a few proposals to read, couple of calls to H.K. I spent an hour studying a catalogue of a Christie's wine sale, wishing I had the wherewithal for some of the really good stuff. Still, I might go. Pick up a case or two. During the slow morning I wished that I, too, could semi-retire. But I can't: not for some years. We're not extravagant, Isabel and I, by any means. Quite modest by some standards. But what with council tax, two cars to run, decent holidays, school fees, all from taxed income, it's hard to feel well off, lucky though we are compared with many. I like working hard: endeavour is not my problem. But the trouble is I'm bored by the import-export business, although I'm known – and privately confess – to be good at it. In an ideal world I'd never again have to think about trading, balancing, the implications of fluctuations of the economy. I'd like to cease to advise the company on the state of world finances. I'm fed up with figures, and forcing myself every morning through the City pages. That's not my natural world. I'm delighted it brings me a decent salary, but money cannot really make up for the hostility I have to my job. In a few years, God willing, I'll join Bert in semi-retirement and write. Every day, all the time.

Ay, there's the rub, as they say. My plays.

I was blighted, I suppose, by a hugely successful start – success of a very minor kind in relation to the outside world, but of monumental importance in university life. As a student of the Classics, I'd just seen *Oedipus Tyrannus* at the Playhouse, and remember saying to Bert I was gobsmacked. He was reading Law, hadn't understood a word of the Greek, so was unable to agree with me. I'd only persuaded him to come with me on the promise of dinner at The Elizabeth. We drank several bottles of mediocre wine, ate horribly creamy chicken, and I declared I now knew my calling in life: I was to be a playwright.

Bert was always one for encouraging his friends – in any direction they fancied going. So he solemnly expressed faith in my ability in this area, despite the fact there was not a shred of evidence that I could write anything, let alone a play. We drank several more glasses to my future success. I wrote a cheque which amounted to three weeks of my allowance, but had not a care. Then we staggered back up St. Aldates. There was a moment when we had to stop and cling to the post office. Bert promised to be there on the first night. As we parted, I gave him one of those gentlemanly punches in the stomach that I had learnt from my father, and said 'God, Bert, old man: life is bloody marvellous'. By now he was past agreeing, and I was too drunk to wonder if he managed the next hundred yards to Balliol.

What Bert never expected, I imagine, was that there would be a first night: that I would write a play. But

I started it next morning within a few hours of the hangover lifting. It was about, I suppose, love and truth and hidden meaning – but lightly conveyed. There were plenty of jokes to adorn the serious base. I wrote almost without stopping for two weeks – well, it was only my second year. Finals were still on the horizon. And anyway I couldn't help myself. I wrote furiously, as if guided from above, as some famous writer once put it. It was the most exciting, stimulating two weeks of my life so far. At the end of it was a neatly typed script, bound in green, all as professional as I could manage. Then I showed it to a friend – no, more of an acquaintance, to be truthful – much involved in student drama. Two days after delivering it to his pigeon hole there was the answer I hadn't even dared to hope for: '*Fantastic*', was Fergus's reply. 'We'll do it'.

My second stroke of luck was that Fergus was a brilliant director. He seemed to know exactly what I was getting at, had no desire to make vast changes in order to put his own stamp upon it. What's more, he had an amazing cast of talented young actors at his disposal. They were all extremely keen to rehearse seven days a week, thus reducing their time for academic work. There were a dozen volunteers for each part. Auditions were enormously enjoyable. Fergus and I found ourselves constantly agreeing, most particularly that Magdalene Brewer should play the lead. Magda, very tall, looked like no other girl I had ever seen: not exactly beautiful, but with a smile so bewitching, and eyes of such penetrating understanding, that I was a gonner from the moment she walked into the room to read her lines. Luckily she agreed with me, perhaps in the exuberance of getting the much-wanted lead, that it would be a good idea to spend some time together talking about the *essence* – I flung out the word, surprising myself – of her part. So we spent a great deal of time in her room or mine. The play was occasionally mentioned. She abandoned her PPE, I gave not a thought that term to Herodotus and co. I was a playwright in love. I'm not so sure about Magda. The following term her ardour cooled. She just might have been one of those women who think it quite in order to go to any lengths to get what you want in a competitive world.

Forward, Forward (by now known to the cognoscenti as simply *Forward*) opened in the penultimate week of the Hilary term. It was a wild success – standing ovation, Magda's dress perilously close to exposing her astounding breasts at the last bow, general delight of an audience which, longing to be pleased, had found reason for laughter between the passages of – in my opinion at the time – profound thought. Bert, swinging a bottle of Krug, could hardly get near me afterwards, so thick were the congratulations, so struggling to show they knew me were my friends. My head was quickly turned: ambition soared.

I had dreaded a sense of anticlimax when the week was over. I read the admiring reviews till I knew them by heart – *here is a writer of truly great potential, comic wit, and wisdom rare in one so young* – was the best (funny how I still remember it today) and wondered what to do next. But just as disaster so often follows disaster so, in that dazzling few months of my youth, success was superseded by further success. A producer – a young man rich in his own right, keen to discover young talent – took the play to the Edinburgh Festival. That was quite a week. Total sell-out. Up every night, all night, drinking. Boasting of the reviews. Much talk of future plays, future productions. Magda, on a complete high, almost exhausted me. How did we do it? How did we manage to get through the days, having stayed up most of the nights to celebrate each performance? Somehow we did. And unanimous, we were, in thinking *Forward* would be one of the experiences we would never, ever forget, one of the best times of our lives and all that (actually, I think most of us would agree we were right there.) The anti-climax came at the beginning of the following term. My tutors gallantly congratulated me on my success in the theatrical world, but suggested that if I wanted to get a decent degree then it might be advisable to return to my academic studies. I heeded their warning, returned to work.

I knew that the whole glittering bubble of time that was *Forward* would flash through my mind when I saw Bert, and it would probably be the same for him. There's nothing like shared experience to ease a reunion after long absence. It's the element that binds friends whose lives have grown apart. It's the engine that powers jokes about youthful folly, and warms one with the arrogant feeling of wisdom now gained. Heavens, it would be good to see Bert again this evening. The day, waiting, went very slowly.

SYLVIE

My parents: Mama and Papa. Actually I call them Mum and Dad at school so's not to be teased. I love them to bits. But they are *weird,* in lots of ways. I mean, take Mama. She has these very definite opinions about all sorts of things, and no one can budge her. Trainers, for instance. She absolutely hates trainers. She says they're so ugly. Shoes aren't ugly or pretty, I tell her: they're just shoes. If I used my eyes, she says, I'd *see* they were ugly (she thinks all sorts of things are ugly that I don't notice, which makes her shopping in High Streets very unhappy). 'So what would you like me to wear instead?' I ask. She can't answer that. She doesn't suggest the sort of sandals she wore back in the Dark Ages, I admit that. But all the same, every time I need a new pair of trainers there's this row … well, argument – usually *in* the shop, which is embarrassing. Though actually, that's the only time she does mega-embarrass me. She doesn't talk in a loud voice at the school gate, like some mothers, or say nice things about me to my teacher, or wear very short skirts, or dye her hair orange like my friend Elli's mother, with all the black coming through. Another of her very firm opinions is that the Beatles were the best at pop music. I admit they're quite good – I like *Lucy in the Sky* – but I wouldn't say they're the geniuses she says they are: she thinks they're the best *ever* – their tunes, their lyrics. I expect she'll go on thinking that till she dies. No one can ever change her mind once it's made up. I asked her what she thought of that old man who's still around – Mick Jagger. The Rolling Stones were rougher, I think she said, than the Beatles. But she liked them too. And a whole load of others who were hits when she was young. I'd never heard of any of them. I sometimes get her to listen to my music. She makes a face and says it's not her sort of thing. Though she does like just one group – Radiohead. Well, yes, they're cool. I suppose a bit like the Beatles.

She's got tons of ideas about what's good and what's bad for me and she's pretty fierce about them. Fizzy drinks, McDonald's food, crisps – all that sort of ordinary stuff I'm only allowed, like, not very often. She's always trying to get me to eat fruit – our kitchen table is like a fruit stall – and fish, which I hate. She's very good at puddings, though. We have chocolate pudding some Sundays which sort of rises up out of a sauce: ace, that.

I can't really grumble much about Mama. She's nearly always *there* – at home, I mean. A lot of my friends' mothers work in offices and companies and they're never there, and they never have time to help or to listen. Mama does listen, always. Elli's Mum, apparently, when she *is* home, is always frantic, and always on the telephone. So I'm lucky, there, having a mother who works at home. Her work is finished by the time I get back from school so we have really nice times at tea. She tells me what's gone wrong and how silly she's been about something, and makes me laugh. She's absolutely useless about technical things. When her mobile rings, which is only when she leaves it on because she doesn't really know how to turn it off, she rushes about picking up a camera or the video thing – absolutely pathetic. She thinks everything to do with computers and the internet and stuff is boring, and hates people talking about it. Well I suppose that's just better than Elli's Mum who gets a hundred e-mails a day and is always surfing the net. Yes: I think it's a *bit* better, Mama's way, though she could try harder about machinery things. I'm always telling her she's an old fuddy duddy, still jellified (one of my best new made-up words) in the past. She says she doesn't care.

Sometimes Mama does drive me bananas, going on about things that she likes, trying to get me to like them. Once she got very cross and said I didn't know the difference between a chaffinch and a daffodil. Which was, like, daft. I know daffodils perfectly well. Hyde Park is stuffed with them, isn't it? And we've got a few in our garden. I said I don't know how you expect me to know about chaffinches if we don't have any here. Next thing: she buys this hideous bird table. 'That's so *ugly'*, I said – and she did laugh. So now what happens? I have these bird lessons at breakfast. What's that, Sylvie? The blue and yellow one? Blue tit, Mama. No: a *great* tit. I keep telling you, the big one is … oh honestly. She's a pain about birds.

But altogether? Altogether I'd say I'm mega lucky with Mama. I mean you can rely on her. She'd never, ever let me down. She's never, ever late. In fact I discovered that when she comes to fetch me from somewhere, she arrives so early, so's not to be late, she has to wait. She says she likes that. Weirdly, she likes being shut in the car listening to Radio 3 or whatever. Then, if something goes wrong, she's the best at giving advice. She always understands, even if she doesn't agree. Sometimes it's quite spooky how she knows I'm worried or not happy or something, and she manages to find out what it is without actually asking me questions. She's not cross very often, and she forgives me a lot. Papa says she spoils me. Well, she does a bit. No so much with presents, though she's very good at surprise presents – she remembers things I say I like and then suddenly they appear. But Elli says she spoils me with *time*. I'm not sure what that means. But I think it means that even if she's tired in the evenings, and busy, she'll always make time to help me with my homework, or my piano practice or things like that. Perhaps I take that for granted, though I don't think I do now I'm older, since Elli pointed it out. Really I think I'm lucky having Mama as my mother. Despite her funny ways I think she's the best. But then I suppose most people think that about their mothers. Except Elli.

Papa! Well, Papa. He's weird, too, in different ways from Mama. His trouble is he concentrates so hard on whatever he's doing that it's very difficult to get his attention if he's in one of his concentrating moods. So he's sitting in the kitchen reading the newspaper about some war or something, and I ask him a question and he simply doesn't hear, which can be annoying. He gets cross about different things from Mama. Like my room. He says it's a tip, and he won't read to me till it's cleared up. Sometimes he says it's a bloody disgrace. When I was young he didn't swear in front of me. Now he quite often does, though not any of the really bad words that Harry told us about at school. He's absolutely wonderful, Papa, at reading to me. He apparently began when I was a baby, and went on years after I could read to myself because I always ask him to. He's so good, doing different voices and everything. I like the Roald Dahl books best, though we're on to *Little Nell* at the moment. I think Papa is very clever. He's got a clever face, especially now his hair is going a bit grey at the sides. He doesn't, like, go on about his cleverness, but I think people can feel it. Sometimes I look at the faces of people he's talking to, and they look really impressed. Once he wrote a play when he was young that nearly made him world famous. He's got framed posters saying all about it on the walls of his study, his name pretty big. I'm very proud of him except when he dances. When my twin cousins had a disco when they were sixteen, they asked people of all ages, even ten year olds like I was then, and everyone was supposed to dance. Mama, luckily, didn't – and she's a proper dancer, goes to lessons. She said she couldn't cope with the music. But Papa! He, like, *squirmed*. He moved about wiggling his arms like an octopus, and humming. I wanted to die. On the way home I said never, ever – please Papa never ever do that to me again. He told me not to be so critical of other people's enjoyment, and anyhow there had been plenty of other fathers dancing. I said yes but you were the *worst*. We haven't been to any more of those sort of parties, thank goodness. I dread Papa making such an idiot of himself again. I expect he will at my wedding or something.

Papa and Mama together are pretty good. I wouldn't want them to be divorced – lots of people in my class have parents who are divorced, and some of them have horrid step-parents. But I don't think Mama and Papa will divorce now. They've been married fifteen years, and they've got me, and they don't squabble much. I think they're happy actually. They laugh a lot, and they thank each other for things, everyday sort of things like when

Papa puts the rubbish out or Mama finds his scarf which he's always losing. They're not at all lovey-dovey which I think is brilliant. I'd hate them to be soppy, kissing and stuff. They agree about a lot, including improving my mind. I tell them when I have children I'm absolutely not going to do anything to improve *their* minds. They said you wait. But to be fair they don't bang on too much. Just subtly try to inform me now and then. I always know what they're up to.

Funnily enough, they don't seem to invite lots of people here. Elli says her parents are always having dinner parties and she has to have cereal in front of the telly upstairs. They go out about once a week, sometimes Papa on his own, a work thing, and I have fun with Mama. She says dinner parties are too much of a palaver, and she hates cooking, so it's very rare that even two people come round. Like tonight. Some old friend of Papa's and horrible Carlotta. Mama looked a bit spinny when I got back from school, shelling prawns and whizzing about, dropping things, so I laid the table for her. I picked all the pansies from the tub and arranged them for her. She likes that sort of thing. She gave me fish fingers and carrots and chocolate yogurt on a tray in the study and said I could watch telly till nine. So that's cool. It's a bit like Elli's sort of evening, but much nicer. I'm even allowed a bit of Toblerone so long as I promise to eat it before doing my teeth. Which I did promise. I'm always making promises. Both Mama and Papa like it when I do, and they believe me.

GWEN

Right from the beginning, with the Grants, it was easy (I was nervous they might not want to take on someone of my age – though I didn't admit what it was). At the interview with Mrs. Grant I made myself plain. 'I'd be grateful if you'd call me Gwen,' I said. 'Everyone calls me Gwen – and I'll call you Mrs. Grant'. She agreed at once. At that very first meeting we discovered we had a lot of opinions in common: the demarcation between employer and employee, for instance, no matter who they are. Mrs. Grant told me that when she was younger she worked in publishing and was very careful always to refer to her boss as Mrs. Whatever, even though they were almost the same age. Course, it's not like that now. Christian names all over the place, today, soon as you meet someone. Call me old fashioned, but my hackles go up if someone calls me Gwen when we've only just met, with not so much as a by your leave. Mrs. Grant feels just the same way.

It was lovely discovering we had lots else in common, too. My previous lady (Mrs. What's-It – I can never remember the double-barrelled bit) in Holland Park, she and I came from different planets. I only stayed the five years because her husband was so ill. But Mrs Grant, she likes a polish and a shine, just like I do. She likes things done nicely. She likes the day to start with a tidy, though she never wants the place to look unlived in like a waiting room. Course, I know just what she means. I never go into her studio, except once a month to hoover: she says it's far too much of a mess and she keeps it as she wants it herself. This may seem peculiar, but I believe it's a good idea to fall in as much as possible with your employer's ways: it must be difficult for them. It didn't work, my method, with Mrs. What's-It and I took a lot of rudeness from her. But with Mrs. Grant, from the very beginning I tried to make relations between us easy for her, and we've never looked back. I said 'Mrs. Grant, if there's anything I do not to your liking, you only have to tell me. I'll not take offence, like some', I said. Turned out she doesn't like the cushions on the sofa standing on their points – like a chorus line of ballet dancers, was how she put it, which made me chuckle. She also doesn't like objects – ashtrays and boxes and so on – placed on the diagonal. She said it disturbs her sense of symmetry.

For myself, I've always rather fancied an ashtray put *not* quite straight – gives it a bit of character, I always think. That's what I do in my living room at home. But of course at the Grants I do what Mrs. G likes. I'm so used to it now I rarely make a mistake.

I've got to know them all pretty well, now. Nine years: you do. In a way I think of them as my family, what with Ernie hardly ever home and Jan up north – not that we were ever close, mother and daughter. Mrs. Grant I know best of course. Sometimes I feel I can read her like a book. She's very quiet, and kind, and, my, she's considerate. A little vague, perhaps – but aren't we all? Forgets things, gets a bit panicky when she's a long list of things to do. When she comes down for her morning cup of coffee is the time she's most abstracted. It's almost as if her mind's still on her business upstairs and she doesn't want the spell to be broken. She never talks about her work, mind. I'm just sometimes shown the finished product before it goes off and I can see what a talented lady she is. Modest with it. I don't think she ever believes my compliments, or anyone's. And then she does move so well, so gracefully. You should see her coming down stairs, a pleasure to watch. Rather stately somehow, even when she's only wearing jeans and a shirt. Very straight back. She once told me that at her school they had lessons in deportment. They had to walk about with a pile of books on their heads. Don't suppose there's much of that around now. She only met Ernie once – he was home on leave and came to pick me up from work in his car, but they got on beautifully. He said I was very lucky to have such a good employer. I said don't be stupid, Ernie: I know that. Jan she's never met and I don't suppose ever will. Jan's not one for making an effort to come and see her mother, and I've only had one invitation to Yorkshire in ten years. But I think Mrs. Grant feels she knows them all, and that includes Bill, though he passed away two years before I came to the Grants. She listens to me chattering on, doesn't say much herself, but always sympathetic. Always interested. The way I know about her is not so much from what she says, but from her body language, as they say. She's very expressive eyes and she's very calm. But just occasionally she frowns, and her fingers play up and down on her mug. Once – I was very late on account of the dentist – I came in and heard her playing the piano. I know she never likes to play to anyone, and she stopped as soon as she heard the door. But my goodness was she storming away! Very loud. Angry, like. I was quite disturbed. I realised later it was about the time she heard her father had cancer.

Mr. Grant I know less well, of course. But from what I can tell he's the sort of man the English do best. A lot in common with my Bill. Very upright, dignified, charming, always a twinkle in his eye. As courteous as you could want. He's not old-fashioned, exactly, but always nicely turned out, none of those T-shirts on a week day that so many men fancy these days. And it's my private belief he's something of a passionate man. Passionate at the desk, passionate in the bed as they say – well, as Bill used to say. I'm never quite sure what it is exactly Mr. Grant does in his office – though it must bring in a certain wage – but up in his study it's my guess he's a passionate at his desk, writing away. When I come on a Monday morning his waste-paper basket is overflowing with bits of screwed up typing paper. It's all over the floor. As for his desk – well. Mrs. Grant says he writes plays, and they're very good. To my knowledge he's only had one put on but he keeps at it. Very determined. Sometimes I go for days without seeing Mr. Grant, he's off so early. But when we do run into each other he's always full of appreciation. 'No one like you for polishing the fender, Gwen', he'll say, 'and definitely no one like you for ironing a shirt'. He's promised that on my next birthday (I think they've guessed what it is – God forbid!) – we'll all go for a meal and see *The*

Mousetrap, something I've been wanting to do for I don't know how long.

Sylvie: Sylvie is something else. A nice enough girl, but moody, headstrong. Not particularly spoilt, though she's got every toy and gadget you can think of. Eighty three stuffed animals in her bedroom – I counted them. As for her bedroom itself, it's a tip. I can only hoover when Mrs. Grant has insisted she clears up, about once a month. She's stuck things all over the walls, too, so you can hardly see the pretty wallpaper which she told me was soppy. Over her desk she's stuck up a list of words. I can't help reading them because they're in such big letters. Apparently they are her made-up words. Mrs. Grant told me she slips one occasionally into her school essays to see if her teacher will notice, and she hardly ever does.

There's no denying Sylvie's a charmer, like her father. One of her smiles, with her head tipped on one side, and she can have anyone eating out of her hand. At the moment she's got those train tracks on her teeth, but I reckon she'll be a beauty like her mother one day, and go somewhere in the world. She's got all these scatty ideas, and more than her fair share of energy and imagination. I reckon Mr. and Mrs. Grant will have trouble on their hands in a few years time, once she's in her teens, just as I did with Jan. But she'll come through. She'll be all right in the end. Once she ran down stairs and flung her arms round my neck and said I was the *best*. You can't help being won round by something like that. I said to her mother, I said 'One day Sylvie'll have her name in lights, mark my word'. Pity she didn't have any brothers or sisters, really. I believe there was some trouble, though I didn't enquire. Still, they're a good family. I'd like to think I can keep working for them till my bones force me to stop.

BERT

God it's good to be home. Can't think why I dithered for so long. New York's all very well for a while. Exhilarating in a way that London isn't. But for real life…

Was a bit depressed when I came into the house. The tenants have taken their toll. Nothing specific – just an air of acute shabbiness which wasn't there when I left. Though I suppose, nearly ten years ago, that's not unreasonable. There was an unpleasant smell – a clash of old smoke and chemical air freshener. I opened all the windows, looked through all the cupboards. In the kitchen everything appeared out of date, overused. I suppose I'll have to re-equip the place: new machinery, new curtains and covers. In fact the whole house could do with re-decorating. And I'll have to buy a car and apply for residents' parking, all very tiresome. It's not that I haven't the money – I've more money than I need to spend. It's just all very boring when there's no one to help, to advise. All the same, I'm overwhelmingly glad to be back.

The first morning home, not a thing in the fridge, I behaved like a New Yorker and went out to breakfast in the King's Road. It was a warm sunny morning so I sat at a minuscule table on the pavement with my cappuccino and indifferent croissant, and felt a bit bleak. I took out my engagement book – nothing but empty pages, of course, since landing in England – and looked at the list of people whose telephone numbers I transfer every year, no matter for how long I haven't seen them. Dan was at the top, his permanent place. He was the one I most wanted to see, I thought. My oldest friend. Great stretches of absence never made any difference to us. We'd just take up the reins again. He was always good at précising the time lost between us. I was never much good at that. I find it difficult suddenly to describe the most important thing that's happened in the last few months, let alone years. So I just murmur about still being a bachelor, hope fading, well-paid job in air-conditioned Manhattan, and he gets the picture. I wouldn't want to bore him with the ins and outs of strategic marketing for the oil company. So from me he gets merely tiny flashes of illumination in my life – an amazing weekend in the Hamptons, or the skiing trip in Colorado. His apparent deep interest sometimes spurs me to a few details.

From him I get a great deal more. Much of it concerns whatever is his current play. It's astonishing, his tenacity and determination. Ever since we left Oxford Dan's been writing plays. Boosted by his stupendous success of *Forward*, he was convinced that he was a born playwright. The fact that not a single play has been produced since doesn't seem to have daunted him. He spends months and months waiting for replies from theatre companies and producers, probably knowing in his heart that the news, if and when it ever does come, is not going to be good. Once or twice there's been a flicker of hope: some director – perhaps out of kindness – suggesting there is a future for a play. But in fact that future is always a return to the bottom drawer. No matter, says Dan. He never blames the state of theatre in general, or changing fashions, or lack of willingness to invest in plays: he blames only himself. 'Well,' he says, 'that one obviously wasn't good enough. So on to the next one.

Must do better.' Thank God he doesn't rely on writing for a living.

I admire his persistence so much. The pathos he exudes moves me frequently, though God forbid he should ever be aware of such thoughts. In the same circumstances, I would have given up years ago. I haven't seen any of the most recent attempts, but he sent me three scripts a couple of years ago. I read them very carefully, wondering what it was that meant they didn't work. I'm no expert: couldn't quite put my finger on it. They're well constructed, witty, usually an original slant on some issue of the day. And yet ... they never quite come alive. In the way that *Forward* most certainly did. So what happened? Is it that some people have within them just a single work? Or, at least, a single work of lasting and profound effect? Like Salinger? I asked Dan about that once. He thought the idea wasn't up to much. 'If you can write one excellent thing,' he said, 'you have the capacity to write another. It's just a matter of unlocking the magic door again.' He always asks my opinion, and I try to be constructive in my answers. He doesn't care that I'm not a professional critic, just wants to know if I *like* a play. That's easy enough to answer. I always enjoy Dan's plays: I can tell him in all honesty. What I can't ever bring myself to say is that I see why they are not put on, though my reasons are so amorphous it's hard to elucidate them even to myself. Whenever I've sent back a manuscript, with some carefully worded letter of appreciation of the good things, I then get to worrying about the whole problem of how honest one should be with a friend about his work. God knows the encouragement of friends is vital to one's life. But is false encouragement or praise a form of betrayal? Would they rather know that something they have produced, in your humble opinion, isn't really very good? It would be patronising, not to say arrogant, to tell a friend you think they have little talent but should carry on enjoying themselves producing whatever it is – painting, writing, composing, whatever. Skilful weighing up, between hurtful truth and hollow compliment, is always called for. When it comes to Dan, I resort to evasion of absolute truth, but my praise for selected parts is genuine. What I always fear is that he knows – as close friends instinctively do – what I really think. I often pray to God that one day, before he's so exhausted by failure that he gives up, he will have another success.

Whatever disappointment he feels, he keeps mostly to himself. I believe I'm the only friend to whom he ever mentions the plays, and when he does it's always with a lively sense of deprecation, thus warning me of what I'm in for. My admiration for his courage and determination is inestimable. I love his company more than anyone else's. He always sees the quirky side of life, the slant on the straight. It was good of him immediately to ask me round when I rang. But it won't be the same, with others. I must get him round for lunch at the club very soon.

I don't really know Isabel. I was posted abroad at the time of their marriage – couldn't get back for the wedding, which I know was a blow to Dan. After the Gulf War I was only in London for a very short time before leaving for New York. I took them out to dinner a couple of times: they asked me round. Sylvie, a winning child as far as I could see, is my goddaughter. Isabel seemed very unlike Dan's previous girlfriends. He used to go for the noisy ones. I remember endless girls tossing long hair into his face and clutching at him in a proprietorial way. But he eluded them all, never declared himself in love except with the wonderful Magda. And she ditched him in a pretty nasty way, once she got the lead in *Forward*.

No: Isabel, in the little I know her, seems to me to exude a kind of calm and peace: perfect foil to Dan's sense of frenzy. And she could look rather beautiful in a sort of timeless way. Rossetti would have liked to have painted her. Dan has never been one for putting his feelings under a microscope – he once said he thought it the height of bad manners – but it's quite plain he loves his wife and they're happy. He would have alerted me if anything was amiss. Be interesting to study everything tonight.

Have to admit I rather wish Carlotta wasn't going to be there. I haven't seen her since she was about fifteen. We often met as children because our parents were friends, but we didn't like each other. She was bossy, a touch humourless, always trying to shock. There was the day in some garden, behind a laurel bush, when she asked me if I'd like to see her knickers. I was fourteen. She must have been about twelve. I said no thanks, and she stomped off in a huff, shouting that only an idiot would turn down such an opportunity. Relations were pretty cool after that, though I seem to remember, in our teens, I did kiss her at a Sailing Club dance in Norfolk, after I'd drunk a great deal of beer and vodka. But Dan has always said I'm wrong about Carlotta: she's got great qualities, he says, though they aren't always apparent. Admittedly, he and Isabel have never tried to throw us together. I suppose they asked her this evening just to balance things. It'll be perfectly all right. All the same, just for this reunion, I do wish they hadn't asked her.

CARLOTTA

Isabel can be absolutely *dementing*. She rings me up *mid-morning* – how many times have I said Isabel please ring me at dawn? – just as I'm about to go into a meeting, and then sounds put out because I have to cut her off quickly. She rang me at the worst time this morning to ask me to supper – there's rarely any such thing as a dinner party, these days, chez Dan and Isabel – and in my hurry I just said yes, because although it's the one night I always like to keep free to catch up with things in the flat, I didn't want to offend her. She mentioned something about Gilbert Bailey being there. Bert! Heavens. Haven't seen him for *years*. Remember him as a rather shy little boy, lanky. Then there was a moment – almost eradicated from my mind, at some teenage dance, and a hopelessly inadequate beer-smelling kiss. Can't say I've the slightest inclination to be re-acquainted, but there goes. He's apparently Dan's oldest friend.

It's ridiculous, really, how little I see of Isabel – not my oldest friend, but one of the very best. We live so close and yet it always seems difficult to find time to meet. Perhaps that's just modern life. I really mind about not seeing her more: she's a wonderfully calming influence, and makes me laugh in her quiet way. God knows why we get on so well: we could not be more different. She's absolutely not of this modern world: has no interest in fashion, speed, cutting edge, excitement, technology – she lives in her own little white tower, working away, enormously talented, and I would think a pretty good wife and mother. She scoffs at my interests, my racy life, the things I find compelling. I've often invited her to come with me to India or Ceylon or America, and promised I'd take care of her, guide her through all the things she seems to find alarming. But she says no, absolutely not. Her idea of a holiday is Wales or Fife or Norfolk or the West Country. Can't understand it myself.

I'm not sure how she ever got to Spain, where we met, by herself. I suppose it was the lure of a painting holiday (in the days when she was still trying to discover what she could do) in Trasierra, a fabulous place owned by a friend of hers. We were somehow always side by side at our easels and talked more than we drew or painted. She was quite good, in fact: on a different scale from me. (I was only there for the relaxation, painting as therapy: hopeless, and didn't even enjoy it). Isabel was of the standard that sells – pretty watercolours competently executed. But she kept saying she wasn't an *artist*. Proper artists are passionate about their work and nothing can keep them from it, she said. And she wasn't remotely passionate about her dinky little watercolours, and couldn't care less if she never painted another picture. But for all our differences we seemed to enjoy talking to each other: she was amazed by stories of my rackety life, while I was equally amazed by the happiness she said her quiet life produced. So our friendship began, ten years ago.

The one subject I avoid with Isabel is Sylvie: she's something of a monster: precocious, spoilt, boastful. Only child-syndrome and all that, I suppose. And Isabel and Dan think the sun shines ... Yes, obviously very bright, and lively, but God she's irritating. I always try to avoid times when she's around. I do admit she can be winning sometimes, and even witty. I'm just not keen on children in general. I'm bored rigid by mothers who go on about them all the time – Isabel, to be fair, doesn't do this – but the domestic problems of women who try to have it all, are deeply tedious and given far too much attention in the media and even novels. Most of my friends are childless.

As for Dan: Dan's lovely. If he wasn't married to Isabel I'd fancy him like crazy. He's a *gentle* man in the real meaning of the word. Bit of a mystery, I've always thought: absolutely obsessed about writing his plays, wonderfully considerate husband, I would think. I've picked up from Isabel he can be a touch moody (she'd never be so disloyal as to complain about anything concerning Dan). But goodness, is he a good listener? – something most of the men I know simply *aren't*. He's wise and learned and marvellously straight. If he was my husband, of course, there'd have to be certain changes in his clothes and ties, though as someone else's husband I find them terribly endearing – his father's suits. He's proud of them. Opens the jacket and points to the date on the inside pocket: '1957 and still going strong', he says, pleased as anything. I daresay I shall never meet anyone as generally desirable as Dan. I often tell Isabel this and she laughs and says what nonsense. I don't think she regards me in any way as a dangerous force: surely I wouldn't tell her how wonderful I think her husband is if I really fancied him.

So I practice a sort of double bluff.

Chapter Two

ISABEL

I've so often wondered why some mornings, outwardly like any other morning, I'm filled with a feeling of unease, pessimism, almost alarm. I can find no answer. But on such mornings I'm more than usually keen to shut myself away in my studio as quickly as possible, hurry through the farewells, the finding of Sylvie's maths book, the straightening of Dan's tie.

It was like that this morning. I ran up the stairs, sat down a little out of breath and rather shaky, looked all round at the familiar things necessary to my trade. For the hundredth time I marvelled about how it had all come to be. Chance, luck, those wayward things that so rarely strike, chose me at a time I was becoming desperate.

I had spent so many years – as a child, an undergraduate, a young woman, trying to work out what precisely I should do. I'd wasted – was it wasted? – so much time experimenting. I did not come into that bleak category of not having *any* clue about what I wanted to do: I came into the next category up of those who have a vague idea but nothing specific gels in the mind. Arts, rather than sciences, was the field I inclined towards. But what, in the arts, that wasn't an administrative job, could I do? As a child I had briefly wanted to be a concert pianist when, after six months of dawn practising, I managed to get to the end of the *Hungarian Rhapsody*, but I knew in my heart I was a conscientious rather than a talented pianist. I could draw quite well, I could write a better essay than most of my contemporaries. But I knew beyond doubt that I was neither a writer nor a painter. Then I took up ballet but quickly had to give it up when I grew too tall. I thought of teaching, but dismissed that idea on the grounds that I was not good enough myself to teach others either English or art in more than a merely competent way. And my belief has always been that teachers should be so passionate about their subject that they can't fail to inspire their pupils. I got a reasonable degree in history at York, but had no thoughts of carrying on with things historical.

Before marrying Dan I went from one dull job to another: working in a gallery, assisting a photographer, organising events for charity. I contemplated going to some third world country and being, at least, useful.

But when I tried to do this I came up against so many stumbling blocks I gave up: apparently energy and enthusiasm were not enough. Qualifications were needed that I did not have. These were years in which I felt wasted and frustrated with myself for not being able to put my finger on what I might really enjoy and be good at. I wrote furious, bad poetry and wondered how this hopelessness might be resolved. It was resolved by getting married, of course. And time was for a while taken up with buying and organising the house, deflecting melancholy about my inability to discover what I really wanted to do. Dan said there was no need for me to work: he was well able to take care of us both. But of course, if it made me happier, he'd support me in whatever it was.

Sylvie was born. I became a full time mother. I loved it. I loved her. The need for a job waned. I seemed to be constantly kept busy by domestic matters. I was happy. Seven years flew by.

Then, Sylvie being at school till mid afternoon, the days began to empty and lengthen, and the old yearning returned: also the old dilemma. What to do? But this time a solution dropped mercifully into my lap.

A friend rang to say she was going to a masked ball and there was not the kind of mask she wanted to be had in London. Could I make her one? I remember laughing. What on earth made her think I could make a mask? She knew I was good with my hands, she said. What proof had she? Apparently I'd once covered a shoebox in sequins and ribbons, and enamelled the inside, and given it to her full of soap for a present. 'Oh *that*', I said. 'Hardly proof I'm a natural mask maker'. But she was persuasive. Eventually I said I'd have a try. I'd nothing else to do…

And then came that molten warmth of challenge, the ridiculous excitement about so minuscule a project. Suddenly the afternoon, full of purpose, was lighted. I hurried off to the Portobello Road, bought a basket full of feathers and sequins and baubles, scraps of ribbon and lace. I bought glue and paint, needles and cotton, and spent a fortune on feathers both upright and shining, and others languidly curling. I found some plastic mask-bases in a theatrical shop, and was ready to begin. That evening Dan came home to find me kneeling on the sitting room floor surrounded by what he called 'mysterious paraphernalia'. What was I doing? Was there anything for supper?

No, there wasn't. Sylvie was with a friend for a night and no thoughts of cooking had entered my mind as I experimented with all my glorious bits and pieces. Dan was wonderful. He took me out to supper so that I could concentrate on explaining what had happened. His encouragement (which, if I'd had time to think about it, I wouldn't have expected) was amazing. He leapt ahead a little, further encouraging. 'If this works,' he said, 'you could set up a business at home: we could convert the attic into a studio, put a huge window in the roof'. He was smiling – was he serious? I didn't know, and didn't ask. 'I don't expect there are many mask-makers in London, are there?' he asked. 'No,' I said: 'none'. My only source of information was my friend who had 'looked everywhere' and found nothing. But by now we were both so caught up in the excitement of the whole idea that her scant research seemed encouragement enough. 'If it works, if you can do it,' Dan said again, 'this might be the answer to what you've been looking for, for so long…'

It did work. That first mask was a wild, beautiful thing, sparkling, catching the light, twinkling with the iridescent colours of a mallard's breast. Now, looking back, I see it was too uncontrolled. It was over the top: I'd thrown everything I had at it in patterns, led by my fingers that seemed to understand. I've stopped using sequins now. These days my masks are a little less flamboyant, though I still aim for measured extravagance, beauty, mystery. But to that 'first, fine careless rapture' of a first mask I owe everything: it set me on my way. My friend was enchanted, triumphant. 'I told you you could do it,' she said. 'You can be grateful to me for enabling you to discover what you're really good at, can't you?' I wouldn't let her pay for it, though she offered me a huge sum. 'I'd rather just lend it,' I said, 'then keep it to remind myself how I started if – that is, if I was to go on.'

Which I was. Someone at the ball, where the mask won first prize, owned an antique shop which needed a decorative mask in the window. From there it snowballed, word of mouth. Dan took me to Venice for a week to research both the history and the art of mask-making by the masters of that art. The attic was quickly converted. I was once or twice photographed for magazines with a selection of my masks. A very rich singer ordered four for his dining-room table. Recently, half a dozen giant masks were commissioned for the carnival in Rio. I'm established now, I think I can say, some seven years after my first attempt.

That first attempt now stands on my desk under a Victorian glass dome. Most days, looking at it, I'm filled with wonder – not at the mask, which is technically pretty crude by my present standards – but at how long it took me to discover what I could do with considerable skill – even art of a minor kind. Chance was my saviour. How reliant we all are on chance. How despairing it is if it eludes us. How lucky I was.

For besides the love I have for Dan and Sylvie, my life now has a point. Half my day is spent creating something wanted by people unknown to me, and those speeding hours, concentrating on the challenge, give pleasure hard to express. Apart from that, I am now a considerable earner. I love being able to contribute financially to our lives, not to have to ask Dan (never anything but generous, but that's not the point) for money for things for myself: able to pay for presents and theatre tickets and surprises, and to give to charities of my choosing. I love all that. And most of all I love the solitude my work affords me. Every morning I bury myself in my small world of fragments that will go to make up a whole, and I'm free to reflect, to plan, to feel thankful in the refuge that my studio has become.

On the morning after Gilbert and Carlotta came to supper I sat for a while doing nothing. The huge skylight was filled with cloudless blue. The parrot tulips on my desk were bent lower over the sides of the glass vase than they were yesterday. Their white petals scratched with fine pen lines of shadow, their edges ruched like the silk of a century ago. I like white flowers in the studio:

colour comes from my feathers and beads and flaring scraps of material. It had gone off all right, really, supper. Very nice seeing Gilbert again, scarcely older looking, a little disoriented having only just got back from New York after so long, and uncertain what he would do next. Carlotta was her usual ebullient self, full of extravagant praise for my cooking though I noticed she left half her cheesecake. When she said, as she was leaving, she had a ticket for a Brahms recital at the Wigmore Hall next evening – her mother had let her down – and would anyone like to go, I would have liked to have accepted the invitation. But it would be Dan's last night before a business trip to Rome, so I said nothing. Gilbert, with no apparent enthusiasm, offered himself. Carlotta was very curt: took his telephone number and said she'd ring him about arrangements. She left quickly. At the front door – Dan was outside trying to get a taxi – Gilbert said if I needed company for an evening while Dan was away, he'd love to take me to a film, or whatever. I said 'Good idea. Lovely. Why not?'

I picked up a handful of old lace trims, very fragile, and began to wonder how to attach them to a band of satin ribbon without damaging them. The melancholy which I'd felt on waking persisted all morning. I wished Dan did not have to go to Rome. Irrationally, unreasonably, I also wished Gilbert had not accepted Carlotta's invitation.

SYLVIE

Mama was in a weird mood this morning. Nothing she said, just the way she moved, sort of vaguely agitated, and glancing at Papa who was buried in his paper and didn't seem to notice. I don't think it was anything serious – I don't mean, like, impending divorce. *Impending* I found by chance in the dictionary and rather like. I've been using it quite a lot recently – but I have to keep an eye on them.

She didn't mention anything about last night, the dinner, how it had gone or anything. I expect they were up very late, or they drank too much for once. So, I don't know. But *something*.

I was still in the kitchen when horrible Carlotta arrived, all out of breath and going on about how *frantic* her day had been. I hate her. I hate her because she's so two-faced. Once when I was alone with her she said I was a spoilt brat. But then Mama came in and Carlotta said wasn't I clever winning the high jump – such a sportswoman we have here, she said, silly cow. Also, she speaks too loudly and stinks of some kind of revolting scent. She makes the whole room smell. You can still smell her when she's gone out. Once I opened the window and she shut it again. When she'd gone I opened it again. Can't think why Mama likes her. Last night she was wearing a skirt much too short for her age and her legs and she brought a box of incredibly expensive looking chocolates and only stopped going on about her new Prada bag when Bert Bailey arrived.

He's my godfather, though I hardly know him. Nice face, twinkly eyes. He's obviously not used to people of my age and asked lots of boring questions about school and things. He rattled about in his trouser pocket and brought out £2 for me – for someone of almost eleven that won't go far. I'd rather hoped it would be a fiver, but perhaps he doesn't realise the value of money has changed since he was last here. Still, it was cool of him. I hope he doesn't fancy Carlotta, or ever get to marry her or anything, because though it's nice having him here it would mean seeing even more of Carlotta, and that would be awful. In fact I don't think there's much chance of that. I didn't see him look at her much, once she'd given him a big sort of show-off hug when she arrived. When I went to say goodnight to Bert he was talking to Papa about fishing in Canada, and he got out of his chair to kiss me on the cheek. Imagine that! An old man standing up for me! Very good manners.

I like Bert. I really hate Carlotta.

DAN

Carlotta's never been blessed with a sense of her own unimportance: humility is not something she understands. She was at her most boringly interruptive last night. Do wish we hadn't asked her. I daresay Bert probably felt the same. Still, she was lively – is she ever not? – and told some quite funny stories about corporate life. When she asked Bert what was it he did, exactly, in the oil company, and Bert with a self-deprecating shrug said just strategy, she became very over-excited. The strategy of marketing is apparently her own forte. Her reaction to finding someone else in roughly the same area was out of all proportion to the discovery, I thought. Bert responded politely to her vivacious interest. He was obviously still suffering from jet lag, energy lacking. But when Carlotta made a few pertinent remarks about the *general failings* of strategy – she emphasised these with an arrogant sweep of a rather pretty hand – he perked up, agreed, laughed. I could see that gradually, through dinner, she was beginning to win him over. Though I don't think he has the slightest interest in her. Just being polite, and the annoyance was drifting away.

God it was good to see Bert again: much the same, a slightly more civic look about him despite his assurance that he ran round a good part of Central Park every morning. His somewhat tubbier ribs were buttoned into a waistcoat with which, he said, he liked to mystify the Americans. And yet he also wore a Brooks Brothers button-down shirt which meant some American influence had brushed off onto him. He didn't talk much about New York but wonderfully described a fishing weekend in Canada: we made a vague plan to go together one day. When I asked what he was going to do in London he said he had no idea: there were practicalities to be settled first, buying a car and getting his house repaired. Carlotta immediately jumped in here. In one of her many careers she had been an interior decorator: she'd be willing to help in any way she could, she offered. She found it all *so* easy to envisage how things could be – an ability not many people had, she added. Bert thanked her for the offer and gave her a look which she probably failed to read: don't crowd me, it said.

After supper – Isabel had done so well, given such short notice – Carlotta stayed sitting at the table, while the other two moved to the sofa. All at once Carlotta became completely different – calm, quiet. Perhaps she was suddenly tired. She asked me how the current play was going. I answered, as I always do, that I had no idea. I loathe talking about my plays. Isabel and Bert are the only ones to whom I've ever expressed the endless despair they cause. Carlotta was silent for at least a minute. She sat looking down into her glass of wine, very long eyelashes (don't think I've ever noticed them before) elongated by their shadows on her cheek. Then she asked, in a voice so low I could hardly hear, when I was writing, did I envisage my characters on a stage, or in real life? 'It's something I've always wondered, when I go to the theatre', she said. How did the writer imagine them?

'It's a question I've never been asked before,' I said. 'I'm not sure I can answer it. I'll have to think about it. The place my characters inhabit is, well, rather cloudy'. 'Please let me know when you find the answer', Carlotta said, eyelashes hitting her eyebrows as she looked up and focused her eyes hard on me. 'I'd be fascinated', she said.

Then she leapt up, claimed she had to be off, she had an early start. Funnily enough, on and off during the night I kept thinking of her question. I was rather surprised that one so apparently unthinking as Carlotta is in many ways, should have asked it.

GWEN

Monday, Tuesday, Wednesday, Friday — those are the days of the week I look forward to. Those are the days I go to the Grants and become — though perhaps I shouldn't say this — part of the family. I've never really had a proper family myself, what with Bill snucking off long before he died, and the children becoming what I call unruly, out of hand at an early age, never wanting to eat round the table. So the Grants represent peace and calm and security. They seem happy. I like their sunny house and feel pride in keeping it up together. I think they rely on me in a way, just as I rely on them.

I only live in Shepherd's Bush — a twenty minute walk every morning, come rain or shine. My heart always lifts when I turn into their road: the plane trees, the blossoms and lilacs in the small but well kept front gardens. When I first came it was a very different place. Shabby. Dirty net curtains in the windows, battered front doors. Now — well, it's a smart road. Not quite Notting Hill, but the sort of place a lot of young well-heeled families like to move. Someone in the corner shop told me houses in the Grants' street were selling for a million or more. You could have knocked me down with a feather. But that's property for you these days: lucky for those who could afford to get on the ladder in the first place.

I could tell soon as I put my bag down in the kitchen that there had been company the night before. There were two empty wine bottles on the dresser, and another with a little under a third of red wine left. No cork. I didn't have to ask what to do with it: throw it out. They leave things like that to my judgment which is one of the things that gives my job a sense of fulfilment. To be trusted to make decisions, and often suggestions, can give you a boost. So I poured the wine – very dark coloured stuff, don't know how they can drink it – down the sink and put the bottle with the other empties in the re-cycling bin. Then I screwed up the used serviettes still on the table and threw them in the machine. Mrs. Grant usually does that when they've been entertaining – she says she doesn't like me to arrive and find a lot of mess. So perhaps they were especially late. It was nice and warm in the kitchen, always a cheery place, what with the yellow paint, even on a grey day. There was a smell of flowers that hadn't been there yesterday: can't have been the old African violet that's been struggling half-dead for years, I thought. Then I saw a pot of gardenias on the table by the fire. Mrs. Grant must have bought them yesterday afternoon, or perhaps one of the guests brought them. Four beautiful flowers, no less, not far open and sending their perfume all round the room. I put my nose to one of them. My, was it heady. A bit too rich for me. I don't think I'd want a gardenia at home. My little room wouldn't be able to accommodate such perfume. I got out the hoover. Its noise is a sort of music to me, companionable. I began. I could hoover every room in the house with my eyes shut, I know every corner so well.

When Mrs. Grant came down at ten-thirty, I could see at once she was in one of her most preoccupied moods. When her mind is still upstairs she puts on a certain little smile, and is as polite and interested as ever, but I know she's not really with me as she is on other days. On the occasions she's distracted I choose only a paragraph or two from the *Daily Mail*: something to make her laugh, and she's drunk her coffee and is up and off in less than our usual ten minutes.

This morning, I'm not sure why, I didn't get the paper out of my bag at all. Mrs. Grant seemed so deep in thought. Far be it from me to interrupt the creative process, I think they call it. I can imagine, when you've a talent like Mrs. Grant, your mind doesn't run at all like other people's, and we more normal people should respect that.

Anyhow, she did say there'd been company for dinner: Miss Cartwright, who I hardly know, and an old friend of Mr. Grant's back from America. She said it had all been very enjoyable and she'd cooked a nice fish. But...I don't know. I had a feeling it hadn't been one of the very best evenings. I had a feeling Mrs. Grant hadn't enjoyed it as much as some. But there again, I'm only guessing. Nine years of sharing morning coffee and you get to understanding your employer without many words necessary. But who knows if my guess was right? She wasn't down long. She said sorry about the mess (there wasn't any mess to speak of) and was back upstairs inside of six minutes.

On the way home – I never enjoy that journey – I tried to think what might have gone amiss. Perhaps the fish. She doesn't like cooking. But it was no use trying to imagine. There are bits of other people's lives you can't begin to picture, no matter how well you know them. That's probably one of the good Lord's wisest blessings. Everyone should be granted some private life and thought. I mean, although Mrs. G. is the most understanding woman I've ever met, I wouldn't dream of telling her about all the hoo-ha with Barry, all those years ago, which still brings tears to my eyes. It's my belief there are things that should be kept in our hearts, not confided. I know that's a very unfashionable belief but I for one shall stick to it. I shall stick to it always. But I couldn't quite get Mrs. G's odd restlessness out of my mind. I felt concerned about her most of the afternoon, till Gary phoned, then of course I had to attend to matters of my own.

BERT

Daresay I can't expect to be completely normal for a few more days. Jet lag's taken its toll. So last night was seen through rather groggy eyes. I know I've got to get down to things this morning. Go and buy a car, for a start. Will I be able just to walk into a showroom and drive one away? Or will there be a lot of palaver about road tax and insurance? I don't know. I don't really feel up to anything much. Might just have a quiet morning. Cogitate. Make lists. Get my bearings.

Wonderful seeing Dan again last night. Made me realise how much I'd missed him. Our weekly jokes. His pertinent comments on whatever was happening in the world. And he didn't seem to have changed much in ten years. Bit craggier, I suppose – rather suits his always handsome face. That infectious laugh undiminished. His kindly eyes and sort of general concern for mankind still seemed to be intact. He exudes a maturing contentment, never lets on about the disappointment he's constantly grappling with – his plays. Man in a million, Dan. Bloody lucky, I am, to be his friend.

Number 18 hadn't changed, far as I could see, either. The rather shambolic, bright kitchen: the bits of furniture, so quietly polished that it's only when you study them closely you realise how good they are. No new pictures: all the familiar Pipers and Nicolsons and the lovely Gwen John Isabel picked up for a song years ago. All very comforting, the sameness. I came through the door wondering what to find. There was no shrill welcome, shouting and hugging: but a quiet sense of pleasure in my return that almost brought tears to the eyes. I felt looked after, loved.

Briefly I was re-acquainted with my goddaughter. Wouldn't have recognised her, of course. She's turned into a tall skinny sub-teenager, rather terrifying, I thought. Daresay she'll be very good looking when she's through the imprisoned teeth stage: Isabel's eyes and auburn hair. Miss far-too-pleased-with herself was my immediate impression. Gave her a couple of quid on an impulse, said go and buy yourself something. By the look on her face it should have been a tenner. Suppose I'm out of touch. But I wasn't drawn to her.

I do wish they hadn't asked Carlotta – not last night, anyhow, our getting together after so long. She always takes over so. Doesn't know when to pipe down, when to listen. She's too full of her own opinions. She's quite sure she knows what everybody is feeling – though if she is so sure, why does she keep asking? She hadn't been in the room for ten minutes when she came up to me, put her face intrusively close to mine, and said *how are you feeling, Bert, back in England at last?* What the hell did she expect me to say? Couldn't she imagine? I mumbled some answer about jet lag which plainly she found inadequate.

Perhaps I'm being unfair. Carlotta is definitely a life-giver, vivacious to a fault. There's something quite endearing about her energy, her enthusiasm, her sudden moments of attention, so acute that they make you feel almost dizzy. Then she pulls away from you, which is very slightly provocative. I have to say I was entertained by her interest in marketing strategy, and her appalling over-use of all the jargon. I teased her a bit about that. I'm not sure she was amused. But she managed to laugh. I quickly changed to the subject of my wretched house, and she offered to help. A picture flashed before my eyes: Carlotta in and out the place being serious about paint and curtains. Not sure I wanted any of that, but I said you're very kind.

Have to say the years have improved her looks. When I last saw her, at that awful dance when we went in for a bit of clumsy fumbling in the bushes, she was plump and unmemorable. Now, what, almost twenty years later, she's a smart London woman. Obviously fashion is of importance to her, and trends and future trends seem to interest her. We have almost nothing in common, so that hasn't changed. And yet I have to admit that she's bright, attractive, beguiling in a noisy way. But not my sort of woman. During the evening my *feelings* for her – wonder if she guessed? – could be charted as some highs, but mostly lows.

Dan produced two marvellous bottles of wine and Isabel, despite going on about being no cook, had done delicious things to a sea bass. I wasn't hungry but declared appreciation. I kept wishing it could have been just Dan and me.

After supper, given some subtle, almost invisible marital sign, Dan made the coffee and Isabel and I moved to the sofa. Carlotta stayed at the table with Dan, which was a relief. I wanted to hear about Isabel's masks – the whole business had not begun when I left England. Diffident as ever, she explained how it had all come about, and when she described how much she loved her work two pink spots appeared on her cheeks. Isabel! *Gil*bert, she calls me. No one else calls me that. Of course I've always thought how lucky is Dan – though it wasn't just through luck he acquired her. He was, is, the right man for her. And she's absolutely the most enchanting creature – unworldly, sweet natured, wise and calm as well as beautiful – even more so, now she's forty (I found this hard to believe) than she was when I first met her. The hour with her passed in moments. When I said I must go, catch up on sleep, she begged me to come round often, now I was back. There was a lot of catching up to be done. 'We must all carry on where we left off,' she said. 'We've missed you. We're so glad you're back'. 'So'm I, so'm I', I muttered, as I got up and I think, though I can't be sure, our eyes met in a kind of mutual pleasure at the thought of the future no longer parted by the Atlantic. It was then Carlotta jumped in with her offer of tickets to a concert tomorrow night. Isabel and Dan couldn't go: what could I do but accept? I hope not grudgingly. But it's the last thing I want to do, spend an evening in a concert hall with Carlotta. Then I suppose I'll have to take her out to dinner and drive her home –

rather, she'll have to drive me: I'm buggered if I'm going out this morning to buy a car.

CARLOTTA

I hadn't wanted to go, but in the end I rather enjoyed myself. I was pretty knackered, and due to the overrunning of the Rumbold AGM I didn't even have time to change into my Manolo's. Still, the Grants are not the sort of people who would condemn one for *that*. I managed to snatch up a box of mega-expensive chocolates, and was only about half an hour late.

Funny seeing Bert again after so long. Think I would still have recognised him. Rather fine steely eyes. I remember their boring down at me as we fumbled about in those far-off bushes. Then they snapped shut when he latched onto my mouth. I kept mine open. One of those odd moments when you're both experiencing it, and at the same time observing it from some distant place.

My feeling is that last night Bert was still a bit disoriented, being back, trying to set foot in a new life. He was sort of there and yet not there. When he looked at each one of us his glance seemed to snag, move away more slowly than he meant it to. It wasn't till I got him talking about strategy in marketing – a subject

he might well know more about than me, though I
wasn't going to admit that – that he began to lighten up,
show real interest. Our conversation rather left Isabel
and Dan out, so after a while I switched to asking
Bert what plans he had in London. He mentioned his
despair (he didn't use the word, but I sussed it) at having
to fix up his house. There, of course, I was able to jump
in quickly with an offer of help. A small house in Chelsea
wouldn't take me a minute to transform. I'd rather enjoy
the easy thought of knocking down walls and choosing
colours again, dashing round to a few of my old friends
in the business, to pick up the latest stuff, before I get
to the office. Bert accepted gratefully. Then as we were
leaving I issued this invitation to the concert at the
Wigmore Hall tomorrow night (Mike, the sod, having
called off). I could see Bert waiting to see if either Isabel
or Dan would accept. I'm pretty sure there was a look
of hope in his eye. When neither Is or D could come,
he accepted pretty swiftly. So it looks as if one way and
another he and I are going to be seeing a certain amount
of each other. Well, I daresay he could take up a bit of
the slack that the disappearing Mike has left. He'd be
an agreeable walker, an easy companion. Sex wouldn't
come into it, having got over all that in the teenage
bushes.

After supper, at the table with Dan, was the good bit. I could talk to him forever. I could see he was a bit agitated and presumed all was not well again with some new play. I know he doesn't like talking about his writing, but I pick up clues from Isabel. So I asked him some question about *where* he imagines his characters when he is writing – on stage, or in real life? Actually, a question that's often occurred to me. That had exactly the response I had expected. He visibly melted in the heat of my sympathy, just as Bert had when I brought up the subject of marketing strategy. Men are such innocents! You only have to fix them with an eye that conveys a hundred percent interest, and ask, and listen, and they think you're amazing – not that Dan thinks any such thing, sadly. Though I could see he was stirred by my question. As for Bert, I think in his present state he's positively a bit hostile. But what with looking after his house problems and plying him with invitations to supper with a selection of good looking, intelligent, available women, I don't doubt I'll win at least a modicum of his affection in the end.

Chapter Three

BERT

The wretched girl came half an hour before she said she would. I was only just out of the bath. Shirt still undone. Still, at least I'd managed to replenish the drinks table. I said help yourself, and went back upstairs.

When I came down I saw she'd spread a fan of small pieces of material on the sofa. There was a pile of charts, paint colours. She said she'd just snatched up a few things which she'd leave for me to study. I said I didn't want to study anything to do with decorating and suggested she should do what she liked so long as she chose nothing red. She took that quietly, then asked if she might cast an eye over the place so that she could get some idea of what needed doing. I said go ahead. While she was casting her eye, I sat back with a whisky and soda, and thought what the hell am I doing? Why is this woman here nosing round my house? Visualising things I can't visualise? There's a terrible superiority about people who can see how things could be. She came back very quickly, saying she'd got the whole picture, it would be easy. Even though there was some major work that obviously needed to be done, it shouldn't take too long, she said smugly. Smugly? Was I being unfair? Yes, the place would be overrun with builders for a while. 'I'll have to move out, then,' I said. She nodded.

She'd come in her Mercedes coupé which she explained away by saying it was three years old. Jolly nice car. Might consider one of those myself. We zoomed to Wigmore Street in complete silence, which was a relief. I wasn't feeling like talking about the budget for the house – which would have to come up sometime – or anything else. Have to admit Carlotta is efficient in all areas – plainly could have been a very efficient chauffeur. She didn't bore on about lack of parking places: simply found a meter and thrust in a lot of coins before I could so much as put a hand in my pocket. But my slight admiration was then stalled by her having got the concert completely wrong. It wasn't to be Brahms, but Mozart. Well, fine by me. I infinitely prefer Mozart. It just irritated me that she didn't… But I'm being unreasonable. Was wonderfully soothed by the piano concertos 21 and 24. Can never work out which is the more sublime.

Re-invigorated by the music, I suppose, I braced up. Being so out of touch with new London restaurants, I'd booked a table at the Savoy for safety. She said she hadn't been there for *years:* she wasn't sniffy about it, but her comment indicated she realised I'd chosen it in order not to have to consult with her where to go. And we had a perfectly agreeable dinner. First omelette Arnold Bennett I'd had for a decade. She burbled on about this and that, asked about my friendship with Dan. I don't think I provided the answers she was seeking. How had my feelings for him survived such a long absence? That sort of stuff. Not the sort of questioning to which I can eloquently, let alone keenly, respond. Then she got onto Isabel: what did I think of her? I avoided that one by asking her the same question. She hesitated, indicating profound cogitation. Then she said she admired Isabel hugely for being so utterly unlike anyone else: her detachment from the modern world, her hopelessness, in some respects, her brilliance as a wife and mother, her talent – though of course, she sneakily added, mask-making was probably more of a high class craft than an art – and her general sympathy and way of enhancing life. By the time she'd got through all that, she'd luckily forgotten that I hadn't answered her question.

She drove me back home. I didn't ask her in, though there was a moment's silence when I might have done. There was a sort of teenage pause when I could feel her waiting for my decision, which made up my mind pretty swiftly. She shrugged: held up her cheek to be kissed. A street light had turned her beige skin into the colour of a white grape. Her eyes were half shut, the lashes thick and long. Appealing. 'Oh Lord,' I thought. 'I know what she's after, but I'm not.' I duly kissed her on the cheek, cold as a grape, too. She smelt of my mother's loose face powder that was always spilling from a Pond's box on her dressing table, and said let's be in touch about the builders. Then I hurried out of the car and into the house.

Yes, there was the faintest inkling – I suppose it's been some months since Minneapolis Mary had enjoyed exhausting me for six weeks - and a man can only go for so long before his thoughts turn to all that. But I have always found availability a turn off. I could see quite clearly how easily I could fit into Carlotta's life. She vaguely mentioned at dinner how some rotter of a man had disappeared without so much as an explanation. Perhaps there was a gap that needed to be filled. I was not prepared to be the filler. But I would like to be a friend. Carlotta's kind of bossy liveliness is enjoyable from time to time.

I poured myself a whisky, took it up to bed. The bed is harder and less comfortable than I remembered. New bed will have to go on the list, I suppose. I don't much fancy asking Carlotta to choose me a decent one. She might come up with some terrible suggestion that we should try it out. A picture came to mind. I smiled.

Then I remembered Dan was off to Rome. I would keep to my word: ring Isabel and suggest some sort of meeting. It would be nice to see her again, alone.

CARLOTTA

I think Bert must have pressed me to more red wine than I'm used to – me, with the strongest head of any woman I know. What was in his mind? It was a Mouton something, terribly expensive and utterly delicious. But this morning it left a rim like a burning wire round my head, sizzling over my eyes. So I was late getting to the office: not a good start to a hellishly busy day.

I quite enjoyed the evening. Bert was easy to be with, not very exciting. Nice hands. Plainly he's a long way to go till he sorts himself out, but I'll be able to help there. His ghastly little house won't take a moment to do, especially as he doesn't want to interfere and money obviously isn't a problem. It means we'll see a certain amount of one another and perhaps he'll slot into being a useful sort of walker, a good spare man. I owe him dinner, now. I'll ask him next week. See how things go from there.

But I shall have to be careful. Driving him back I was acutely aware of an amorphous question between us. For my part, the answer was plain: no. He sat with his hands on his knees, keen as mustard, I reckoned. When we stopped I flashed a cheek at him, the conventionally polite thing to do. He paused for a moment, I daresay wondering why I hadn't turned to him with eager eyes and parted lips. Then he just brushed my cheek with his and got out of the car with the speed of one who is fighting to control various urges. I drove away very pleased. The last thing I wanted was more fumbling with Bert. He behaved perfectly. It means there'll be no complications in our future business of the house ... or friendship.

Odd, then, that driving home a sort of weakness fluttered through my whole body. I felt the chill that descends when something that might have been possible didn't happen.

I'll ring him, but not for two or three days.

GWEN

Thursdays are what I hate: Thursdays are the days I most dread. There's not the safety of going to the Grants for the morning. Gary knows I don't work Thursday mornings and then takes his chance, takes me unawares.

This morning I'd just slipped down to the shop to get the paper, looking all about me, as I always do, when I saw him across the street. I quickly looked away, but not before he'd smiled at me, knowing I'd seen him, and my heart started its beating. I gave up the idea of going on to Tesco's to get a few things for my lunch: Gary's sometimes trawled the aisles, a few yards behind me. It gives him a kick to see me in a state. Sometimes he goes ahead of me, lingers in the cereals or the washing powders, knowing I need to be there. He gives me one of his sickening smiles and goes off to buy himself a packet of Marlborough while I'm paying at the check-out, my fingers all of a fumble. Then he's waiting for me outside. Follows me home, about ten yards behind me. He doesn't try to get in, these days. But he just stands watching, knowing he's got me all shaken up.

I still can't work out how I came to my decision three years ago. But I suppose we all sometimes do things that seem right at the time, then live to regret them. He'd been following me for months. Never attacked me, just unnerved me. Then that day I thought maybe he's a troubled soul, maybe I can help. Maybe if I just talk to him, listen to what's on his mind. Maybe he'll realise I can't help and he'll stop bothering me. So when I got to the door – he was just a few feet behind me, closer than normal – instead of hurrying in without looking back, my usual way, I said would he like to step in for a cup of tea? It didn't occur to me I might be inviting an attack of some sort – me, an elderly woman with a scarf and my perm coming undone: not exactly your Nicole Kidman. You have to trust people. Instead of smiling, he just nodded and followed me in. He sat at the kitchen table, didn't seem interested in his surroundings, never mentioned my nice clock or anything. Then he began to talk, all about his childhood and that, all very sad. I felt so sorry for him. If he cleaned up a bit and had a haircut he could be quite a presentable man, despite missing a few teeth. I don't know why, but when he started talking I forgot all about the annoyance and frights he'd given me. 'I forgive you, Gary,' I said, when he got up to go. He apologised very gently. He said he hadn't meant to scare me, just found me a lovely woman who he hadn't dared approach. 'Let's be friends,' he said. I had the feeling I'd be his only friend in the world.

I don't know how it was, he only ever came in for a cup of tea, never brought me so much as a pot plant, but I fell in love with him (I'd never have guessed you could feel so dizzy at sixty). I never breathed a word of this, but I think he knew. Then one afternoon, I remember I'd just disinfected the sink, he came round and the way he looked at me I think he could read how I felt. So he had his way with me – there we were, at three o clock in the afternoon. We had several such afternoons in my small bed. I've never enjoyed the physical side of things very much, but he was gentle, got it all over nice and quick, none of that slow messing about that Bill used to called 'forward play'.

I remember Mrs. Grant, around that time – she notices everything – was concerned about a rash on my cheek. It was Gary's stubble agitated the skin, I knew, but of course I couldn't tell her. She gave me a lovely tube of cream: didn't do anything, though I pretended it did. Mrs. Grant would have been horrified to think I'd taken up with a man who followed me – an unknown man – a stalker, no less.

I may have been kidding myself about being in love with Gary, of course: it's nice to think you're in love with someone, though. In honesty our friendship was going nowhere, he only talked about football. It became quite boring. Then one day – one of the days it was tea only, bed had been petering out – he said goodbye Gwen in an odd, gruff sort of voice, and went. And never came back. I didn't see him anywhere in the streets or the local shops, for two years. Disappeared off the face of the earth. In my heart of hearts I was relieved.

But a couple of months ago, just as I was taking out a pack of peas from the chiller cabinet, I heard this voice behind me. 'Gwen,' he said. I froze cold as the peas in my hand. I turned. There he was, same stubble, teeth still missing. 'I'm not interested in any more cups of tea and afternoons in bed,' he said. 'That's not what I'm after. What turns me on is finding out what's going on, the *unlocking* of mystery, know what I mean?' The unlocking of mystery? Whatever was he talking about? I swear he had murder in his eyes. Before I had time to say a word, ask him what on earth he meant, he'd gone. My knees were shaking so much I had to lean on my trolley. God knows how I managed to get to the check-out. I felt sick, cold, terrified. What was he going to do to me? Why had I ever let him in?

I got home best as I could, tried to turn my mind to comforting things like doing out Mr. Grant's study next day. But I was really unnerved, and there was no one I could talk to, was there? I thought of going to the police, but they wouldn't be very sympathetic to that sort of domestic matter, would they? 'What, once your lover, now he follows you about? Never hit you?' They'd laugh in my face.

This afternoon I took a peep behind the curtain to see if the way was clear. I needed to go to the shops to get something for my supper. Blow me down, Gary was still there, other side of the road, looking about. So I stayed indoors, heart beating, hungry, cursing Thursdays. He stayed where he was, hands in his pockets, whistling. He was still there at tea time. I sat at the table, not up to anything, full of regrets. Over and over again, I thought, what a fool I'd been. What a fool I'd been to let him in in the first place.

ISABEL

Goodness knows why, but the thought of Gilbert and Carlotta at the Wigmore Hall occupied an unreasonable amount of my thoughts last night. At supper Dan and I speculated about how they were getting on. Dan thought she would irritate Gilbert so much he'd probably never go out with her again. I didn't know what to think.

And now Dan's on his way to Rome. High among the clouds. I know he thinks it's silly, but I always pray that the journey will be safe. I never feel totally easy till he's rung me to say he's landed. I hate it when he goes away, even for a few days.

All morning I worked hard on a bird mask – glorious blue black feathers spurting from a golden heart (a rather ingenious upside down heart, so that the point would touch the forehead and the two curves would fit each side of the nose). Then I went down to the telephone in Dan's study – unusually tidy, wastepaper basket empty. Gwen had obviously had a good go at it this morning. The room was full of sun. I sat for a few moments in the swivel chair, swinging from side to side, warm, comfortable, wondering if I should. I picked up Dan's favourite photograph in its tortoiseshell frame – the three of us, Sylvie must have been about five. Dan and I definitely looked younger, though indefinably so. I dialled Carlotta's number.

Naturally she was in a hurry. I could tell that from the way the mobile was snatched up, even before she spoke. 'You're ringing to find out how it went with Bert,' she said. 'Thought you would.' She laughed a short bark of laugh that wasn't wholly amused. 'I'm in a dash, but I can tell you, it went bloody well. Really good evening. And, no: if that's what you want to know. But could have, easily. He was raring to go. Much livelier than the night we had supper with you. Jet lag over, I'd say. Peaceful through the Brahms – Mozart – whoever, randy but gentlemanly at the Savoy ...'

'The Savoy?' I said.

'Randy at the Savoy, and absolutely all for it when I parked at his front door.'

There was a brief silence between us. 'But, hell, you know me,' she went on. 'I'm thirty-six, not the spontaneous woman I once was. I wasn't interested. I'd like Bert to be a friend, a useful spare man. I'm not up for any more complications, not after Andrew.'

'Quite,' I said. And then I added that I hadn't rung up to find out whether or not she had slept with Gilbert, but whether she had liked him and whether she had enjoyed the evening. 'Oh *that*,' she said airily. 'Of course I liked him. I only didn't like him decades ago when he jumped on me in the bushes. I nearly always like your friends, don't I? I like Bert, I enjoyed the evening, I shall enjoy doing up his house, OK? Now I've got to go. Speak to you soon.'

So there was no time to ask more, and anyhow to have done so would have been intolerable, even in a jokey way.

Now I sit in the empty kitchen, listening to the pounding of the grandfather clock, awaiting Dan's call to say he's safe in Rome.

DAN

Stifling, Rome. Carlo, my only friend here, is in Capri. 'Come and join us for the weekend,' he said, when I rang. What an idea. But Isabel would be miserable at the thought of my extending my trip. So would I. I wouldn't enjoy Capri without her. I rang her. Didn't mention the invitation I'd refused just in case, in the sweetness of her heart, she tried to persuade me to go. Then had dinner by myself in a *trattoria* down the road. God it's good being surrounded by Italians again. Their emphatic way of speaking somehow endows every moment of every ordinary day with a sense of importance, something I love. It would be exhausting in England, but it works here. Over my *tagliatelle alle vongole* I cast my mind back to my year in Florence after Oxford, a kind of post-university gap year, and the best of my youthful decisions. The hours – careless of time, money, the need to be productive in some way – just looking at pictures, at sculptures, at the Arno, at the cypress trees black against skies familiar from the small background space they were afforded by Botticelli *et al.* I remembered that Bert came out one weekend. The thing that got him were the hot *bombolini* in – what was it called, that tiny dark street? They zoomed down from an upstairs window in a chute. You'd pick them up with a paper napkin, heat still burning your fingers. The dense sugar stuck to a huge area of mouth and cheek. Fingers could only be de-stickied by washing them. Never had such doughnuts. And the Dante and Boccaccio. I'd wake at dawn and read before breakfast. A couplet, just as I dug into a nostalgic *zabaglione*, came to me unbidden:

Chi vuol esser lieto, sia -

di doman non c'e certezza...

For how many years had that lain buried in my sub-conscious? It's something I must pass on to Sylvie in a few years' time.

The telephone was ringing when I got back to my hotel room: the office to say I was wanted in Nairobi on Monday. Did I want to come home first, or fly straight from Rome? Isabel, as I knew she would, said of course... it would be mad to return home for half a day. Oh hell: we'd been looking forward to the weekend. I was going to suggest Bert came round again on Saturday evening, on his own. So we were disappointed, but resigned. *Di doman...* No certainty of to-morrow, indeed.

Now I sit gloomily in my air-conditioned room, dejected by the narrowness of the hotel desk. The shutters are half-shut. Sky, the colour of wild salmon, pushes in through the shut windows. I fling onto the floor the plastic hotel blotter and all the bumf about hotel services. They make a clatter. It jars my head, previously calm, now muddied by change of plans. I set up my word processor.

My last play, finished two months ago – a more lively piece, than usual, I'd thought – is whirling round that silent outer space in which theatre managements reside and never respond. So it's time to stop fretting about that one, and all the others, and to start something new. This time I feel more than usually enthusiastic – or do I always feel that? I've a suspicion I do. Anyhow, it's to be about rejection. Something I'm familiar with. Something we're all familiar with. Something we should all be taught to deal with as children in order to soften the inevitable blows as grown-ups. I've many thoughts on the subject. And I've a cracking good opening, I think. So here goes.

Act One. Scene One.

Now, late into the Roman night, I begin.

ISABEL

When Dan rang late last night to say he was going straight from Rome to Nairobi – sensible, of course – I expressed the normal sort of disappointment, and cheerfully agreed it wasn't that long till he'd be back on Wednesday evening. In truth I felt a profound sense of gloom which I could not understand. Dan is often away for anything up to ten days. I miss him no end but can cope perfectly well, enjoy spending more time than usual concentrating wholly on Sylvie. So why the shadowed feeling after his call? Perhaps it was simply because it was late and I was tired, and the envisaged weekend was shattered. I put out the light, very awake. Then the telephone rang again: Carlotta.

'Hope I'm not calling too late,' she said – she would have been scathing if I had said she was. 'But I just thought you'd like to know my plan about Bert. Would you?' I didn't know what she was talking about but said I'd listen. 'Although I've agreed to do up his house,' she said, 'I don't want him to think of me just as a decorator.'

'I understand,' I said, after a long pause.

'I'd like him to be a proper friend,' she went on. 'Now I've ditched Mike, there's – well, a bit of a gap. It'd be nice to think I could – you know – ask Bert round sometimes, take him to things, generally ease him into my life in the most innocent way. What do you think?'

I said I didn't know what to think. I seemed to remember she'd said a few weeks ago that Mike had walked out on her. Perhaps I got it wrong. Or perhaps she'd changed her story. I felt no inclination to sidetrack her onto that subject. I didn't really understand what she was on about, this plan about Bert. Where was it leading? Why did she have to ask my advice if all she was plotting was an innocent friendship? My long silence, tacked on to my lack of opinion, plainly disappointed her.

'So what I'm going to do,' she said, '*despite* having rushed about getting samples of goodness knows what, is to keep him *dangling* for a bit. I mean, I don't want to sound too keen. I don't want him to get the wrong idea. So I'm not going to ring him *at least* till the middle of next week. By then, he might have become impatient. He might want to get the house started. So he might even ring me. – Isabel?'

I said I thought she was being oddly devious about a plan which was directed at simple friendship. Why didn't she just ring him when she was ready to explain her decorating ideas? Besides, I heard myself saying – and it was a cruel thing to say – knowing Gilbert was not the sort of man who would ever be aware of the state of *dangling,* there wasn't much point in putting it into practice.

Carlotta gave a long sigh. 'I might have known it wasn't worth talking to someone who's been happily married for fifteen years,' she said. 'You've obviously forgotten what it's like, negotiating the single world. Nothing is simple, not even a quest for friendship.' She sounded forlorn. Before I could apologise for my lack of sympathy, she put down the telephone. We do sometimes end conversations like that – out of sorts, ruffled. Luckily the chill quickly melts. I'll ring her tomorrow, apologise.

I was awake much of the night, thinking of her, of Gilbert, of Dan. In my confused reflections only one thing was clear to me: I did not want Carlotta to become too close to Gilbert. I wanted him for *my* friend: mine and Dan's. Horribly selfish, that: Carlotta needs him far more than I do. For all her toughness in the business world, she's extraordinarily insecure when it comes to men. Most of her disasters have been because, too eager to gain their love, she's gone at them too fast – offered everything. She never believes me when I say men don't want everything: they only want selected parts. I hope her foolish plan won't lead to another disaster. Perhaps, devious woman that I am too, I had better warn Gilbert. Tell him, simply, if he doesn't want to be engulfed, he should keep his distance.

GWEN

This morning, I don't know why, I went down much earlier than usual to the post box. Usually all I get is bills and junk mail. But there was a real letter among them in a grubby envelope. Not what I'd call 'educated' writing.

I sat down at the kitchen table – the place where I've received so much bad news over the years, and very little good – and opened it. Just a couple of lines, it was. *I know your sort* it said. *I know what you're playing at Gwen. There are forces out there who know more than you think. You should take care. Yours, Gary.*

I read it over several times. Chilled, I was. If it had been from anyone else I would have thought that it was just some crank, and probably thrown it away without another thought. But from Gary... What was he on about? Was it a threat? Was he saying he knew something about me that he could use to hurt me? Was there any such thing? I tried to think. I've made a lot of bad mistakes in my life, but as far as I know there's nothing wicked I've done, nothing I'm ashamed of. All the thinking put my head in a whirl. I saw my hands were shaking. I didn't fancy my cup of tea though I took a sip or two to get down a couple of aspirin. Perhaps I should speak to Gary next time I see him lurking. Trouble is, he's always just out of hearing: I can't shout across the street, and if I approached him he'd be off quick as anything. It's horrible of him. I've got my life up together, straightened it out, I'm as happy as anyone could be, given all the circumstances: I mean Ernie's not a bad son and, though Jan's a rotten daughter, I still love her, she's still mine... And now this dreadful man comes and unsettles everything. Haunts me, threatens me, takes away the feeling of safety.

At one point during the morning I found myself so upset I decided to ring Mrs. Grant. But then I quickly went against that idea. I've never talked to Mrs. G about anything much in my life, for all our closeness. Besides, it would be too long to explain, the background. She'd be horrified by my story of having taken up with Gary in the first place. No: I couldn't bother her with all that, not on a Saturday morning, busy with taking Sylvie swimming and so on. Mr. Grant back from abroad, Mrs. G getting muffins out of the freezer and the sun coming in through the windows. I can see it all. Their house is always in my mind. It's not a place I want to bother with my problems.

BERT

Still accosted, I am, by an unusual restlessness. Perhaps in middle age one takes longer to re-adjust. It will all be better when I've decided what to do. Next week I'll sit down and seriously consider the offers that are coming in. How do these companies suddenly know I'm on the market, back in London? All very odd.

It occurs to me Carlotta, who assured me she'd be in touch immediately about her decorating plans, hasn't rung. Tremendous relief, actually. I'm not up to her barrage of suggestions just yet. So I'll carry on with the rackety old fridge and oven for a while: only ring her when things actually collapse.

What I feel like is a peaceful evening with Isabel. Which reminds me, Dan is in Rome. I said I'd ring her. If I don't do it now, Dan'll be back. I'll make my way to the Garrick for lunch, then go hunting for a car. It'd be fun to roll up to number 18 in a Lamborghini, see Isabel's face. I know she thinks Dan's taste in cars is fairly unadventurous. What would she think about mine? I'm prepared to be berated.

SYLVIE

I don't like it when Papa isn't here on Saturday morning. He usually drives me to pick up Elli, then drops us at the pool. At breakfast this morning Mama said Bert had rung and was coming round this evening. Again? I said. I mean I like Bert, but I wanted a nice evening with Mama playing games and stuff. But she was extra kind – to make up for having to share her, perhaps. She let me have a fantastic new yummy ice-cream for lunch, and said Bert – why does she always call him *Gil*bert? – might be coming in some swanky new car, and if he did we'd all go for a ride in it. So? – I mean, that'd be cool. But no car would be as good as Papa's BMW. Then she said, perhaps we should take our chance and go and get those new *trainers* (she didn't even purse her mouth) you've been going on about. Cool, I said. Thanks. Whatever's got into her? She walked about humming, and chopped stuff for salad into very small bits. Sometimes she's so weird.

Chapter Four

ISABEL

I heard an unusually melodious hooting of a horn outside. I looked out of the window. Parked outside the house was a great bird of a car, vast and silver. If it had raised invisible wings and risen into the air I wouldn't have been surprised. It carried on with its cooing noise, like a plaintive dove – surely no warning to errant traffic. I laughed. There was a moment's silence, then Gilbert got out of the car. From his puffed up gait and jaunty swagger I could see he was tremendously pleased with himself.

He explained he had only just managed to get the beast in time – and, what's more, he hadn't paid for it. No: it had been *lent* to him for the weekend to try out. He'd already been to Windsor and back and then had had a very entertaining time trying to get to grips with the inbuilt satnav. 'What made them trust you?' I asked. Gilbert just shrugged, suggested it was his honest look … Oh, *and* he had left a deposit large enough to fill the boot with Chateau Mouton Rothschild 84 …

He couldn't wait for Sylvie and me to test it. The inside was a cave of bleached leather. Sylvie climbed into the back. Having been thoroughly snooty about the whole idea of this ride when I put it to her earlier, she was now clearly in some awe, but trying to hide her perfidious reaction. Her loyalty to Dan's BMW is total.

I swung into the front seat. Gilbert shut the door from the outside. It made that soft clunk that's the nature of really expensive car doors, the re-assuring noise of leather slippers on stairs. Then we were off – Hyde Park, Constitution Hill, St. James's Street, Regent Street and back down the Marylebone Road to Shepherd's Bush. Wonderful: I suddenly understood Dan's thing about cars, though his BMW had never actually inspired me with this feeling. Gilbert said as soon as it became his – and there was no question of it being returned – he would take us for a spin on some motorway very early one morning so that we could get an idea of its speed – 'Might even let Dan have a go at the wheel,' he added. When we got home he asked Sylvie her opinion. 'Cool,' she answered, '… but nothing compared to ours.' She's so predictable.

She didn't want to eat with us. I gave her a tray of supper to take up to the television. When I went to say goodnight to her later, her lights were turned out and she was asleep, or pretending to be. Odd. Her moods are constantly fluctuating. Her age, I suppose. But Gilbert was probably relieved she didn't join us for supper. He's not brilliant at conversation with children.

He was the one to bring up the subject of Carlotta. She hadn't rung, he said, and was somewhat relieved. So, I thought, she was putting her plan into action. And my prediction was right: Gilbert had absolutely no idea that in the silence she saw him as *dangling*. 'What do you make of her,' I asked, 'after all these years since your childhood?' I pillowed this question very carefully. *What do you make of?* is somehow less crude than the straightforward *what do you think?* Less blunt, less challenging. Usually produces a more considered reply.

Bert shrugged, gave a flick of a smile that indicated he wasn't much interested in the subject of Carlotta, but he'd do his best before we moved on to more compelling matters. At least that was my initial interpretation. A second later it occurred to me he had become smitten by Carlotta in the two evenings they had been together, and I was the last person to whom he had any wish to confide his feelings. A blade of ice ran down my spine.

'Well, of course, she's changed out of all recognition – hardly surprising. Better looking. Much better looking. Lively, noisy, doesn't know when to keep quiet. But plainly a good friend.' He could quite see my fondness for her, he said. Though what exactly it was that drew us to each other, he had still to decipher.

He said all that so easily, so honestly, it was hard not to believe he spoke anything but the truth. A silence fell between us. I finished my glass of wine, loathe to ask more questions. Then he said, very quietly: 'but she's not my type. So please, you and Dan – please don't go trying to match-make. It wouldn't work ... for either of us,' he added. 'I'm sure she's not got designs on me. I'm not nearly exciting enough. I'm not cutting edge – can a man be cutting edge?' We both smiled, laughed, and the almost indecipherable moment of awkwardness was dispelled. 'I don't think we had any ideas of match-making,' I said with what was meant to be a kind of mock affront. 'Obviously it wouldn't work. Much though I love Carlotta, she's something of a control freak. You'd be consumed. She'd exhaust you. She'd...'

'Yes, yes, I know,' he said. And re-filled my glass.

There was a long silence between us. My head spun with alternatives. Where to go from here, I wondered? I'd become too heated about Carlotta. Too disloyal.

Had he noticed? The subject of her should definitely be closed, or he might say something I had no desire to hear. Eventually I asked whether he would like fruit, cheese, anything? 'What I'd like,' he said, 'is to see your work.'

To see my work? I heard my own gasp. 'But nobody ever wants to see masks in progress,' I said, 'there's nothing much to see.'

'Please,' he said. 'I'd like to see the place where you spend your days.'

'Mornings only,' I corrected.

I could not remember anyone else ever following me up the stairs eager to see my studio, my work. It was both a pleasing and an alarming prospect. Very few people are interested in someone else's work if it's not in their own field. I understand that. There's something rather alien about being a curious spectator, asking questions, knowing the answers are unlikely entirely to clarify. I never ask Carlotta about the nature of her work: in truth it doesn't interest me. She certainly doesn't ask about mine, though on occasions, when she's seen a mask downstairs waiting to be delivered, she comes up with extravagant praise that means nothing to me. I never ask Dan more than functional questions about his business because that holds little interest for me, either.

I'd like to enquire about his writing, but know better than to do so. Writers, artists, musicians, shouldn't be interrogated. Their work is their answer. I believe that firmly. I suppose it's all right to question someone like me, a simple craftsman, on how we do it: 'I pick up a minuscule bead with a pair of tweezers, dab it in a speck of glue.' To questions about technique I've given such answers, and I don't mind, because I know I will never be asked what it's all about to me. I doubt anyone would ever guess the maker of masks finds herself *marinating* her masks with hopes and fears – unease at times, and vast happiness at others. I knew that Bert would never ask questions about that side of things, so I felt quite safe. But puzzled. And a little… Had I drunk a glass more than usual? Why was my heart so beating?

I opened the door. Went to my work table, switched on the shaded light. There were many other lights I could have put on – ready for the rare occasions I can get away to work in the evening – but I did not want to. I think I must have wanted Bert to be a little puzzled by what he saw … mystified. I think I wanted him to sense, just very faintly, what I try to do.

I turned and saw him standing in the doorway. His arms hung at his sides. His fists were clenched. Even in the dim light I could see his knuckles, two small arcs of white pebbles. I didn't look at his face – not wanting, just yet, to see his reaction. But I saw him swallow, and take a cautious step into the room as if he was treading water.

BERT

I fell in love with Isabel at that moment.

That moment when she switched on the light and turned to me, not meeting my eye, and stood by her table slightly quivering as if touched by the merest breeze. In the imprecise light I could see nothing clearly, but was aware of swarms of empty faces, their hollow eyes upon me. Many of them sprouted plumes and ribbons and clumps of frothing materials sparkling with crystals no bigger than a wren's eye, and beads. I was aware of bright, glorious colours struggling against the dimness of the room. I felt a sense of curious life, there, a kind of soaring, as in music.

'This is all it is,' Isabel said at last. God knows how long we had stood in petrified silence. It may only have been a second or two. 'There's nothing much to see,' she added.

That was not true. She knew it was not true, but it didn't matter. I nodded, not knowing what to say.

I hadn't expected any of this, of course. In the single evening spent with Isabel, Dan and Carlotta, I'd felt a kind of ease with her, a joy in her presence and her laughter. But perhaps that was just in comparison with Carlotta, for whom I felt nothing but vague gratitude for her offers of help. This evening, in the car, Isabel's delight had stirred me a little further. But I swear the drive was no more than a confirmation of my liking. Had I thought there was any danger of being assailed by more potent feelings for my best friend's wife, I would never have agreed to spend this evening alone with her. And indeed at supper all was normal. Quiet, enjoyable. She talked a lot about Dan. She loves him. They're as happily married as any couple can hope to be – I sensed that. We talked about the changes I'd been finding in London since I left. She gave me news of mutual friends.

It was when conversation turned to Carlotta I felt a sense of puzzlement. Isabel's feelings for her friend are ambivalent. While plainly she loves and admires her, she also disapproves of her values, her bossy control, her arrogance. Was there, I wondered, also a tinge of jealousy in the mix? Surely not: Isabel would hate Carlotta's life. She loves her own. What on earth was there to be jealous of?

Clearly Isabel was warning me off any serious involvement with Carlotta. I assured her that wasn't necessary – last thing on my mind. But I wanted very much to stop talking about Carlotta. She holds little interest for me. I wanted to know more about Isabel, and here was my chance. So to kill two birds with one stone, as it were, I asked to see her studio, her work.

I'll never forget the look of total horror on her face when I asked this question. It was hard to know why her reaction was so extreme, and for a moment I felt like the most crass of intruders. Then she gave me a half smile, and with relief I realised I'd done no wrong. Merely surprised her.

All the way up the stairs – three floors, following a little behind her long skirt of swaying blue silk – I suspected nothing. I can assure you, Officer, no such thought was on my mind. I was absolutely innocent. Then, the opening of that door to her secret place. The turning on of the light. The apotheosis.

'All about hiding,' I said … when eventually I could speak.

'I suppose so,' Isabel answered – so dully, I thought, perhaps she didn't agree and had no desire to argue such a matter.

'I imagine you've been through all the metaphorical thoughts about masks,' I went on uncertainly. I added a slight laugh to convey that I was being pretentious on purpose.

'Oh yes,' she answered with a shrug. Then: 'do you like them?'

'*Like* is hardly the word I'd use,' I replied. 'I can't see them very well. I'm bewildered by what I *can* see.'

'Good.'

'They're beautiful.'

'I'm not going to put on any more lights.'

'No.'

I moved closer to a shelf where three feathered masks were placed, and was suddenly gripped by the illusion that they were preening themselves with invisible beaks. I turned to Isabel so fast that for a second all the masks in the room seemed to stir. I would not have been surprised if with one accord they had spread their wings and flown out of the open window. I could understand why some people suffer from phobias about masks. This was some kind of madness more disturbing than jet lag.

Isabel suggested we return downstairs and open another bottle of wine. Her voice was firm now. I could see she had no intention of explaining anything. I could also see she had no idea of what was happening to me. She hurried from the room. I quickly followed her, shutting the studio door behind me. Relieved to be leaving. Going down stairs I waited for normality to return, the moment of loving Isabel to be gone. But that did not happen. The thick stair carpet silenced our descent: the clatter of our footsteps on the bare boards of the kitchen floor were then cruel in their noise. Somehow I had lost a skin. I was raw, exposed, horrified by my state.

'I know Dan would want us to choose something good,' Isabel was saying. But she knew nothing of wine. Why didn't I come with her and make the decision?

Once again I followed her. This time down steep steps to the cellar, a place on which Dan had spent a great deal of money to make it fit to accommodate his marvellous collection of wine. But for all the expensive air vents, there was a cellar smell – a sweet mustiness, the amorphous scent that's a combination of old glass bottles, cobwebs, and labels fixed with ancient glue. Unlike most cellars, it was not lighted by crude neon strips but by copious down-lights scattered across the ceiling. Isabel turned on just two of them. Did she intend to leave so much shadow between the discs of light? I don't know… Probably not: probably my fevered imagining. She put out a hand to lead me to a particular shelf. I took it, gripping her fingers. When she paused, saying

'I think this is it, Gilbert…,' I snatched her to me. Her body bent, unresisting. With my free hand I touched her hair, to brush away a cobweb. To what? In truth, there was a trace of a cobweb, but it was also to kiss her. I felt her breath in my face for no more than a second. I saw – I think I saw – her lips were parted. Never in my life have I wanted a woman more. I was about to give in to my terrifying desire, clutch her to me with all the love that had gathered over the years and had had nowhere to go, when she screamed.

ISABEL

I knew what he wanted, what I wanted. In one of those appalled seconds in which huge quantities of life and reason are concentrated down into a pinprick of realisation, I screamed. Not out of fear. But to stop him. The sound was flattened by the low ceiling, but piercing. With no forethought, I slapped him hard on the face. He drew back, tongues of red from my fingers leaping up his cheek.

I will never forget his face. It had broken up, fallen into more fragments than I could count: astonishment, regret, fear – was it fear? Anger? I couldn't read them all before the pieces closed back together making his face whole again. He didn't put a hand to his cheek, as do people in films when they have been hit (why did such a thought come to me at such a moment?). He put a hand on my arm. This time I didn't back away. I kept my voice very low.

'I love Dan,' I said. 'Never, in a million years would I …'

'Isabel,' he said, 'I was trying to brush away a cobweb from your hair. Not for anything in the world… would I, either. Look.'

He took something from my hair, showed me on his fingers the shattered part of a small cobweb. It glittered like the trail left by a snail, then was gone as he rubbed his fingers together.

He had been speaking the truth, then. A kind of truth. Shame at my behaviour suffused me: I knew my cheeks were scarlet. I felt idiotic, foolish. How could I have supposed…? How could I have thought his intentions were different? Could I have imagined my own nefarious feelings that had flared up just a moment ago? Even now, I longed for him to hold me while we both apologised for the silly misunderstanding.

I said I was sorry. He said he was, too. Then he took a bottle from the shelf and we went back upstairs. We drank half of the wine, talked easily of Dan and Sylvie and his desire to be settled – 'whatever that means,' he said – very soon. Between us loomed a semi-truth, and a deeper truth that was unacceptable, inadmissible – a truth I couldn't help believing, for all his declaration of innocence.

It was past one when Gilbert left. When I opened the front door there was a blast of surprisingly cold air, and he hurried down the steps. I was denied a normal kiss on the cheek. Did he fear to touch me again? He said nothing about a future meeting. He went off in his ostentatious car with a squeal of tyres, like a teenage joy-rider. I scarcely slept for the rest of the night, re-living the moment of confusion in the cellar, wrestling with the truth – his and mine.

GWEN

Gary's note must really have got to me, for I knew I couldn't sleep if I went to bed. I watched rubbish on the telly, tried to take my mind off it. It was very hot in the flat. I felt stifled. I was afraid. I thought a breath of air might calm me down.

As I put on my jacket I knew I was being foolish. Women should not walk alone in London late at night. Even elderly women in headscarves are vulnerable, especially somewhere like Shepherd's Bush. But I couldn't stop myself.

Where should I go?

I didn't know when I shut the door behind me – I didn't think … I couldn't think – but I found myself on my normal route to the Grants. My feet took me. It was a kind of instinct. And once I was on my way I felt happier. I'd just take a look at the house, all in darkness. Imagining its rooms, which I'd be safely in, in a few hours time, would be comforting, I thought.

I didn't let myself look for Gary in corners and shadows. He'd never think I'd be out on the streets so late. I just hurried along, head down. There were few people about. No one seemed to notice me. I hardly looked the kind to attract a mugger – didn't even have my bag. A police car zipped by, siren screaming and lights flashing. That gave me confidence. I thought if something's happened and police are about, well, there's protection for the likes of me walking alone.

I reached the Grants' street in my usual time, just under twenty minutes. There were hardly any lighted windows in the houses. Then, I must have been ten yards or so from number 18, when I saw all the downstairs lights were on and the curtains weren't drawn. I stopped.

Very unusual, I thought. When Mr. Grant is away Mrs. G likes to go to bed very early.

I stayed standing by the gate of a house across the road. A lot of greenery tumbled over the high fence. I stood in its shadow, wondering. Then I saw the front door open and a gentleman – a tall man – came out. He seemed to be in a hurry. Ran down the steps and into a great swanky silver-coloured car, and drove away with a squeal. Then I looked back at the front door and saw Mrs. G standing there. Her arms were folded under her chest as if she was feeling the cold – well, there was a cool night breeze even though it had been warm all day. She just stood there, looking after the car, frozen like a picture. I got the impression she was puzzled, even upset. The thought struck me that I should go over and say something. But what should I say? She'd be amazed I was out alone so late at night, and whatever concerned her was not my business. Just as my problems were not her business, and it was best to keep going as we always did, very friendly but knowing the dividing line. So when she turned and went back into the house, I left to walk home. All the time the picture of Mrs. G standing there was bright in my mind and I didn't think about Gary any more, or the danger of being on the street so late. Eventually, I slept.

CARLOTTA

What's going on? Bert hasn't rung. Really annoying. I don't quite know why I feel so annoyed, but I do. I've got masses of stuff to show him. But I'm going to hold out a bit longer. Then I shall just *go round,* unannounced. I mean, my patience is running out. Whose wouldn't? I'll wear that new black thing that shows off my cleavage. I'll sit next to him on the sofa going through samples, and he won't be able to contain himself. Meantime, Isabel might know something.

I rang her on Monday morning. There are always a few moments just after eight thirty when I know she's free, after Dan and Sylvie have left and she hasn't yet gone up to her studio. Absolutely dementing, the way she still refuses to have a telephone there. She was out. Gwen said Mr. Grant was still abroad so 'Mrs G,' as she calls her, was taking Sylvie to school.

Hell. I do hate the whole thing of having to make so many calls to get someone. I missed her mid-morning – she hardly took a coffee break this morning according to Gwen – but managed to get her at lunch time. She was in one of her non-communicative moods, I could tell. She said Dan had had to go on to Africa and wasn't coming home till tomorrow evening. She'd been alone all weekend, 'catching up' – whatever that means. I said 'you should have rung me. Or asked Bert round to keep you company.' She said 'As a matter of fact he came to supper on Sunday night.'

He went to supper with her on Sunday night. Did he now?

I know Isabel. I don't think she flirts in a calculated way, I really don't. But I know the way she can look at men who interest her. A sort of gentle pressure of attention comes from her eyes that men can't resist. Then there's her walk. I tease her about it. She says it's all because of deportment lessons which were mandatory in her school. Whatever: she *slinks,* in a much more subtle way than Marilyn Monroe, and those long soft skirts she will insist on wearing lap round her in a way that could drive a man to distraction. Maybe I'm exaggerating. I know she sends out a red light signal that tells everyone she loves Dan, and Dan only, and perhaps her beguiling ways are unconscious (actually, they couldn't be, could they?), so there's no point in men approaching her because they'll be severely rebuffed. But I've seen men dream. I've seen them bewitched by her natural allure – which most of us women have to try to create … and that's no substitute for the real thing.

'What's he up to?' I asked, flat as anything, sounding as uninterested as you can get.

She said she didn't know. He hadn't made up his mind what to do, or been to see any of the people who were offering him jobs. Then she asked how I was getting on with doing up his house? I told her that I was engaged in the plan we'd talked about and, although I was ready to go, I hadn't rung him. Her question provided a good reason to ask if he'd mentioned my name – wondering why I hadn't come round with pots of paint, perhaps?

There was a fractional pause. Somehow a spark of just discernible friction tightened the line. Then she said no, my name hadn't been mentioned. 'It was a pretty uneventful evening,' she added, 'why?' Did she suppose I might think they'd been up to something? I laughed – tried to laugh, not sure how convincing it was. 'He's a pretty uneventful man,' I said, and changed the subject to Dan's trip to Africa.

The way she said it, un-ev-ent-ful, breaking up the syllables, made me see red. I don't know why. But when I put down the telephone I raged round my office re-arranging chairs and shuffling through files. I couldn't bear to think of her, innocent Isabel, my friend, helping Bert to one of her cloudy puddings and talking away about everything under the sun. Eventually I calmed down, told myself I was being ridiculous. I put my mind to the afternoon meeting. But I couldn't get the picture of them out of my head. I know nothing would ever happen between them. Dan is Bert's oldest friend and a man of high principle. Isabel is the last person on earth ever even to consider infidelity. So why am I so disturbed by the thought of their innocent evening? I suppose, pathetically, it's because it's something I can never have – an evening at home alone with an agreeable – attractive – man, protected by the state of marriage. Isabel's ease of acquiring what she wants has always annoyed me, unreasonably, because I'm sure that both wanting and then getting don't enter her head. So I'm being a cow about Isabel and despise myself for it.

Driving home, I wondered if Bert had got his version of my car by now. No harm in ringing up and asking, I thought. Perhaps it was silly to keep him dangling any longer if he doesn't realise he's being dangled. I thought of several ways in which I could spur him to action, make him need me as a friend. That's all I'm after, really … isn't it? Acknowledgement. I'm not kidding myself that love would ever be involved.

So: onto the case, Carlotta. Action.

And if none of the plans work, as a last resort I could always… But no. For the time being I shan't let myself think of that.

SYLVIE

I woke up very early, drew back the curtains. I crept to the chest of drawers, opened the sock drawer. After a bit of shuffling about I found the lipstick. I took it back to bed.

I hadn't even tried it on. Not even on the back of my hand. It was a lovely bright red, like Carlotta wears. Mama would think it was awful. Elli's got masses of lipsticks hidden in her drawers. She says they're the easiest things to get, though you want to keep changing the hiding places. She's the one who made me do it.

She was right, it was easy. There were lots of people up and down the aisles but no shop people anywhere near, just at the paying tills. I picked up lots of different lipsticks, opened them, and put them back. Then I quickly took this one, slipped it into my pocket and didn't open it till I got home and locked myself in the bathroom. But the way I'm different from Elli is she says it's all good fun and not serious stealing. But I haven't found it good fun at all. In fact I've cried two nights running, now, thinking what an awful, stupid thing to have done. Knowing what Mama and Papa would think of me if they knew. And having no idea how to get it back – I got it from a Boots when I went to tea with Elli, and her mother was in the shop next door buying shoes or something. She was ages and Elli said here was our chance.

Anyhow, now I've decided on a plan. I'm going to tell Mama, and put it back, and not tell Elli what I've done. She'd just think me a feeble wimp. So I'm going to try to do that this morning on the way to school – good thing it's Mama taking me. Papa never has time to stop anywhere.

Two hours still to breakfast. I feel all shivery and cold.

ISABEL

I woke very early, having only slept a couple of hours, and lay in the dark. I thought first of Dan, in some imagined hotel bed in Nairobi. Then of Sylvie, next door, all askew in her bed, duvet half on the floor, innocent, innocent.

Absence is a secret presence. I've so often thought that. When Dan's away I feel he's only half away. His voice is constantly in my mind. His belongings, in the same place as when he's there, re-assure. I only have to open the cupboard where his clothes hang, and I can smell the smell that's on his skin: a mixture of thyme and good material, the paper of old books – how can one define smell? If I had to open a hundred men's cupboards, blindfold, I'd know which one was Dan's.

So with all the re-assurance of his coming back soon, and the presence of his things, the way I miss him causes no heartache. I just miss him in the same way that I miss shade on a hot day, knowing its absence isn't going to be for long. It's more of a fact than a feeling.

It was no different, this time, until last night. Since the weird episode in the cellar – and the strange, ungrounded look on Gilbert's face in the studio – I've longed for Dan's return in a wild, unnerving way. He will never know about this, just as he will have no idea of the re-assurance that'll return with his presence. Just two days to get through. And Gilbert – will he ring? Should I ring him, so that he knows I believe him and want everything to go on as usual?

I got up soon after six, lightheaded from lack of sleep. I knew it was going to be a lost day. I would make a stab at finishing the gold lace mask that was to be delivered by the end of the week, but I knew that whatever I did wouldn't be much good, and I should have to do it again on a more ordinary day.

I stood in the kitchen – our large, friendly kitchen which is just as it was when we painted the woodwork ourselves fifteen years ago – looking around at the miscellany that goes to make up the familiar pattern in my mind's eye that travels with me everywhere. I boiled the kettle for coffee, and put the two wine glasses, still on the table, into the machine. Then, surprising myself, I hid both empty bottles of wine behind a pile of boxes in the cupboard under the stairs. I didn't want Gwen to think that I'd been drinking with Gilbert – I'd mentioned he was coming round to supper – however innocent that was. In our guilt, planned innocence is blighted.

Sylvie came down a little late, her usual cheerful morning face disgruntled. She ate her cornflakes in silence, then said she had something to tell me. She pulled a lipstick from her pocket and said that 'somehow' she had taken it when looking at a rack of lipsticks with Elli, and she wanted to get it back. 'Somehow' it had found its way into her pocket. She had opened it. She didn't like the colour. Of course she hadn't tried it. What should she do?

Then she put her head in her hands and I could see tears running down her wrists, though she remained silent.

I wished I had not felt so rough. I could have dealt with Sylvie's dilemma better. I simply said if she hurried up I would drive her to the chemist on the way to school and wait while she went in, handed it back, and apologised. She lifted her head from her hands and looked horrified. If she admitted what she'd done, she said, they'd call the police and she'd go to prison. I shrugged, but said I doubted it.

On the way to school I briefly expressed how appalled I was that she should steal, or even think of stealing. She cried again and said over and over again how sorry she was, and explained if she hadn't taken the lipstick Elli would have thought her a wimp and probably not been her friend any more. I parked in front of the chemist and dried her cheeks with my handkerchief, wished her luck, and said I trusted she'd do what I said.

She ran off, was back in so short a time I doubted she had kept her word, but decided not to ask. She thanked me many times and begged me not to tell Dan. I said I wouldn't.

At the school gate she hugged me and said I was the best mother in the world, which she says whenever I'm able to rescue her from scrapes. I said: Never again. She said: Promise. Then she ran off exuberant with relief, and I drove off into the usual traffic jam, wondering.

DAN

The plane was two hours late, the taxi took forever from the airport. We'd planned to have lunch then I'd have a couple of hours sleep. All plans smashed.

I rang Isabel from the airport but she was in the studio. Sometimes I wish she'd have a telephone up there, but nothing can persuade her. Luckily Gwen was still there. I left a message saying I didn't know how long it would take me to get home, and how sorry I was. In the stifling taxi, air soured with a previous passenger's over-sweet scent, impatience rattled me. I'm always impatient to get home, but the feeling of odd urgency made my fingers sonata on jigging knees.

I flung far too much money at the taxi driver and ran up the steps, calculating it would be quicker to use my door key than to ring the bell and get Isabel down from the studio. I had a sort of half hope she might be in the kitchen, and would run to the door.

The hall was silent, tidy, as it always is when Gwen leaves. There was sun on the polished floorboards, a faint smell of herbs and roses: everything as always. I dumped my luggage and ran up the stairs. Hardly ever do I visit Isabel's studio. But in my hurry to see her I couldn't wait for her to hear my shout and come down.

I flung open the door and saw her – in a freeze-frame that lasted less than a second – sitting at her work table, head bent over a handful of pale ribbons, sun gilding a lock of hair that fell over her face – before she saw me. Then she looked up, threw the stuff aside, rose and opened her arms. As she moved towards me I saw astonishment in her eyes, or perhaps it was puzzlement. Again, the impression cut into me only for a second. Then she was laughing, we were clutching each other, our voices chiming as we declared our happiness at my being back, being home.

'I imagine you hardly slept on the plane,' she said at last.

'Hardly,' I agreed.

We drew apart and I looked round the studio, a room I hardly know. It seemed to me that there were many more finished masks than when I had last been here. There was a shelf crowded with beautiful, multi-coloured things, their cut-out eyes smiling, it seemed. What an extraordinarily nice place in which to work, I thought vaguely. How agreeable she's made it. No wonder she's keen to come up here as early as possible every morning.

'Something to eat? Tea?'

I shook my head.

'You look exhausted,' she said. 'Why don't you sleep for a couple of hours, before Sylvie gets home? She's at Elli's house.'

Again I shook my head. I was curiously awake, I said. Was there any news? Anything been happening?

Those eyes, the tawny pupils striped with green – I know every stripe so well – locked with mine.

'Absolutely nothing,' she said. Her smile petered out and she suggested we went downstairs.

We didn't reach the kitchen. Our bedroom door was open. I was curious to see it. It's not often one goes into a bedroom mid-afternoon: the rumple of getting up has been straightened out, the night time lights and drawn curtains are a distant world. In the mid-afternoon the bedroom is a strange place, sun slanting across the white bedcover – how sun seems to rampage through our house, it's everywhere on a day of early summer like this.

'Just take off my shoes,' I said, sitting on the bed. Even through my socks I could feel the heat of the rug beneath my feet. Isabel stood looking at me, arms folded, anticipatory laughter – I think it was – now in her eyes. Then she sat beside me. In a moment we both toppled backwards, the bed warm beneath us as a patch of southern sea. We did not bother to draw the curtains, or shut the door, but spent an hour or so in our strange, sun-filled bedroom.

When we got up to straighten the bed and ourselves for Sylvie's homecoming, Isabel said 'Thank God you're home,' and ran both hands through her hair, so that its lights scattered like fireflies.

SYLVIE

Mama and Papa were in the kitchen having tea when I got home. I couldn't think why Papa wasn't any browner than when he went away. I mean, there's a lot of sun in Nairobi. He said he didn't have time to go out in it.

He hugged me and gave me a giraffe carved out of wood and said he'd been too busy for serious shopping. Later, when I took it up to my room – and I do like it even though it's a funny sort of thing to give someone my age – tears came into my eyes. I don't know why. Perhaps because I still can't quite forget that whole lipstick thing. Still, Mama obviously hasn't told him. She's kept her word.

She didn't ask me if I'd kept *my* promise – if I'd apologized and everything. She just trusted me, which was just absolutely awful. I'll never forget how she looked when I got back into the car. I just *couldn't* tell her I hadn't dared speak to the horrid-looking lady behind the counter. I hope she never guesses the truth … and, if she does, she'll understand. And I hope she'll never, ever tell Papa. I wish none of it had ever happened. I wish it would all go out of my head. I wish Elli didn't make me do things I don't want to do. I don't really want her to be my friend any more. But I don't know what to do about that, either.

CARLOTTA

Right: it's going to be all go. Time to make a move. I can't imagine what's going on in Bert's mind. Why hasn't he rung me? I offer to help, take him to a concert, show nothing but friendliness. Instead he just ignores me ... and goes round to supper with Isabel. I suppose I'd had a vague hope he might be different.

Huh! All men are the same, as the universal untruth goes. But it's seriously strange how alike they are in not picking up on opportunities. Bert must know I'm not after his body, only his friendship. Somehow I've got to make that quite clear – obviously I haven't made it clear enough to date – or he'll want to avoid me. Oh God: it gets so tedious, the analysing, the plotting, the wondering. I'm not going to give Bert another thought once I've rung him. And this evening I'll go round with my file of stuff and show him just a few things so as not to confuse him.

I've even got my builder sorted – ready to start next week if Bert gives the go-ahead ... if he isn't utterly amazed by my efficiency.

Chapter Five

BERT

I went to the City by bus. I hadn't travelled on a bus for years. It was rather agreeable, trundling along the King's Road in the sun. I was observing the changes in London – curiously, the sameness of so much. The same shops appearing again and again in different streets. The same clothes appearing in the same shops. A feeling of horrible uniformity, as if everyone was constricted by fashion, rather than daring to be different. I didn't much like the look of the new London.

I thought the bus ride would give me a chance to cogitate, though I wondered how I would begin to do that, on the subject that consumed my mind, affecting every hour of the day. One comforting thought: still unsettled by the move back to England, I was suffering some wild illusion. Except I know all about illusions. And this wasn't one. I had been thunderstruck by Isabel, and my love for her was real. She epitomised the vague picture I had had in mind for so many years of the woman

I might eventually fall in love with … and marry. How weird, how inconvenient that the beam of hope should fall on an unobtainable woman. How difficult would it be to extract myself from the agonising tangle I was now in? 'God give me the strength to do the right thing,' as my mother taught me to pray. Of course I shall do the right thing: I like to think of myself as an honourable man. The right thing is to do nothing, to say nothing, to carry on as normal in my friendship with Isabel and Dan. I will never give Isabel a clue to my real feelings … and perhaps, starved of possibility, they will go away.

But for the moment – for every waking moment since I left her on the doorstep, her face has been there. As I sat in the chrome and leather office of a genial banker, his desk shorn of signs of vital work – virgin blotter and silver paper-cutter the only ornaments – her face hovered like a laser picture in the air. The banker's enthusiastic murmurings about my own desirability sounded a long way off. He offered me a ridiculously large salary. What would I do with all that money? I had more than enough already. He emphasised his eagerness to employ me by pushing down the cuticles of his puffy white fingers. I resisted, though a fleeting thought came to me about how, twenty years ago when I was starting out in the business world, I dreamt of being persuaded to join some distinguished firm who would pay the earth to acquire my talents. But now:

'No thank you,' I said.

'And may I know why not?'

'It's occurred to me, sitting here in your delightful office,' I said, 'that perhaps office days are over for me. I don't want to be bound any more by the clockwork days of long hours, travelling to and fro in overcrowded tubes…'

'Tube?' he interjected, incredulous. 'My dear fellow, we'd provide a car…'

'Or in traffic jams in a car,' I went on after a pause long enough to show my appreciation for this offer. 'Perhaps I want to do something quite different. Even retire. I'm sorry,' I added, 'for wasting your time. It honestly had not occurred to me, until I came here, that it wasn't what I wanted.'

The banker, still genial, stood up. Should I ever change my mind, he said, he would like me to remember that I was a man the bank would do anything to take on board. We shook hands. I imagined his afternoon in the stuffy, lifeless office. I could see him going home to Esher in a company car. I could see his house, probably genuine Tudor bought with a single bonus. It would be neither in town nor country, but in that ubiquitous place that journalists call 'leafy.' I could see his wife, of large hip and tight hair, ready with the ice for his gin and tonic. I did not want to join him in the thump, thump, thump of his financially-centred days. I did not want to earn a salary that would support an entire village in the third world. I wanted … God knows, I thought as I said goodbye.

I took the bus home, too, and reflected no more on the banker or the job I had turned down in such cavalier fashion. Maybe I should live to regret it, but I don't think so. My regret is of a different kind.

Home, I looked round the dreary little room, poured myself a glass of wine. I had not telephoned Carlotta, as I'd meant to, because there seemed to be no pressing need to get on with the restoration of the house. I was already used to it as it was, found its imperfections rather soothing. Besides, I hadn't the energy to face Carlotta's relentless liveliness just yet. I needed quiet … in which to think of Isabel.

I had not rung her, either. I was anxious to make sure she had believed me. But perhaps to her the incident in the cellar had been so trivial she had forgotten it already, and to start explaining it again would give it an importance that could actually undermine my assurances. The arguments swilled around in my head. Time went by, I did not make the call. I could only hope she believed my explanation. The puzzlement was – and I've been through all this so many times – that I could have sworn that, just for a second, something had flared within her, too. Some recognition. Had I not been aware of that, I would not be as confused as I am now. Perhaps, when I see her next, there will be clues.

When I let myself into the house the telephone was ringing. There was no answering machine – another mod con I suppose I'll have to get – so it rang and rang … persistently. I took off my interview tie, undid my collar and answered it with the kind of physical reluctance that makes your limbs clumsy. I fell over a chair.

Carlotta.

She listened impatiently to my apologies for all the huffing as I tried to untangle myself from the telephone cord, and pick up the chair as well as myself from the floor: sympathetic she was not. Then she barked the news that unless I was positively not going to be there, she'd take the opportunity to come round this evening. She had a lot to show me, and as builders were lined up to start, I had better start thinking about where I could move to for a few weeks. This threat rendered me silent. I had no desire to move anywhere. I might have to inform her that I'd become very fond of the William Morris curtains, and the general shabbiness, and re-decorating would have to be postponed. But all I said was that I'd expect her at seven.

The telephone rang again. Dan, this time. First moment of pleasure of the day. I sat in the one armchair – savouring possibly its last moments of sagging seat and threadbare arms – and listened to his accounts of Rome and Nairobi. Dan only has to go a hundred yards down the road and can come back with a good story. Forced abroad, his richesse of anecdotes requires much of a friend's time, and he knew me always to be a keen and sympathetic listener. Perhaps he had missed me as an audience all the time I'd been away. Now he described to me a dozen small details that no one but he would notice, and made me laugh and raised my spirits. In return I told him about the interview, and was pleased he agreed I'd done the right thing. I told him Carlotta was coming round to sort out the house, and I rather dreaded all that. His – jokey, I think – advice was to keep her at a distance: with the best of intentions, she was known to take over peoples' lives. But he assured me she'd do a good job on the house, and talk about Carlotta ran out. Then Dan said Isabel was planning to go down to Dorset for a few days to visit her parents. He suggested we should have lunch in the next day or so, and I could fill him in with the way my life was going. I agreed, wrote down the name of an Italian restaurant in my empty diary.

We'd been talking for almost an hour when I put down the telephone. I pictured him going downstairs, perhaps, telling Isabel of our lunch plan. I could not imagine her expression. Noncommittal, I suppose. Not a very exciting piece of news.

I wished she wasn't going away. I wish so much she wasn't going away.

GWEN

When you've been working for people for several years you can't help but pick up on things. With Mr. Grant back, I could see Mrs. G was much happier. She's used to his coming and going, of course, but she always misses him. Though she never says anything, I can tell. Something about her.

At our coffee break the morning after Mr. Grant got home, she told me about Mr. Bailey, their old friend, coming round on Saturday. He'd taken her and Sylvie for a ride in his new posh car, she said. So that solves that mystery — the mystery of the tall man I saw hurrying down the steps. I don't know why, but I'd had a nasty feeling that there had been some kind of a ding–dong. Some kind of unpleasantness. The way Mrs. G had stood so straight, stiff. But it must have been my imagination. I couldn't see very well through all the greenery and that.

As for myself, I've put Gary out of my mind. There's no point in letting him haunt me, disturb my nice quiet life. On Monday morning, giving the front hall a special polish for Mr. Grant's return, I felt so safe it was hard to believe that Gary and his nasty ways existed. I felt confident, happy in my work. And a good idea did come to me: I'd buy a mobile telephone. I'm not at all a gadgety sort of person, and I don't like to see people in the street with their blank eyes and their phones clamped to their ears, and ... why on the bus do they have to ring someone just to say they're on the bus? Beats me. All very unnecessary, to my mind. But when it comes to danger, to protection, I'll have to admit a mobile telephone is a very good idea. So I'll get one and keep it in my pocket. Then if Gary gets up to any more tricks, I'll ring the police.

Once I'd made up my mind about all that I felt much happier.

CARLOTTA

Hey ho, I was off. In low-key mode, I decided. Not too much of the old vitality. I had a feeling Bert could be intimidated by liveliness.

I swapped my briefcase for a rush basket – more user-friendly, I thought. In it I put some – but not too many – samples of materials, mostly plain bleached linens … nothing too cutting-edge to alarm him. I took a couple of paint charts and also three or four small sample pots of paint, and a new brush. In the likely event of Bert not being able to envisage a colour I suggested, I would open a pot and brush a few sample strokes on the walls. I thought he might find that *fun*. He might even see the point of the job I used to do – though thank goodness I'm no longer officially in the business, clients constantly changing their minds and builders letting one down.

As for the matter of builders – rather depending on how our meeting went – I thought I might mention that if Bert'd like to camp out *chez moi* just for a couple of weeks … well, that'd be no problem. Then I decided I'd change 'camp out' – which he might associate with discomfort and student-type quarters – to 'stay.' I'd quickly assure him of his own bathroom, linen sheets, and my absence from home all day. Then I'd shrug, indicate it didn't matter to me one way or the other – it was just a thought.

I found Bert in distracted mood (when is he going to stop doing all this tiresome distraction and pull himself together?). There was half a bottle of wine and a glass on the table beside the revolting old armchair. He just stood in the middle of the room scratching his head and saying was he expecting me? I reminded him of our telephone conversation this afternoon, and he apologised. Said it had been a day of quite important decisions. One of them had been to turn down the offer of a job in banking. He didn't mention the others. With huge willpower I managed not to enquire further, and hoped he'd appreciate my reticence.

Then he said, looking at my basket, 'Have you brought me eggs? I could do with some eggs.'

'No,' I said. I'd brought samples. Stuff for the house.

At this he looked so forlorn I almost suggested I should come back another day when he felt more up to the business of renovation. But I said nothing. He fetched me a glass, poured me wine.

The part of my plan to sit next to him on the sofa – and I'd decided in the end against wearing the sexy black top – went up in smoke because Bert chose to return to his vile chair. Bit of quick thinking called for here: I sat on the floor at his feet, chose samples of material from the basket and held them up like offerings.

Bert was profoundly bored by the whole process, but made a great effort – I could see – to take from me a single piece of duck-egg blue linen and declared he liked *that*. 'Could be curtains in here,' he said, enthusiasm waning as he spoke. Then he saw the sample pots of paint and observed they wouldn't go very far. I wasn't sure if this was meant to be a joke, or if he was plain stupid. I laughed a bit and explained that I could try them out – here I picked up the brush and waved it – on the white kitchen wall so that he could get an idea. But he interrupted firmly. 'No, please,' he said, 'I'm not a colour man. I wouldn't want to have to choose from stripes of paint. Please, please, Carlotta – do as I said before, choose whatever you want. I've absolute faith in your taste.' Then he tilted back his head and shut his eyes.

'O.K,' I said after a while.

'Thank you for your efforts,' he said, eyes still shut. 'I do appreciate them.'

Eventually he opened his eyes, and I sensed we were both floundering in the uneasy silence. He patted my hand. Avuncular. I could see he was making another effort to stir himself and concentrate on the tiresome business with which I'd come to him. He re-filled my glass. Gave the briefest tweak of a smile, I suppose to tell me it wasn't my decorating plans that were bugging him, but life in general. Very gently, I broached the subject of the builders, and the need for him to have to move out for a few weeks.

He sighed and said he'd rather anything than try to live with them. Resignation clouded his face. I said he'd probably hate the idea, but he could always use my spare room (which on the spur of the moment I calculated would be the least alarming way of saying 'Come and stay with me.'). I listed the benefits. I assured him we'd hardly meet, there'd be no having to make conversation at breakfast because I left for the office long before I presumed he'd be up. It was just a thought, I added, and I could quite see it might not appeal to him.

There was a long silence. Again he patted my hand. Then he said, 'Carlotta, you're looking very pretty.'

Was that an acceptance? A compliment in lieu of an acceptance? A refusal? I'd no idea.

'It's a very kind thought,' he added. 'I'll think about it. I need time to think about what's best to do.'

I suppose I'm impatient, but I'm irritated by men who need time to think about very simple matters. Infuriated by his lack of decisiveness, I looked up at him with calm and understanding eyes. My reward was his promise that he'd move out next week so, yes, I could give the green light to the builders.

It was at that moment – a resurgence of his distracted fatigue – that I realised the evening was going nowhere. He was plainly not going to ask me out to dinner. And even had he done so, I would have said no. In his boring, self-preoccupied mood it would hardly have been a lively evening. So I stood up, looked at my watch and said I had to go. I was due … he didn't ask where, and I daresay he knew I wasn't due anywhere. He came out to the car with me and promised he'd ring me with an answer to my kind invitation in a day or two. We pecked each other on the cheek, he patted me on the shoulder – added bonus, that, I suppose. Then I got in the car and swooped away without looking back.

He was going to be a challenge, Bert was. God, he could be unrewarding, though. My demure, sympathetic mode seemed to have got me no further than my alluring vitality. What should I try next, I thought? And what were the chances he'd come and stay?

These questions frothed back and forth over a sense of pretty acute failure. I needed to talk to someone who could see the whole thing from an objective point of view. I couldn't face going home to eat the remains of a packet of Parma ham with a slice of past-its-prime melon. I decided to drop in on Dan and Isabel. I knew they'd ask me to stay for supper, and afterwards, when Dan had gone back to his play, I would call upon Isabel – always wise – for advice.

I might even find out a little more about her evening alone with Bert.

DAN

I hate it when Isabel's away. I know it's absolutely essential for her to go to the country from time to time, and she doesn't do it often, so I can't really complain. But I still hate it. The house, denied her presence, is bigger, emptier. The chill of stillness goes through me.

I'm being ridiculous, of course. Sylvie is marvellous on these occasions. She seems to sense how much I miss Isabel, and keeps close to me. I cooked her spaghetti which she ate with bottled tomato sauce, and said yes to two helpings of caramel ice-cream (Why, I wonder, are we so foolish as to bribe or comfort our children with unhealthy food?). Then we got down to *Jane Eyre*, which she seems to be enjoying. I read it quite slowly and she interrupts every now and again to ask a question – usually the meaning of a word. When I've explained it to her, she writes it down in her book, her private collection of words. If nothing else, Sylvie will have an exceptional vocabulary and I shall be delighted. This love of words has nothing to do with Isabel or me: her curiosity was entirely her own – from a very early age. Of course we encourage her, but we also encourage many other things that she ignores.

I turned out Sylvie's light and went down to the kitchen. It echoed in a way it never does when Isabel's at home – or perhaps it does and I don't notice. I was going to finish the bottle of wine in the fridge and heat up a fish pie that Isabel made yesterday. She always leaves me well provided for, but I still never manage to carry out all her instructions. 'Scrape some baby carrots,' she said, 'and make a salad: there's masses of watercress and endive.' But I couldn't be bothered. I wasn't hungry. I'm domestically lazy. The vital feeling was to get back to my study as soon as possible and carry on with *Rejection*. I have a feeling it's going quite well. I'm enjoying writing it, it buzzes along. But then I often feel that, and what happens? I send off a handsomely laid out edition of the finished product, with a statutory SAE overloaded with stamps for safety, and the result? Nothing. The envelope is not made use of. The script never returns. I never hear what the faceless man behind the desk in the office of some provincial theatre thinks of it. I'm left tormented, and the torment never quite dies. What's so puzzling is my constant eagerness to return to this form of self-torture. Perhaps one day I shall force myself to realise that I'm no bloody good at writing plays, and I might as well give up. Then, I'd be free.

But I don't want that kind of freedom. I want to go on trying.

I was reflecting, as I often do, on such painful matters, when the doorbell rang. I finished pouring myself a glass of wine, annoyed. I'd no desire for any kind of interruption. My evening was pleasurably planned. I didn't want to talk to anyone but Isabel, when she rang later. But that's the trouble with living in a street of friendly neighbours, and indeed friends: they drop in.

Carlotta, it was. Backlit by the evening sun, a halo of hair frizzed by the strong light. She apologised for not ringing to warn of her arrival but said she'd had a dreadful time with Bert, was fed up, and didn't think we'd mind her coming round for a drink. When I explained that Isabel had gone to her parents, Carlotta's face clenched … appalled, disappointed. She backed away − another inch and she would have fallen down the steps. I put out a hand, pulled her through the door. 'In that case I must go,' she kept on saying with the hollow firmness of one who has every hope of being persuaded to stay. And what could I do? She looked so forlorn. What had Bert been up to? I was faintly intrigued. All these thoughts skittered through my mind and I saw my quiet evening of writing float through the air and break like a bubble. 'I'm all alone, for God's sake,' I heard myself, saying 'please stay.'

'If you really mean it, then,' she answered, making her way towards the oven.

Carlotta knows our house, our kitchen, well. Often she's helped Isabel cook. She knows where things are. She's efficient. She doesn't have to ask questions. 'You've got eggs,' she said with a decisive glance at the basket, piled high. 'Omelettes, then. Salad and cheese and – look – Isabel's left a mass of raspberries. You can keep the fish pie for tomorrow.'

She was in charge, I could only thank her. I gave her a glass of wine but she shook her head, and instead put on Isabel's old apron to protect her tight black dress. Had this been chosen for Bert's approbation, I couldn't help wondering? If so, it should have had effect. It showed her small waist and very rounded breasts to great advantage. What I found confusing was that from the waist down, in the disguise of the apron, she could have been my wife. I smiled. 'Missing Isabel?' she asked. I confessed I was. I wasn't much good without her, I said.

Carlotta's one of those natural cooks who fling in a bit of this and a bit of that, and suddenly something that smells deliciously of herbs and garlic is there, ready, perfect. My darling Isabel is not in this category, far from it. I don't mind, but it's hard not to admire someone to whom it all comes so easily. She tossed a salad of glinting leaves, threw in chives, cut a tomato into transparent slices so fast that all I could see was the flash of the blade. I was aware that, in the admiration I felt for her speed and skill, resentment also lurked: that she should be exhibiting this talent in *our* kitchen, that she should be so much better at all this culinary stuff than Isabel, was unreasonably irritating.

'Good thing I came,' she said a long while after we had spoken. I wasn't sure whether she meant because she could cook for me, or whether she thought that she might make up for Isabel's absence. I nodded agreement and laid the table.

Over supper she confessed the trouble she was having with Bert. He was so hopeless to deal with, she said – and I was to understand she meant on a professional basis. She wanted to make it quite clear that all she wanted from Bert was friendship. She was in no way ready for another relationship with some dithering man: she had had procrastination, indecisiveness up to *here*

– her hand swooped across one breast rather than her temples – since she'd had to tell Mike to bugger off. I said I quite understood. Fond though I was of Bert, I added, he'd be a tricky number to be involved with. It was not for nothing he was still a bachelor. I'd forgotten about the warmth that intense agreement so often, and confusingly, induces. I could feel this warmth, born of our agreement: it was almost tangible between us. But in a moment it was blasted by guilt. How could I have suggested to Carlotta that Bert was tricky? That was an act of unforgivable treachery. I tried to change the conversation, but Carlotta would not be deflected from her theme: Bert was a loser. *Basically* – here she shook her head so fiercely that her dotty hair shimmered like the leaves on a *tremula pendula* – Bert was nothing more than a hopeless loser. And she had made up her mind that all she was going to do was to re-furbish his house, because she was not a woman to break her word, then make no further effort.

'Quite,' I said. Then added (perhaps to make up for my previous betrayal) that I thought it was possible he hadn't found his feet, yet, back in England. This idea produced a sneering laugh. Found his feet? He'd only come from New York, for heaven's sake. He'd got bags of money, a house that someone else was going to take trouble over, and plenty of friends. So if he hadn't found his feet he was, in a word, *pathetic.*

Then, suddenly, Carlotta ran out of steam. Her sigh, followed by a silence, was a relief. I noticed her glass, and the bottle, were empty. She looked rather endearing, sitting there, chin in cupped hands, staring out of the window, indignation filtering away.

'Why don't we go down to the cellar,' I suggested, 'and choose ourselves a bottle of something memorable?' At the word memorable she looked up at me and nodded.

Carlotta is knowledgeable about wine. She drinks a certain amount and, when we have dinner with her, always produces a very good bottle of something she thinks I haven't discovered. I don't think she'd ever been down to my cellar before. I felt it might interest her. She would probably appreciate the money I'd spent on its design – the lighting, the layout, the exact temperature – all things that hold no interest for Isabel. I think she's only ever been down once since it was all finished.

I went ahead. As Carlotta was wearing high heels, I gave her a hand down the last few steep steps. When we reached the bottom she continued to clutch my hand, tightening her grip. Then she shook herself free and went over to a corner where my most valuable and prized bottles await the right moment. She still wore the apron. Its strings made two patterned snakes over her bottom. Her head was on one side as she tried to see labels without removing bottles. Then she turned to me.

'Goodness,' she said. 'Lucky you. What a cellar.'

At that moment she looked desperately sad, vulnerable. Looking back I realised I was stirred by the pathos of her. At the time I was unsure what it was that made me want to cross the two yards that parted us, take her in my arms and rid her of whatever it was that had drained her of her usual high spirits.

I quickly took a bottle from the rack next to me and suggested we go back upstairs. She gave a small shudder – throwing off whatever had assailed her, perhaps. Because when I offered a hand again up the stairs, she shook her head and bounded ahead of me. The odd moment, I realised, was a figment of my imagination. I had mistaken passing thoughtfulness, which had crossed her features like a shadow, for melancholy. Carlotta, shouting from above that she was going to open the French windows because the evening was so warm, was her normal bossy self again. I had misread her, and was shaken by my misreading.

We sat on the sofa by the open windows that leads onto one of those small terraces that are common to Edwardian houses in London streets. From the garden came the faint smell of lilac: the blooms were just past their best. By day they had that cindery look that comes when some of their flowers have turned brown. But by night they still, just, held their scent.

We both kept to our far ends of the sofa. We'd sat here, in just these positions, dozens of times, while Isabel was cooking, or upstairs saying goodnight to Sylvie, and in a way it was no different from any of those other times. Except there was, I think, the faintest trace of expectation between us. Not of anything nefarious. But I think I half hoped Carlotta, alone with me, would reveal something she had never before revealed – though perhaps she had to Isabel. She looked at me with smiling eyes and said she promised she would say no more about Bert.

On the low table in front of the sofa I'd put two new glasses – our most delicate ones, kept for rare occasions – and carefully poured the Burgundy and handed her one. Then the telephone – on the table – rang.

Isabel.

She sounded cheerful, as she always does when in Dorset. Easy drive, lovely weather, and her mother had left the deepfreeze full of wonderful things so she wasn't going to have to be bothered with cooking. I laughed, thinking of Carlotta's heavenly omelette. How was Sylvie? How was I? About to go up and carry on writing, I said: I'll ring you tomorrow evening. 'Miss you, love you,' I added. We always say that when we're away from each other, small pebbles of words so well used I doubt either of us dwell on their meaning. They're just habit, but I daresay we'd be alarmed if we forgot them.

'You didn't say I was here,' Carlotta said when I'd put down the telephone.

'No.'

'Why not?'

I sighed. Took a sip of wine, needing a moment in which to answer the question to myself.

'I don't know,' I said eventually. 'At least, I don't know exactly. Something to do with not wanting a long conversation, and with knowing I really do have to get down to work…'

'Would she have minded?' Carlotta asked. 'Surely she wouldn't.'

'No, of course she wouldn't. I suppose I just didn't want to get into the whole explanation, Bert not asking you out and so on. It's up to you to tell her all that, not me.'

All expectation – if that's what it had been – between us had now disintegrated. We were left stranded, silent again.

'Try the wine,' I said at last. Carlotta leaned forward, hair falling over her face. She tasted it, said it was sublime, and returned her glass to the table. Then she rested her head on the back of the sofa, shut her eyes.

I had never seen her like this before. Vulnerable, quiet, heavy. Nor had I realised that she was, well, quite so oddly attractive: long eyelashes, two dark curved smudges on her cheeks, the two small peaks of her top lip precisely defined. I had always thought of Carlotta as over-made up, eyes lined too harshly, lips too dark. This evening she seemed not to be wearing much make-up. Or maybe it was a crepuscular illusion. Apart from a candle on the kitchen table there were no lights on in the room. The sky outside was that pale darkness, watery from streetlights: the customary early summer night sky over London.

I sat looking at her for a long time. Then two single tears, one from the outside corner of each eye, appeared, and ran a hesitant race down her cheeks. I was fumbling for my handkerchief when she jerked herself upright with a loud, animal-like noise, and began to sob. Instinctively I moved towards her, held her to me while her body heaved and the cooing noise of her weeping was alarming in the air.

I don't know for how long we sat clasped to each other. It reminded me of occasions when Sylvie was small: clutched together, swaying back and forth, I would try to comfort her. I stroked Carlotta's curls, said nothing. She smelt of roses – tuberoses, perhaps: the scent was too strong. When eventually she disentangled herself from me, I gave her my clean handkerchief and she wiped her eyes. Mascara ran in black streams down her face. I couldn't help smiling, and she returned the smile.

'Thank you,' she said.

'Anything I can … help with?' I asked. But she shook her head.

'Just, sometimes,' she said, 'living alone – seeing your friends happily married, children, house, family life … Just sometimes you despair … But mostly not.' She gave another half smile. 'I think it was Isabel ringing you,' she went on, 'that started me off. The idea that after fifteen years your wife goes away for a few days and misses you, and rings you, and really wants to know how you are. I've always imagined that one day I might have that sort of thing. But this is self-pitying rubbish,' she added. 'I'm sorry.'

She was scrubbing at her face with my clean handkerchief, making it a worse mess.

'You're striped as a tiger, now,' I said. 'Tiger face. And of course, one day …'

She gave a small snort of derision.

'No, probably not. But thank you, Dan. You've been so kind. Such lovely wine.'

She picked up the glass, took several sips. Then she handed back the handkerchief.

I remember thinking it was imperative I get away from her. I took the handkerchief to the sink, ran it under the cold tap, wrung it out and returned to her. I had a distant sense that what I was going to do was dangerous, foolish. She stood up. I tipped up her face and began to wipe it clean. I tried to look fatherly.

'Thank you,' she said again, when I'd finished. 'You've been…'

She couldn't finish because I was kissing her. She was kissing me. My hand was full of one of her breasts. My inner eye was confused by scarlet flares and miniature fireworks. Carlotta was responding to the slightest movement of my free hand. Then a sudden paleness swarmed behind my closed eyes, bleaching out the colours. With one accord we pulled apart. I saw that the light in the hall had been switched on. I heard the dim slap of bare feet on the floorboards.

Turning from Carlotta, I saw Sylvie standing at the kitchen door, looking at us.

'I can't sleep, Papa,' she said ... and ran towards us.

ISABEL

I can't think why I felt so tired. Usually I'm full of energy. Suppose I've been working very hard, trying to complete that large order for the opera. And now there's this order from New York: a dozen masks for Saks Christmas window. But I can't face beginning until I've had a few days' rest.

So here I am in what I still think of as home: house of my childhood. It's a little odd, being here without Ma and Pa. God knows why they'd rather be in Madrid than Dorset at this time of year, but in their retirement they've gone a bit travel mad. Rio, next, apparently. Strange I haven't inherited their love of seeing the world. Britain holds quite enough for me.

It's all as it always was: the grandfather clock in the hall still half an hour slow, its loud tick providing a reminder of rhythm as you flit across the hall – persistent, its mellow voice, but not intrusive. There's a smell of dog – Chancer, my mother said, would prefer to be with me than be sent away – and everything sags and bulges in the sitting room: flowered chair and sofa covers are so blurred that there's no distinction between flowers and leaves. The arms of Pa's usual armchair are threadbare. As for the curtains: fifty summers have left their linings in rags. However gently you pull them small pieces of blanched cotton flutter down. Their edges long ago relinquished their pattern, and now match the bleached patches of carpet near the windows, which was not the idea when Ma chose everything so carefully from Peter Jones half a century ago. There's no point, as she keeps saying, in re-doing it all now. 'We're used to it, we don't notice the wear and tear,' she says. 'We'll leave it to you and Dan to do what you like – if you keep the house, that is, when we're moved into some Home, or we die.'

'Of course we'll keep it. I love it, I love it.'

I went for a short walk: examined the garden – more ardently cared for than the house – and went on up the hill so that I could look down on the hamlet, the church spire, the roof of the house, the fields that swirl down into the valley – a place I've been to a thousand times to listen to the silence. A place so minutely recorded in my mind that to return is merely to confirm: the transparent mental picture is simply coloured in by reality. I took deep breaths, expiring London from my lungs, my heart, my whole being. Then I walked quickly back down the cart track of reddish earth, a path that can't have changed since it was walked by Hardy.

Ma, as always, had left me well provided for. In the dusky kitchen – stuff on the shelves, a muddle of things that could have been thrown out years ago, shopping lists of yesteryear, their ink now brown and making me smile – I grill lamb cutlets, and tomatoes from the garden. There's a silver-framed photograph by the stove, placed between bottles of oil and vinegar so that Ma can see it while she's stirring: it's Dan, Sylvie and me some years ago, Sylvie still at the gap-toothed stage. We're here in the garden, lupins behind us – I can't remember which summer, exactly. They roll so quickly into each other, melting into a whole ribbon of summers knotted with similar memories later only recognised by Sylvie's height, or Dan's greying hair.

I think of them, now, without me. Dan will have read to Sylvie for a long time, as he always does when I'm away. Sylvie will set her alarm: she's always afraid Dan won't wake her in time for school. Dan might remember to heat up the fish pie, then he'll be off up to his study. *Rejection*, I understand from the few hints he has dropped, is going rather well. He's still trying to think of a good title. I must try to think for him on my walk tomorrow. Sometimes, titles just come to me: he's used several of mine. When I rang him at nine thirty he said he was only just going up to work. He must have read to Sylvie for ages, and then been very inefficient about heating up the oven and the pie. But he sounded fine – he's always fine when I'm away so I don't know why I'm so often pricked by a nameless anxiety. In what is now Dan's and my room when we're here I get into the double bed and pick up my book, but I'm too sleepy to read. My head is cleared of masks. Through the open window I stare back at a full moon. Dan and Sylvie are safely there, is all I think, and I'm here. We're all fine. Perhaps I'm the last one to fall asleep.

SYLVIE

I couldn't go to sleep ... because. Well, just because. I haven't a clue why. Some nights it's just like that. Probably because I spent too long on my maths homework and then got spooked by Mrs. Rochester.

Chapter Six

GWEN

My mother used to say she was a woman of nervous disposition. She said this with such pride it sounded like a boast. For years I'd no idea what she meant, but I would nod in agreement as my mother was someone who didn't like to be contradicted. Now I know what it means, I'm afraid I might have inherited that same nervous disposition.

I wake up, nights, in such a sweat, fretting away. Nothing to do with the menopause – that was over long ago, thank the Lord. Sometimes I think I hear someone in the kitchen, though I know I'm imagining things, but I daren't get out of bed and go and look. But mostly I wake with such a spinning head I can't stop it. What is Gary up to? Is he trying to scare me? Is that his plan? And if so, why? What have I done to deserve such menace?

He's a lonely man, of course: not much to do. I don't recall he had any friends. Not that he talked about himself much. Didn't let on about whatever was going on in his mind – not that I asked. 'There's a fine line to be drawn between interest and prying,' was another of my mother's sayings. She warned me to keep questions to myself in case I should be thought nosey. She herself went overboard in this respect. She never asked me anything: whether I'd fancy another cup of tea, or a new pair of shoes, or how I was getting on at school – nothing. All this not-being-nosey seemed to me like a great lack of interest. My mother had her mind on quite a few things, but they didn't include me. I remember yards and yards of silence as a child.

One of the nights I woke up alarmed, thinking of Gary, something occurred to me: I thought perhaps it was *revenge* he was after ... simple as that. Revenge for his own inadequacies. He had a good many of those, but I daresay the one that disturbed him most was the one I was privy to discovering. Yes, the truth of the matter was he was no good in a certain area. Rotten – I would go so far as to say he was on the road to total impotence. Without spelling it out, I did try to make it clear to him I didn't mind about all that. The physical side of things has never been that important to me, I said – though not in so many words – and after one particularly embarrassing afternoon between the sheets, our so-called 'sex life' fizzled out. But perhaps what got him was the fact that

I was a witness to his failing, and he wanted to punish me for that. Yes, I thought, that must be it: Gary's after revenge.

But having worked this out, I didn't feel much easier. I was only able to put it all aside when I was at number 18, knowing I was safe there. Knowing he couldn't get me. I'm damned if I'm going to let this silly fear, this nervous disposition, get me down. But it is hard, knowing someone's out to get you. Stupidest thing I ever did in my life, befriending Gary. But there's not much to be done about regret. Regret is a canker in the soul. But at least I've got my mobile now. That was a good decision … makes me feel a little bit safer.

DAN

Did Sylvie see us?

The question will haunt me until there's some proof that she didn't. Her furious eyes were concentrated on Carlotta, who said something about it being late and dashed from the room. I said to Sylvie I'd take her back to bed. I was smoothing my hair, conscious of a red face. I got her a glass of milk which is what she usually has when she comes down at night. She took the milk but said don't bother to come up. 'I'm fine,' she said looking at me hard. 'I'd rather you didn't,' she said and stomped off with hunched shoulders: a sure sign she's put out.

I spent a wakeful night, cursing myself, cursing Carlotta, trying to work out what had happened. Drink, I assumed. We'd drunk quite a bit during the course of the evening. But I knew that wasn't the answer. I wasn't drunk. I'd simply been overcome by a moment of pernicious lust for someone I didn't even much like. I haven't been so blindingly struck since I was in my twenties. Protected by my profound love for my wife, fancying other women – however delightful – has never been something I've contemplated. Carlotta isn't even a delightful woman, despite being able to switch on the charm. And I certainly didn't *contemplate* anything. I just found myself leaping upon her, almost out of control – boyish. The extraordinary and surprising thing was her response. Had she indicated an iota of distaste at my boorish behaviour, I would have stopped at once. But perhaps *she* had been contemplating, and things were turning out just as she envisaged they could. God knows what might have happened had Sylvie not appeared. I like to think we'd have come to our senses. I like to think we'd have defied weakness of the flesh. But perhaps that wouldn't have been the case. Even now, as I think of Carlotta, breast malleable in my hand, hips writhing …

The thought also sickens. I feel the profound chill of shame, regret. I loathe the knowledge that for ever more the familiar trio of Isabel, Carlotta and I will never be the same. Carlotta and I are now bound by a secret that Isabel must never discover, though the idea of my wife being the ignorant party is too appalling to think about. For my unforgivable betrayal I'll be punished for years to come.

Dazed, shaken, I got up very early, tidied up the things from last night. I didn't want Gwen to think I'd been entertaining while Isabel was away. Sylvie came down at her usual time. Intent on finding some lost book, she pointed out that it was odd to find her father putting a bowl of cornflakes on the table for her – not a normal practice. I managed a laugh, relieved to see she appeared her normal self. All the huffiness of last night seemed to have disappeared.

I switched on the radio, so there was no need to talk. When I dropped her at school she gave me a particularly firm kiss on the cheek. What, if anything, was going through her mind?

Home, I took a couple of aspirin before going to the office, and remembered that today I was to have lunch with Bert. Should I, in the most oblique way, tell him about the disaster last night?

'Of course not, you fool,' I told myself. Men don't have those kinds of conversation. Bert wouldn't want to hear of my idiocy any more than, in truth, I would want to confess. And besides, confession is an unreliable way of easing guilt. No: we'd talk about his life, his plans, laugh about some of our misdemeanours in the past – funny how, recalled, elaborated, they still amuse us. Part of the pleasure, of course, is recognising each other's embroidery.

Lunch with Bert would be the one cheering thing in the day. What a bugger is remorse.

ISABEL

I'd forgotten the kitchen clock was permanently ten minutes slow, and mistimed my call. Dan was leaving the house. Sylvie was already in the car. So only a brief word, but he was fine. No news. We'd speak this evening.

The long day rolled emptily ahead. Being a creature of habitual discipline, I find a curious kind of alarm underlines the pleasure of such days. Mornings are the problem. Mornings, in my scheme of things, are for work. I like the routine of early rising, getting down to my masks as soon as Dan and Sylvie have gone. I like keeping at it – the four hours pass so fast – till lunchtime, when I feel I've earned the slacking off in the afternoon and the change of occupation. What a ridiculous, puritanical concept, I tell myself so often. Were I not bound by it, I would enjoy holidays much more. As it is, during the obligatory holiday in France … or Italy – or wherever – in a rented house or hotel, mornings confound me. What can I do with that stretch of time if I can't work? I join in with whatever the plan for the day is, of course, but it never feels right. And the afternoon, unearned, is less rewarding. But obviously I can't take all my mask-making stuff with me, or even bring it here for a few days. So I'm left with the problem of unstructured hours till lunch. Alone in my parents' house, there's no need to shop. On my own, I scarcely eat. The relief of not having to think about food is immense. I promised I'd take Chancer for a walk twice a day, and deadhead the roses if I felt like it. When I came down for breakfast she was asleep under the kitchen table. No need to disturb her just yet. I went to the drawer in the hall chest where the secateurs were kept. In it I found a couple of metallic marbles, a single gardening glove in a state of such *rigor mortis* it could never be worn again, various lengths of string and a pre-historic torch. They were all there when I was a child. My mother never throws anything away. But she would scoff at the obvious idea that things past their prime might come in useful one day. Her reasons for her serious hoarding are far more inventive, convincing, funny. And somewhere within me, too, lurks her disposition for hanging onto useless things. I understand the feeling. It's a sort of security: material links with the past. Reminders. My mother's habit encourages friendly scoffing from those who love her. Sometimes I even join in the laughter myself, but really I'm on her side.

I took the secateurs and went into the garden. It was a fine morning, sun not yet warm, traces of dew still silvering the lawn. To reach the roses I had to go through a small garden enclosed by beech hedges. Here an intricate pattern of box hedges divided beds of white flowers, my father's proud achievement. In its centre was a small but clever fountain of his own invention: a stone bowl, punctured with random holes, which produced feathery arcs of water. Designing this fountain had afforded him hours of entertainment. It was several years in the making, and by the time it was finished he'd become not only a skilled stone-cutter, but an expert on complicated drainage systems. The day it was finished, I remember, we drank glasses of pink champagne to match the pink evening: the bottle in its cooler stood in a bed of white pansies, squashing some of them flat. There was always an element of carelessness in whatever my father did which counteracted the enthusiastic energy he put into his projects. Praise for his fountain meant far more to him than did the medals he received after the war, or the praise accorded to him when he retired from his job as chairman of a company that made farm machinery. And, heavens, did my mother smother him in admiration that evening. There was no inch of the fountain that escaped her marvelling. I can see her now, in her old garden hat (still, thank God, hanging in the cloakroom), head thrown back, pretty eyes screwed up in laughter after her third glass of champagne, moved beyond words at my father's achievement. In return he muttered about it all being 'nothing much'. But I guessed he sensed that once something is finished the effort it has taken turns to dust. It's hard to remember all the hours of striving. 'Achievement,' he once said, 'is not half so sweet as trying to achieve.' For all the laughter and the drink, there was a sense of anti-climax that evening. There were unspoken questions: what next? What now?

But, years later, the fountain still bounces out its water just as merrily as it did that first night. I stood watching it for a while, listening to its arcs splattering against the garden silence. Suddenly an early swift swooped down, darted so fast between two curves of water that it was scarcely visible, then soared back to the safer expanse of sky. It had dared, I thought, in order to know. A sense of both wonder and absolute inadequacy swept over me. I moved on through the enclosed white garden to the coloured roses.

Somewhere deep in the leaves of a bush of Maidens' Blush, reaching for brown withered heads, avoiding the few remaining petals of fragile pink, a picture of Bert came to me. Bert and me in the cellar. And, again, the question: what had been the truth? My truth? His truth? When would the questioning stop, the picture fade?

A walk up the hill with the dog, I thought. My father always said that when you've something on your mind that needs working out, don't waste your money on bloody therapists, go for a walk. And don't tire yourself thinking too hard. 'Nature'll do its work,' he said. That belief, inherited from him, has been of immense use to me.

I called Chancer and set off up the hill. By now the sun was up, but a breeze up-turned the silver side of the poplars, and against my bare legs the long grass of the orchard was warm and dry.

CARLOTTA

I'm gutted. Utterly and completely bloody well gutted. What an evening! I get nowhere with Bert, go round to Isabel and Dan to find Dan on his own. Do my best to fix supper for him and have a nice evening, good wine, then – I tell myself – he goes and spoils the whole thing by leaping on me for a quick snog. Dan! Of all the faithful husbands, he surely takes the prize. Don't know what I was thinking of, really. Nothing, probably. I was a bit pissed. I got a bit maudlin, needed an arm round me. Dan provided that … and more. It was quite comforting, though. I could have gone on. If he'd said how about it? I daresay I'd have followed him upstairs, no thought of Isabel. But then that wretched little snivelling Sylvie appeared and we jumped apart like shot rabbits.

I've no idea whether she saw us kissing and I don't really care. At the moment I'm in such a rage about everything I don't care about anyone. I suppose I should feel guilt about snogging Isabel's husband, but I don't … possibly will later. The interesting thing now is, what will happen? What will happen when the three of us meet again? Will Dan, the most honest man in the world, feel bound to confess to Isabel, thus exorcising his guilt? Or will he say nothing, but avoid my eyes, hide from me what he would really like us to do? Then, will I tell Bert? Ha! I can just see that. Bert in a sea of colour charts. Me on the floor flicking though the Provencal blues. Me: 'Bert, after I left you the other night I went round to Dan and we went at it hammer and tongs all night.' No: I think not that. Bert would be shocked. He would see it as gross disloyalty. Rather than fire him up, the thought of me and Dan, it might have the opposite effect.

I suppose what I must do is to ring Dan and see how he stands in the accusing light of day. I mean, if he's planning to confess to Isabel, I'd better be prepared. My story will be to blame the drink – a silly moment fired by the wine. I'll try to laugh it off, say half a dozen times I'm sorry for urging him on. Though I'm not at all. Two things Isabel must never know: Dan wanted me like crazy, and I wanted him back. Because now I come to think of it, it didn't spoil the evening and it wasn't a one-way thing. Bugger it, I loved every moment. I've fancied Dan for years.

I rang him – trembling, I admit. It was a horrible conversation. I can't get it out of my mind.

'Dan?'

'Carlotta?'

'Look, I'm sorry.'

Pause.

'So'm I. One of those crazy things. We'd drunk a certain amount.'

'Quite.' Another pause. 'Are you planning to tell Isabel? I mean, obviously you'll say that I came round. But … nothing else?'

'Planning to tell Isabel?' He sound terrified. 'Are you mad?'

'I just thought, having heard your views on the need for *total honesty* so many times … you'd want to.'

'Well I don't. Of course I don't. And I hope you're not planning to, either.'

'Of course not.'

'No good could come of telling Isabel. It was just a stupid moment we should forget as soon as possible.'

'Quite.'

'And next time we meet, everything'll be as always, right? No exchange of looks or anything…'

'Dan, what do you take me for?'

'Look, I've got to go. I'm meeting Bert. D'you think Sylvie saw us?'

'I don't know. Sylvie was the last thing on my mind.'

'You can be a real cow, sometimes, Carlotta …'

'But you wanted me. Don't ever pretend you didn't.'

Dan put down the telephone.

SYLVIE

This morning I got into trouble with Mrs. Beale. She said I wasn't concentrating. She said why are you staring into space, Sylvie, not thinking about *mathematics*? As she calls it. I said I didn't know.

I was thinking about last night. When I came into the kitchen it was so weird. Papa was red in the face and his hair was rather skew whiff. He turned to me and looked *flabbergasted* (that's my newest word. I like it. I've used it twice this week). Carlotta looked rather sort of sleepy and, like, dopey. They were standing apart but rather close, for people just standing, I mean. There were empty glasses and bottles of wine on the table by the window. They'd had quite a lot, I suppose. Mama and Papa never drink that much.

Actually they both looked really goofy. But then I realised they weren't just goofy, they were angry. They must have had a row. What about? I don't know or care but I don't like the idea of Carlotta and Papa having a row in our kitchen when Mama's away. I *hated* that. Papa said he'd take me up to bed. I said *I'd rather you didn't, thanks*, which is a very grown-up way of putting someone down. I didn't mean to sound cross, but Papa was so peculiar I didn't want to have anything to do with him. On my way upstairs I heard Carlotta banging the front door behind her. I don't just not like her, now. I hate her. For ages I couldn't go to sleep, wondering what they'd been rowing about. Perhaps when Mama comes back I'll ask her what she thinks.

BERT

Cricket, London, New York, Oxford, *Rejection* (I'm secretly worried this is another of Dan's attempts, one that won't have producers clamouring) – we ambled through subjects easily enough. But Dan seemed a bit down. Perhaps he's always like that when Isabel's away, loving spouse that he is. I offered him the best claret that I could find on the list, but he declined. Said he rarely drinks at lunch any more. So we both had mineral water.

He'd cheered up a bit by the time we got to the coffee. It was then he told me Isabel was coming back this evening. She loves the idea of getting away for a day or two, but she loves coming home even more, he said. She was meant to stay in Dorset till Friday, but… He tailed off with a small smile. Had it been anyone but Dan, I would have called him *smug*. 'Isabel said you went round one evening when I was in Rome,' he then said. 'Thanks for looking after her. She doesn't like it when I'm away…' he tailed off again. 'That's all right,' I said, lightly as I could manage. 'She cooked me a perfect dinner.'

The subject of Carlotta followed, as I knew it would. I suppose I was feeling faintly guilty about her, vaguely keen to share the guilt. It was I who brought her up, as it were. Confessed I'd behaved rather badly last night, not taking her out to dinner when she obviously wanted an invitation in return for bringing round all her decorating stuff. There was a long pause while Dan stirred his coffee more than a small cup of espresso needs stirring. Then that smile again, and he said I needn't have worried – she'd dropped in, not knowing Isabel was away. 'Had to ask her in for a drink, really,' he said. 'In the end she stayed for something to eat. In fact she even cooked it – she's rather a good cook.' I said I'd probably find that out quite soon. There was another pause. I hazily imagined their evening: Carlotta being kind and efficient, Dan perhaps feeling faintly uneasy due to Isabel's absence – though after years of friendship with Carlotta, that was unlikely.

I was bored of thinking about Carlotta. I didn't want to talk about her. But there was just one thing on which I wanted Dan's advice. I told him she had suggested I go and stay with her while the builders were in my house. Dan's eyebrows raised so slightly the skin of his forehead scarcely creased. 'I don't have any views on that,' he said. 'Daresay it'd be all right. You could keep your distance if you really don't want to be involved. Should you change your mind – well, easy access, under her roof, and all that.'

My turn to smile. Dan began his hectic coffee stirring again. 'Isabel did mention to me you'd need somewhere for a few weeks,' he went on at last. 'We've got a perfectly good spare room. We'd love to have you. You could weigh up the various advantages and disadvantages – Carlotta, or us? Couple of good offers to choose from…'

I thanked him. I wanted to say much else, of course: ask for more advice. But it's not the sort of talk men like Dan and I would ever consider.

'I'll be interested to see which you go for,' Dan added. 'The hurly-burly of Carlotta, or the unravished quietness of Isabel and me?'

He gave me one last smile and I signalled for the bill.

Chapter Seven

SYLVIE

Mama was there when I arrived back from school. Yippee.

She'd brought baskets of stuff from Dorset as she always does. There were lettuces and mint and vegetables all over the table. They made the whole kitchen smell kind of green. I took one of the apples and shined it on my knee.

She wanted to know what I'd been doing. I said nothing much. Yes, it had all been fine. We'd missed her but we'd managed OK – she likes to hear that sort of thing. The only odd thing, I said, was that Papa and Carlotta had had a row.

What? she said. She didn't know Carlotta had been round.

Just dropped in, I think I said, expecting to find both of you.

Mama was pulling leaves off a basil plant. She began to pull them a bit quicker and a bit more fiercely.

Something was bugging her but I don't know what. I mean, I specially didn't mention that Carlotta wore her apron. She can't possibly have been cross because horrible old Carlotta came round. Anyway, I went up to her and put my arms round her waist and my head on her chest. She smelt as she always smells, of some kind of wild flower. I hate Carlotta, I said. She pushed me away at once and looked at me so sternly I was really confused. Somehow it had all gone wrong and I hadn't' even got round to asking her what she thought the row might be about. Better not do that now, I thought. You can't possibly hate Carlotta, she said. She may be a bit overpowering at times, but she's kind and generous and clever and funny. And what's more she's my *friend*.

I *know* she's your friend, I said, and walked away. But you don't like some of my friends, so why should I like yours?

I just hoped that when Papa came home and we all had supper together everything would be all right.

ISABEL

Good to be home as always. I'd only got half the fruit and veg put away when Sylvie got back from school. She seemed as pleased to see me as I was to see her, and sat eating one of the orchard apples. She said Carlotta had come round last night and stayed for supper. Then she said she thought she and Dan had had some sort of row, or argument. I was sure she'd got that wrong, I said. It couldn't have been anything serious, but they're always bantering. They don't share many of the same views. Then Sylvie declared she hated Carlotta and I snapped at her. Her all too apparent and intense dislike of Carlotta annoys me. Of course you can't expect your children to like all your friends, but Carlotta's never done anything to upset Sylvie as far as I know. Anyhow, she stomped off out of the room in one of her sulks. A taste of what we'll be in for all too soon, I suppose – a few years of those boring teenage moods.

She was fine at supper, though, and Dan was in good spirits. My chicken salad was praised – much better than whatever Carlotta had cooked last night, put in Sylvie. Dan and I chose to ignore her.

'Sylvie told you, then?' Dan said. 'Carlotta came round and was disappointed to find you away.' I'd told her I was going. She never remembers other people's plans.

'I'd been looking forward to a quiet evening,' Dan went on, 'but it'd have been churlish not to ask her to stay. She offered to cook. Something with eggs – pretty good, actually, Sylvie,' he added reprovingly.

'So what did you have the row about, then?' Sylvie asked.

'Row?' Dan looked bemused.

'When I came down, you'd obviously been having a row,' Sylvie said. There was a spitefulness in her eyes I don't like. Where does this streak of meanness in our daughter come from?

Dan then gave the merest smile. Bewilderment cleared. 'Not a *row*,' he said, 'just a difference of opinion – about Bert.' He looked at me to signal he'd give details later.

I was intrigued. But as we never discuss our friends' private lives in front of Sylvie, and it was time to change the subject, I went to the fridge to get the strawberries and cream. Dan and I began to talk about the new computer he was planning to buy.

Sylvie's sulkiness returned until she went up to bed.

CARLOTTA

Jesus Christ. Cat among the pigeons. Dan whirling about in a ridiculous state of guilt. Does he honestly think a man can go for nearly twenty years lusting *only* after his wife? I've absolutely no feelings of guilt. I thought they might come, but they haven't. It meant little – I mean, in terms of any feeling other than sex. I didn't suddenly think I was in love with Dan just because he kissed me, or any of that rubbish. I fancy him, I like him, but our tiny indiscretion could not be called anything but innocent, certainly not a threat in any direction. My only regret is that there wasn't time to go further. I could have killed that bloody child coming down to spy on us.

I suppose I might have guessed Dan wouldn't come clean to Isabel. Well, yes, it might have complicated things a bit. There's a chance Isabel would have taken it too seriously, though I doubt she would have actually believed it was anything more than an under-the-mistletoe sort of kiss. Anyhow, his decision relieves me of not having to lie through my teeth to Isabel about the insignificance of the encounter ... plus, should she confront me with one of her unbelievably smug *I'm-so-happily-married-Dan-would-never-look-at-another-woman* boasts, I could always call on my tiny mite of stored ammunition. Serve her right for having it all.

So, what? Bert?

I'm *furious* with him, the ungrateful shit. But at the same time I want him under the net: his friendship, his companionship. I see him as a useful man in my life. I see us going out *à quatre* with Isabel and Dan. I can imagine a holiday – some sunny place abroad. I've got much better breasts than Isabel. While she'd sit pale under a sunhat and parasol, I'd put on my scantiest bikini and see if I could torture Dan a little, and at the same time inflame Bert's jealousy.

What am I saying? I think I'm more shaken by the whole thing than I realised. I also think I know what to do. I'll ring Bert and withdraw my offer of his coming to stay. Make him wonder if he isn't being foolish, hesitating about turning down so good an offer.

As soon as this idea came to me, I rang him. He was out. I couldn't leave a message as he still hadn't replaced his Stone Age telephone. All day I jittered about – cross, sad, I don't know.

He didn't call.

DAN

There were several moments during lunch with Bert when I almost gave in to weakness and told him of the incident with Carlotta. But of course I didn't. And by the end of lunch Bert had cast his usual spell of sympathy and humour, and it was all as easy as our lunches in the old days. When he began to talk of Carlotta I had the impression he was genuinely irritated by her kindness and persistence. I doubt he'll agree to go and stay with her. I hope very much he'll come to us.

As for Isabel's return, it all went off much better than expected. It is, of course, only guilt that made me suppose she might have been uneasy about Carlotta's visit. Carlotta's always dropping round – she didn't know, or had forgotten, Isabel was away. I think she was positively grateful to hear Carlotta had offered to cook, and keep me company.

Slight panic when Sylvie came up with her row idea. Also relief: she definitely thought our possibly ruffled appearances were the result of some kind of disagreement. I was pretty quick off the mark with the Bert explanation, though my heart was thumping fast as I produced it. Isabel, of course, completely understood. She looked intrigued. Later, in bed, we discussed what, if anything, might happen to Bert and Carlotta. Then I mentioned the possibility of his coming to stay for a time while the builders were in his house. There was a fractional pause, as I knew there would be. I could see Isabel's practical mind racing round the idea of one more to cook for, extra cleaning for Gwen and so on. But she said that would be a lovely idea. She was lying on her back looking at the ceiling. She put out a hand

and touched my wrist. I moved towards her. She took me with particular eagerness.

Now, I think she's asleep. The moon comes through the window flinging its wide band of silver across the carpet, up on to the bed, over the mounds of our feet. All's well again. We're back on track. I love my wife. Never again will I betray her, or think of betraying her. I can only pray Carlotta is to be trusted and will never, ever give the slightest indication to Isabel of what happened. But the fact is, Carlotta's not to be trusted. She can be a vengeful bitch if things don't go her way. I wouldn't put it past her, if there was some row between her and Isabel, to blurt out what happened in a fit of jealousy of our married life. So I suppose that – though I've got over the first hurdle and will try to put the whole thing from my mind – I can't be absolutely certain Isabel will never know.

Does that mean the old innocent peace is forever to be disturbed? If it does, it's my own fault. How could I have been such a bloody fool?

Oh my Isabel: waking, sleeping, I love you...

GWEN

So I got it. Surprisingly cheap. The man in the shop was very kind. He tried to show me how it worked. But I could see he was very busy. There were a lot of people in a queue all wanting to buy phones. Everyone in the world wants a mobile today.

I came out of the shop feeling quite in the fashion. Gwen Bishop with a mobile! This time last year I would never have believed it. I felt quite excited, and thought I'd try ringing my daughter some time.

But when I got home I was confused. Everything the man said went out of my head. And those little things you have to press – they're too small for thumbs like mine. But I did press, here and there, and read the things that came up on the screen once I'd found my glasses. It made little squeaks and squawks – made me jump. I don't know what it was trying to say but I daresay I'll get used to it in time.

I took it with me to number 18. Every now and then I got it out of my pocket and just looked at it to see if I could understand it better. But I couldn't. So I showed it to Mrs. G. at coffee time. She laughed at me. She said she'd never have guessed I would succumb. She herself has a mobile though I've never seen her use it, or heard it ring for that matter. It lives on the top of the fridge.

She took mine and went through it all with me. Very kind of her. Then we both returned to our work and I put it back in my pocket. I don't suppose it ever will ring, of course. I mean no one has my number or even knows I now have a phone. In some ways it was a waste of money, but I've done it now. Maybe it will come in useful one day.

Some time later – perhaps half an hour – I was at the kitchen window when I saw a man on the opposite side of the street, hands in pockets. He was staring straight at me.

It was Gary.

My heart didn't just miss a beat, it gave a ruddy great leap. I heard myself give a small cry. Oh no! Instantly my hand went to the phone: I would ring the police.

But then I thought: I can't do that. Gary's done nothing wrong. He's at liberty to stand where he likes, look where he likes. Besides, by the time I'd managed to get my glasses on and fiddle about with all those small buttons, and call the police, he'd be gone. And the likelihood was if I did get through to the station they'd think I was a nutter and wouldn't come round. So I picked up the hoover and went upstairs. Mrs. G's bedroom's over the kitchen. I peeped out of the window. Gary had gone, so I was right to have done nothing.

Heart still racing, I got on with my work.

BERT

Lunch with Dan still on my mind. I'd thought it would be easy enough – Dan and I such old friends, we could chatter on forever. In fact it was hard. We weren't at a loss for things to talk about, of course. Went through all the usual old stuff. I managed to make him laugh. And then brought up the subject of Carlotta. He didn't seem much interested in talking about her.

All the time I was in half a mind to confess, clear the air and say, 'Look here old man, the other night things got a bit out of hand with your wife, with Isabel. I, well, to be blunt I tried to kiss her. Never in my life have I wanted a woman so much. But, don't worry, I kept control.'

Of course I said none of that. Wouldn't have done so in a thousand years. As I listened to his problems about the opening of Act 2 of *Rejection,* I couldn't help wondering what would have been his reaction if I *had* spilled the beans. Perhaps, being a man of such goodness and understanding, he would have taken it on board calmly enough. Laughed it off. Forgiven me, forgiven her. Not wanted to know how she felt. On the other hand it might have been the end of everything – our friendship, their marriage. Bearing all that in mind, not for anything would I have taken that risk.

And never will Dan know, or have reason to guess, how much I love his wife. That is something I have to deal with on my own. God knows how.

There was only a piece of cheddar and a cucumber in the fridge this evening: supper enough, with a bottle of wine. We'd eaten a huge lunch.

Then I sat in the old chair that Carlotta will want to throw out, or re-furbish beyond recognition, and thought yet again about the aimless muddle my life had become since returning to London The drink hadn't helped extinguish Isabel from my mind. If anything, with the picture of her in the cellar, head tipped back, her face cloudy pale in the dim light, my desire for her was increased. Not just to make love to her, but to be with her. Always.

I stood up. And it came to me – the obvious answer: I would accept Dan's offer to stay. Then, at least, I would be able to *see* Isabel every day, be in her presence. Her proximity, alongside never being able to touch her again, might ease this pain. No hope can kill forbidden love in the end, I believe. It was worth a try.

I stumbled about the room in search of another bottle

to celebrate the excitement of this idea. I switched on a second light. Seeing more clearly the shambles of the room, the wretched Carlotta came to mind. Hadn't I promised to ring her? Let her know my decision about staying with her? Suppose I probably ought to offer some kind of apology for having been a bit churlish the other evening, too.

I looked at my watch. 11.30. She was probably out. Perhaps she'd be out all night, pleasuring some young man who would later become one of her anecdotes. I picked up the telephone. Had some difficulty finding, then reading, her number written on a scrap of paper. Then I dialled. The familiar scrapings of the old Bakelite telephone came back to me. Doubtless it was another thing she'd want to change for a newer model. I'd put up some resistance, there, I thought. I'm used to my old telephone. It's done me well.

CARLOTTA

The telephone rang. I'd just put out the light. 11.30pm. Bert.

'Didn't think you'd be in,' he said. 'Just ringing to say I'm going to stay with Isabel and Dan. I think that'd be easier. But thank you for the kind thought …'

'Easier than what?' I asked.

Bert didn't answer that. He mumbled something about being in low spirits the other night when I came round, and he was sorry.

I put the phone down, not waiting to hear his apologies or anything else. Then, very unlike me, I cried myself to sleep.

ISABEL

Much of my life is spent picking up beads the size of a pinhead with tweezers. I've been doing that since nine this morning. Once the beads have been stuck in a neat little pattern on the end of a ribbon, it's time to add a few small feathers. They catch the light when the ribbons move – though not in the same way as the beads, of course. They pick up a gentler light. It's this contrast in a tiny space that I aim for ... and hope to achieve. Not an achievement, I acknowledge, that many would either aspire to ... or notice. But our own small, secret pleasures are essential to our wellbeing – no matter if others are innocent of their existence.

This morning it's hot in the studio. The window is open. The fretwork of leaves on the plane tree outside is absolutely still. Not a cloud trespasses the sky. The white parrot tulips bend too far over their jar on the desk: no one looked after them while I was away. I can see that their water in the glass vase is a slimy green. On the top shelf of the dresser a butterfly rests on a mask of silver and rust spots, as if it had found a place of camouflage. Dead ... or sleeping? I can't tell. But it gives me an idea. I'll put a fake butterfly on one of the quieter masks – just one, high on the cheek. It might work. I'll try that, once I've finished the next commissioned masks on my list.

I pick up a length of invisible thread. I love this stuff: it's like a piece of real cobweb, but strong – Cobweb? Quickly I put that thought from my mind ... that cobweb in my hair.

As I hold it up and move my hand, its transparency flashes with colours – mauve, green, gold. I wonder at the marvels there are to observe in ordinary things: in our hurried lives so much goes unnoticed. One of the reasons I love my private world up here is that, not only can I make the masks that float into my head unbidden (and sometimes turn out to be more beautiful than I had imagined), I can also quietly observe the minutiae that, in the greater passage of life, go unappreciated: the scratches of shadow on a white tulip, the dull clash of antique colours in the Kilim rug, the sizzling lights in a pot of gold paint ...

I thread the needle with invisible thread – becoming increasingly invisible to me with every week. Soon I shall have to give in and get glasses.

There are footsteps on the stairs leading to my room. Odd. No one ever comes up in the morning.

Dan puts his head round the door. Mornings, Dan always has the look of a well-scrubbed schoolboy. Each night seems to wash away his real age. By the time he comes home in the evening, it's caught up with him again: battered by his day at the office, he's returned to his middle-age.

'Sorry to disturb you,' he says, 'but Bert has just rung. He said he'd love to come and stay. Were we sure?'

I put down my needle, still free of the thread. It swung round on the table, pointing at Dan.

'Of course,' I said.

The invisible thread had now vanished completely. I felt a stirring of irritation.

'I don't think he'd be much trouble,' Dan went on as if I needed convincing. 'Out most of the day, generous to Gwen and all that …'

'It's fine,' I said.

Dan was still merely looking through the open door. He would deem stepping over the threshold a gross intrusion, whereas breaking his news from the passage he'd judge hardly counted as a disturbance. I said I'd get Gwen to make up the room.

It seemed Bert's plan was to move in tomorrow. I nodded again. I shuffled things around: ribbons, cards of buttons, small pots of glitter, skeins of ribbon. The needle, now, had disappeared too. How I hate interruptions.

'Darling: if it doesn't work, if it's too much, we can always ask him to go,' Dan was saying. 'He'd quite understand. And I daresay Carlotta's invitation remains open.'

I looked at him, knowing exasperation was in my eyes. I said I rather wanted to get on now, but he should tell Bert we were expecting him tomorrow, and looking forward to it.

Dan backed away, apologising for this visit, and shut the door.

In long and happy marriages such short, edgy exchanges after a loving night are the norm: a mere flutter against the great backcloth of mutual understanding. My annoyance was nothing to do with the content of our conversation, but about the breaking of work that had been going well. The spell was now broken. I lashed irritably about in search of more thread, another needle, and feathers no bigger than a thumbnail. I wondered if I should give up for a while, change the water in the tulip vase. Still ... all this annoyance, I vaguely realised, did keep me from wondering what it would be like, having Bert in the house.

In the end I went downstairs for coffee earlier than usual. The kettle hadn't boiled. Gwen was apologetic. It occurred to me she looked unusually pale. But she didn't say anything and I didn't enquire. Gwen never says much about her life and I don't like to appear curious. I do sometimes wonder, though. What does she do alone in her small flat after she's left us? What equivalents, if any, does she have to my secret life in the studio? One day, I must gently enquire how she spends most of her time.

I asked her if she would make up the spare room bed, explained about Bert. 'The green sheets, it'll be,' she said, nodding.

I couldn't read her look. It was a combination of acceptance, puzzlement, reluctance. But perhaps it just conveyed the same sort of irritation I'd so recently felt. Happily engaged in polishing the kitchen table, she would now have to leave that job to prepare the spare room. I couldn't tell her I understood. I simply told her there was no hurry, and apologised for this extra job.

CARLOTTA

At lunchtime I rang Isabel. I had to talk to *someone* about Bert.

'I hear he's chosen to come and stay with *you*,' I said … nicely, calmly, I thought.

Isabel agreed that was so. She, too, then suggested it would be 'easier.'

'Easier than *what*?' I snapped, irritation blasting all my good intentions to stay calm.

Isabel, sounding a touch weary, suggested it might be a bore for me, having a man around the house who hasn't got a job. I pointed out that I was at work all day and in fact it would be rather agreeable, coming home and finding someone there each evening.

I could hear Isabel's sigh, her effort to find the right thing to comfort me. In the end she said she was sorry but there was nothing she could do. It was Bert's choice, though she herself was wary of a third presence in the house. 'You must come round often,' she added. 'We can all go to the theatre, films.'

Huh! Some consolation.

'Thanks very much,' I said. 'And meantime things have got to such a bad state between Bert and me, I'm nervous of ringing him even to talk about the business

I'm doing for him – getting him to agree to a slight change in my budget and so on.'

'I'll talk to him,' Isabel assured me – so damn soothingly I could have strangled her.

Then, in my outrage at the unfairness of it all, I went too far.

'Well, it'll be nice for you and Dan having Bert there,' I said. 'But if I were you I'd try to remain ... you know, on the alert.' I said this jokily, I thought.

'What do you mean?'

'Single man under same roof as beautiful sympathetic woman. Single man with no woman in his life. You can never be sure', I said.

'Don't be ridiculous,' Isabel snapped back – angry, now, I think. 'Bert's Dan's oldest friend. Never in a million years ...'

'Don't you be too sure,' I heard myself saying – out of control by now, the words rushing ahead of me. 'You know what men are, *all* men.'

The utter stupidity of this remark further enraged Isabel. But I went on: 'I wouldn't put it past Bert ...'

'What are you saying?' Isabel asked very quietly.

There was a long furious silence between us.

'Intuition,' I said at last.

Isabel snorted. '*Intuition?* You're a pathetic judge of character, and your powers of intuition are absolutely nil. You're a devious mischief-maker, and I can't think … why you're my friend,' she petered out.

In all the years we'd been friends, I'd never known Isabel so angry. I felt a surge of tears again. Wondered how to make amends.

'I'm so sorry, Is,' I said. 'I don't know what's got into me. I'll ring you later.'

Isabel didn't apologise for the foul things she'd said. I stayed on the bench in Hyde Park (where I'd been eating my lunchtime sandwich) wiping my eyes, regretting the whole conversation. Then some nefarious spirit came to my rescue. Tears disappeared suddenly as they'd come. I knew what I'd do. When the time was right, I'd make a move that Bert would be unable to resist, and also find a moment alone with Dan.

Isabel deserved her bloody smooth life to be shaken a bit.

GWEN

When I came out of number 18 I looked up and down the street. No one there. No sign of Gary. My heart was still beating: thump, thump. I knew I hadn't much in the fridge but I couldn't face Tesco's. Gary could well be waiting for me just by the organic sliced bread, where he knows I always go – organic being my own extravagance in life. I didn't feel safe till I'd shut my door behind me. Locked it, bolted it. Then I sat down in my usual chair, no appetite for lunch. I turned on the radio to try to take my mind off things.

Once, once long ago in Blackpool – I must have been nineteen or twenty, long before I knew the children's' father – I met a boy who I think really loved me. Barry. He was nothing special – I'd be the first to admit that. Not much more than a lad. He worked as a porter up at the posh hotel where they had the political conferences. Sometimes he would get big tips from Conservative MPs, just for carrying a suitcase a few yards. 'I'll never vote Labour,' he said. 'Socialists don't believe in tipping.' When he'd saved a few bob he'd treat me to fish and chips and a couple of lagers. We'd have them on a bench opposite where the sun goes down over the sea. Sometimes there was a brass band playing, and seagulls circling over our heads. 'Like confetti,' I said once jokingly – not that he took the hint. One day he said 'Gwen, you're a wonderful girl. A girl after my own heart, I've never met such a girl.' And he held my hand. But there was no hanky panky between us. Never. He was a shy one, Barry. I don't think he'd ever tried that sort of thing and I never pressed him (I hadn't gone all the way in those days, either. Looking back, I do wish my first time could have been with Barry). What I cared about was the love that came from him, and I gave him in return. He was so kind and thoughtful, one of nature's gentlemen. I really imagined that one day we could be together: a small flat in Blackpool and I'd proudly watch him rise up through the ranks of hotel staff. End up in some senior position, I was sure.

The holiday came to an end. I had to go home with mother. She said Barry was no more than a holiday romance, and nothing would come of it. I said it was much more than that, we loved each other. Barry said he'd write. He did, once or twice. And I wrote back, pouring out my love for him. I've never been good with words but they just flew from my heart. Then came a letter saying he'd been sacked from the hotel. Sacked? Barry? I couldn't believe it. Him, always so conscientious. He said it had been a nasty business. He'd been falsely accused, but he didn't say what of. It haunted me, that, for years. Still does. But even in the best people there's something dark, I suppose. Then he sent a card saying he was off to Canada and a new life. But he'd come and fetch me one day and we'd have a family.

That was thirty years ago.

I suppose it was Barry who warned me to be suspicious of men, and I was to discover there was something about me that attracted the bad ones. I never met a good man after Barry. But at least for a few weeks I knew what it was like to love and be loved, so I'm lucky there … and still hopeful.

I expected this morning to see Mrs. G. with a bit more colour in her cheeks after her two days in Dorset. She was quite pale, but then I know she has a lot of work on. I didn't say anything, of course. Not my place. She seemed pleased to be home, filled the house with flowers from her parents' garden. She told me Mr. Bailey was coming to stay for a few weeks and would I mind doing the spare room?

I didn't mind at all. I finished my polishing quickly and went up there with a pile of sheets and towels. It's a lovely room for visitors, though we don't have many. Overlooks the garden. White walls and white curtains covered in little blue pictures – shepherds and that. Rural scenes. You can get quite lost in them if you look at them for a long time. It's special French material, Mrs. G. told me. I didn't catch the name.

I thought how good it would be for one night, just one night, to sleep in that room. When the Grants are away on holiday, of course, I could do that. I could take the chance and they'd never know. But I'd never do it. Never, never. I shall probably die never knowing what it's like to sleep in a lovely bed, linen sheets, overlooking a garden. Perhaps if Barry had come and fetched me we might have gone back to Canada and had a big bed with nice sheets. But there again, it might not have worked out.

The funny thing about my mobile telephone is that it'll never ring because no one in the world knows my number. I don't even know how to find it out myself. Still, I'll leave it on from time to time. Just in case.

And also it'd be ready to dial the police if Gary gives me any more bother.

BERT

I think I've made a great mistake. It's going to be intolerable.

I arrived yesterday evening. Isabel was flurrying about the kitchen, Dan took me up to my very agreeable room. It has a large desk in the window, and the overflow of books from downstairs are in shelves all along one wall. I certainly shan't be short of reading matter.

I went back to the car to collect half a dozen bottles of

Mouton Rothschild '82, which I thought would please Dan. Dumped it on the kitchen table. Isabel thanked me with a kiss on the cheek. She smelt strongly of mint, which she had been chopping. She said she hoped I had everything I wanted...

At supper – the three of us and Sylvie – all was outwardly easy, normal. Dan was teasing me about my current lack of direction. Sylvie giggled a lot, friendly. Earlier I'd slipped her a fiver – it was plain I was going to have to pay my way to her heart. I looked mostly at Isabel's hands, pale as skimmed milk, a tracing of pretty blue veins round the knuckles. She wore a very obvious engagement ring, an aquamarine surrounded by sapphires. What wouldn't I do to give her endless aquamarines. I thought of her and Dan in some shadowed jewellers' shop with its padlocked glass cases, choosing it together. Young faces lit with anticipation of the married life to come. Young postures – that slightly bent way of standing that youthful couples employ. Or perhaps Dan brought it home in a leather and velvet box and surprised her. There were so many things I would never know about their past. I could feel my heart racing ... yes, racing. Luckily I wore a jacket or it might have been visible.

After supper Dan went up to read to Sylvie. I helped

Isabel clear the table and stack the dishwasher. We didn't speak for a while. Avoided each other's eyes. Or at least I avoided hers. Then she asked again if I had everything I wanted (innocent, I suppose, of the irony of this question) and said I must help myself to anything. I assured her I'd be out most days at interviews for jobs I had no intention of taking – though this I didn't tell her. I said I'd like to take her and Dan out to dinner and the theatre from time to time. 'Lovely,' she said. I hoped I wouldn't be a nuisance, I added, and it wouldn't be for too long.

It was then she gave me one of her ravishing smiles and said how good it was to have me there. I had to make my hands into fists so that I would not touch her. I really believe she believed my cobweb story was true, so in her eyes our friendship is innocent as always. How can I bear it? Will I break down one day, confess? I hope not. I must not.

I thanked her for supper and said I'd go to my room, get over the chore of ringing Carlotta and telling her to give the go-ahead to the builders.

'Ah, Carlotta,' Isabel said. 'I must ring her sometime, too. Our last conversation ended badly.' I didn't ask why.

In my room the white walls were shadowed with blue. Fresh evening air came through the open window.

I pulled up the armchair so that I could look into the garden, dominated by a vast chestnut tree. It was good, here, the room. Bad – and yet good – being so close to Isabel. I lit a small cigar, thought of her hands, her smile.

Eventually I rang Carlotta. She seemed to have calmed down. Didn't ask how or where I was, though she must have known. She suggested we'd meet at the house in a week's time when I'd be able to see some progress. I resolved to be nicer to her. She's trying to help, after all. But I'm very glad I chose not to be her guest. I know exactly what would have been expected of me to show my gratitude, and I couldn't have faced that. Not in my present state of love for Isabel. But if I can stop myself being quite so churlish to Carlotta, perhaps we could be reasonably good friends.

Isabel, Isabel: just yards away in the marital bed with Dan.

I took out my flask of whisky. Best not to think.

SYLVIE

Bert has been staying with us for about a week now. He gave me a fiver on the first night and today he gave me another ten. He said he realised the first £5 wouldn't buy a video. He's cool. It's nice having him here. He makes

Mama laugh and listens very hard when Papa bangs on about his play. So far he hasn't brought horrible Carlotta round, so maybe they're not going to be an item. So it's all OK.

I think he'll probably give me some more money in a week or so, if I keep being nice to him.

Chapter Eight

DAN

Good having Bert here. The perfect guest, I'd say. Keeps out of the way. He produced a tin of caviar last night, a week after the generous wine we're happily getting through. He's pretty vague about the interviews he goes to: I've a feeling he's no intention of taking any of the jobs he's offered. I think he spends a lot of time re-acquainting himself with The National Gallery and the B.M. – and he admitted the Tate Modern took him a whole day. I like to think he's happy here. He seems more relaxed than when he first arrived back from America.

I gave him Act II of *Rejection* to read. He made one or two small suggestions, said he was no expert on reading plays but there were various things he liked or that made him smile ... or think. I respect his opinion, as I always have, so took encouragement from his comments. But I don't know what he really thinks. He didn't show any great enthusiasm – perhaps he doesn't want to encourage false hope. But it was kind of him to read it, give me his thoughts. So I'll plod on ('plod' being the apt word at the moment. Act II has yet to come alive). One day I'll say to him, 'Bert, tell me honestly, do you think my writing's crap? I haven't got what it takes? I should give up trying?' And I know, confronted, he'll give me an honest answer. But I won't ask him just yet. Perhaps when *Rejection* is finished. I have sleepless nights trying to think of a proper title.

Carlotta he never mentions, nor do I, although I know he has a meeting with her arranged in his house. I don't think she occupies much of his thoughts.

I don't dwell on her much, either. The incident seems far away, reduced in size to a bantam's egg. Odd, mind pictures: visualising it, I see us both the size of eggs, in the same way that I think of people in the ancient world as very small, toy-sized figures. Historical perspective has always played tricks on my mind.

I still can't begin to understand what demon got into me – or Carlotta, for that matter. And when I do let myself think of it, it's with infinite regret. More worrying – and the anxiety is larger than an egg and won't go away – is the fear that one day Carlotta will hint to Isabel what happened. Years from now she might – even accidentally – refer to it. There have been moments in the past when she's let Isabel down by revealing something she was sworn not to reveal. But there's nothing I can do about that. Just hope. If my stern warning to her could trammel up the consequences... But I can't be sure of that. I can only live trusting that one day the whole regrettable business will fade.

CARLOTTA

So. The evening of the meeting at last. I sent Bert a card saying please be there at six. I don't want to ring him again. My plan is to get there at 6.15. That will give him time to take in the progress so far on his own. He can gather his thoughts, put them to me when I arrive. It can all be over very quickly. I shan't hang around looking for an invitation to dinner. I shall act as if he's nothing more than a client.

All the same, I've been thinking constantly of the move I might make that would stir things up one way or another. Should I, or shouldn't I? Would it be completely mad? Certainly it would be a risk. Think I shan't decide till I get there. See what sort of mood he's in. Act spontaneously if there's the slightest indication...

I arrived back early from the office, had a bath. When I got out of it I stood for a long time looking at my naked body. Not bad, I have to admit. Amazing breasts, small waist, narrow hips, long legs. Sexier than Isabel, surely? – I know Bert admires Isabel hugely: does he fancy her, I wonder? I put on a black cotton shirt that does up with a spine of tiny pearl buttons. Left a few undone at the top, but not too many. No intention of cheap provocation. Then I took up my Bert file and set off in the car.

With some trepidation, I have to admit.

ISABEL

A week to the day after Bert moved in I ran into him on the stairs. I hate meeting people on stairs. It's always hard to find something to say as one is going up, the other down: not the place to stop for a proper exchange.

I knew he was off to see what Carlotta had done so far to his house. He'd said he wouldn't be in for dinner – he thought he'd better take out 'the decorator', as he called her, to make up for his previous bad behaviour. If she refused, he added, with a sparkle that indicated this would be unlikely, then he'd look after himself.

Bert was coming down, I was going up. We stopped simultaneously, he just one step above me. Our eyes met. I blushed, then regarded my own hand, a distant thing, nothing to do with me, tighten on the banister. There was a timeless silence, a mutual rush of unspoken words, flaying questions: how to begin? I think both of us wondered.

'In an ideal world,' Bert eventually said, 'I wouldn't be doing this, going out this evening to waltz my way round Carlotta's sensitivities. I'd be here sharing the fish pie with you and Dan.'

'That would have been nice,' I answered, helplessly.

He stepped down onto my stair, said he wouldn't be late. He moved as if to kiss me goodbye. Then he flicked back his head before our cheeks had a chance to meet, and looked at his watch without conviction: I knew he didn't give a damn about the time.

'Must be going,' he said, and hurried down. I could see he was disturbed.

When he had gone, I lowered myself onto the stair. Often, as a child, I would sit on the old mole-brown carpet of our stairs at home, trying to puzzle out the worrying preoccupations of childhood.

The habit hasn't left me. I still do it when no one's around. I rested my spinning head on my hands. Had Bert said anything about our...whatever it was, our moment of madness, to Carlotta? God forbid: surely not.

But how could I know? I'd vowed to myself never to mention it again. Like that, it might go away. But it was terrible not knowing.

Worse was the thought of their evening. Carlotta taking him round his own rooms, explaining things. Giving him those patient little smiles that she knows can captivate, her front teeth just visible on her bottom lip. I know her come-hither stance so well: head on one side while she does her listening act. For all his irritation, Bert might find this too much to resist. It must be some time since he had a woman – I could tell.

The thought of them brought deep unease. I stood up, went to the kitchen, took the fish from the fridge. It would be awful when Bert left, in a couple of weeks or so, but his presence here is an odd strain. I half wished something would happen that would mean he had to leave early: no more slight dread of meeting him alone on the stairs.

I searched for a sharp knife. Dan banged the front door, home later than usual. He put down a bag of lemons I'd rung and asked him to buy. 'For all Bert's talents as a guest,' he said, 'it's lovely that we've got an evening to ourselves again, isn't it?' He took me in his arms, kissed me on both cheeks.

Then he held me a little away from him, and looked at

me so intently my guilty heart couldn't help wondering if it was an enquiry.

BERT

I had to drive very slowly to give myself time to calm down. That moment of unplanned proximity with Isabel on the stairs had had its effect. I must be very careful in future: make sure I don't run into her alone again, be so close.

Carlotta's car was parked outside the house. I drew up behind her. Heard myself sigh. It was a great effort to get out, let myself through the front door.

The sitting-room was transformed by exactly the kind of mess I'd imagined. Furniture was humped under dustsheets, islands of various size on the carpet white with dust. Pictures were stacked on the floor, wallpaper was stripped from one wall. Didn't seem to me much progress had been made.

Carlotta was sitting in my old chair – perhaps she didn't plan to throw it out after all – whose shape I recognised even in its disguise of a gingham dustsheet. 'Don't worry about the carpet,' she said, looking at my footsteps in the dust, 'it's going.'

She stood up. She seemed to be wearing less make-up than usual: bare lips, not much stuff on her incredibly long lashes. Bare legs, too: flat shoes. A black shirt done up by dozens of minute buttons. I had the impression she had deliberately not tried with her appearance.

'Those must have taken you ages to do up,' I observed, with a nod towards her shirt.

She smiled politely at my pathetic observation. 'Yes,' she said, 'but they don't take a moment to undo.' I reckoned we were about equal in our feebleness. She suggested a tour of the house.

I followed her: kitchen, study – chaos everywhere. I was thinking of Isabel and Dan at supper. It was hard to take much interest, but I managed to sound appreciative. We went upstairs. She bounced on each stair, bottom swinging from side to side. In my mind's eye was Isabel – the fluidity of her ascent to the studio that night. The shifting of her long modest skirt. So different.

My bedroom, too, was covered in dustsheets. There were streaks of pink plaster here and there on the walls that covered familiar cracks. On the window ledge a white board had been propped up. It was painted with stripes of various greens.

Carlotta wanted to know which one I liked best. I stood looking at them in uninterested silence. If she had asked me how I would have liked this room to be done,

I would have said with white walls and the same curtains as there are in my room at number 18. But she would never have asked, having decided I was as hopeless as all men when it came to decorative matters, and I would never have said. As it was, the greens all looked so similar it was hard to be struck with a preference. I didn't know, I said at last.

'Bert,' Carlotta suddenly snapped, 'do *try*. Please.'

She swung round to re-study the samples herself. In the hunch of her shoulders and the tightness of her back I read her impatience.

There was a sudden, startling noise of ripping. Her hands were outspread, holding the front panels of her shirt apart. I had a momentary sensation that I was seeing the wings of a rook about to fly.

She pivoted round to face me, more challenging than irritated now. Her shirt, parted wide, revealed her bare breasts. She looked at me looking at them. Smiled.

'See, I told you the buttons didn't take long to undo,' she said, and quickly closed the wings of material and fumbled to do them up again. I don't know for how long it was she had allowed me to gaze at her nakedness. It might have been a second, it might have been an hour. Whichever, the impact was so astonishing that there was not an inch of those exquisite breasts that was not imprinted on my mind. I defy any man, even Dan, not to have been thrown by such a surprise, such a sight. I was speechless.

'Joke,' Carlotta said, head down, still concentrating on the buttons. 'Joke, joke, joke. Please Bert, take it as a joke. Probably a very silly one. But I had to do something to wake you up, stir a fraction of interest in green paints. Besides, I wanted to lighten things between us, not to seduce you.'

She made a sudden move towards me, gave me what I took for a conciliatory kiss on the cheek. For a second those heavenly breasts were divided only by our shirts from my own chest. I fear I quivered. She backed away. Suggested we should progress to the bathroom, where she talked with incredible speed about brass taps and orchestrated lavatories, wall mirrors and the possibility of a power shower in the corner. It was the weirdest evening I'd ever spent in my own house.

Beyond any coherent thought, I could only keep agreeing with her plans.

GWEN

'Can you tell me *exactly* what happened, Mrs.?' A nice voice was in my ear. 'Can you remember?'

I couldn't remember. I was muzzy with the pain, and whatever they'd given me. I couldn't remember the children's names, or their numbers or where they lived. So I gave them Mrs. G's number. Somehow that seemed stuck in my head.

Now, I'm lying in a hospital bed. It must be the middle of the night. A bandage and a wodge of something covers most of my head. It goes right over one eye. With the other eye, which I open just for a second, I can see other beds. I must be in a large ward. Streetlights come through thin curtains across the windows opposite. Someone groans horribly. My left side hurts if I move, even very slightly. My right arm is heavy when I try to lift it. It's covered in bandages, too.

I shut my eyes again. Try to remember. After a while, things come back to me. I do remember bits.

I left number 18 this morning − was it today or yesterday? I can't be sure − with head held high. I wasn't going to be cowed by the thought of Gary any more. I couldn't let him haunt me. I walked home quite fast, looking neither right nor left, and I didn't see him.

Late afternoon, after I'd had my tea, I decided I'd treat myself to a cinema. I hadn't been out of an evening for I don't know how long, and I'd seen there was an old

Carry On film at Shepherd's Bush. That might give me a laugh, I thought. Take me out of myself.

I set off at six, or thereabouts. I enjoyed the film – laughed out loud with the rest of the audience. I should do this more often, I told myself, as I came out. I was struck with that funny feeling, as I always am after a film, of how small we all are. I suppose it's after looking at those much larger than life people for a couple of hours. 'How small I am,' I thought, 'and how unimportant.'

I wasn't twenty yards from the cinema when I saw a man running very fast along the crowded pavement towards me. People were pushed out of his way. I had the impression he was either being chased, or chasing someone. I saw his face only for a moment, twisted with anger or fear or some such. But the light was bad, it being dusk, semi-dark. And it all happened so quickly I couldn't be sure of anything. Except that the running man was wearing a pale blue anorak with a black stripe down one side. It struck me: Gary has an anorak like that. I can't be sure if he was wearing it when I saw him outside number 18. But then it's a mass-made garment. Thousands of men must have them.

As he passed me I felt my bag being wrenched from my arm. I felt the sting of its sharp clasp cutting into my wrist. I was spun round, almost knocked off my feet.

I think for a split second I was face to face with my attacker, but by now I was so dizzy I don't know. Then he held up a hand. He was holding some hard implement, I don't know what. He hit me on the face. I felt no pain.

I do remember falling. As I went down I felt as if I was disintegrating, my whole body coming to pieces. I felt I was falling in flakes, like snow. I felt the pavement beneath one of my hands. It was oddly gritty as if there was spilt sand. My fingers came across a sticky paper, and a patch of soft stinking rotten banana or something, and I thought I was going to be sick. Commotion, I was aware of. Such commotion.

Then darkness. Darkness, and a face came into that darkness. Gary's face – just like it does in my nightmares. Was Gary checking I wasn't dead just before he ran off, or was it an hallucination? I'll never know. The wailing of an ambulance siren was going up and down in my head like a see-saw. Hurting so much, I think I cried out. Then nothing.

Next thing I knew, Mrs. G was by my side. She was holding my unbandaged hand. She was saying something but I can't recall her words. It was nice having her there, against the throbbing pain in my head. At one moment I saw Mr. G beside her. Then a nurse came and gave me an injection and I must have slept.

So now I do remember most of it. I'm glad of that. Besides, it could have been worse. In the morning I'll be able to tell them what I know. Perhaps I'll have to describe it all to a policeman, not that they're very interested these days. Too many muggings to cope with. But I won't give them Gary's name. I'll keep my suspicions to myself. If Gary thought I was the one to have put the police on to him, Lord knows what he might do. So I'll not mention Gary, not even to Mrs. G.

I'll ring for the nurse, now: see if she'll give me a bit more of that whatever it was for the pain.

ISABEL

Dan was rather quiet at supper. Tired, I think. Perhaps we'd become used to Bert being there and had to accustom ourselves to being on our own again.

About 9.30 – I'd just finished clearing up and had settled down with the paper – the telephone rang. The hospital. A Mrs. Gwen Bishop, they said, had been mugged, and was admitted a couple of hours ago. They understood I was her next of kin. She was asking for me, could I come round? She was in shock, but conscious.

Dan said he'd wait till Bert returned so that Sylvie would not be left on her own. Then he'd join me.

I drove very fast, goaded by the swarms of terrifying thoughts that leap into action on hearing bad news. Shamefully, one of the thoughts was – what would we do without Gwen? God make her all right. I never like to think of her having to leave one day. Now that possibility twisted through my mind … alarming.

I ran through corridors, was confused by lights and notices.

Lost. At one moment, crossing an internal bridge with a bright blue rubber floor, I sensed it was coming towards me rather than I was moving along it. Despite my hurried walking, I appeared to be standing still. But I can't have been, for eventually the bridge was crossed and I found the ward.

Even faced by the plight of others, I thought, we cannot banish ourselves. I despised myself.

Gwen was in a bed at the far end of the ward. Her head was bandaged: one eye only visible, and beneath it a bruised and swollen cheek. Her left arm, lying on the bedclothes, was bandaged to the elbow. The other, which seemed to be all right, was bent. Her hand moved up and down a few inches of the pillowcase as if testing and disliking the rough cotton stuff. Her uncovered eye was shut. I moved her hand down from the pillow, held it. I felt the roughness of her skin – well, I thought, ridiculously at such a moment, she always refuses to wear rubber gloves. The feel of her skin on a hand I knew so well was shocking. She didn't stir.

I mumbled something about how she was going to be fine. Even as I said the words I wondered at their pointlessness: cliché comfort surely deceives no one, and yet the victim would feel deprived if no consoling words were offered. Human inadequacy, at such times! 'You're not to worry about anything,' I added. 'We'll take care of you.'

I've no idea if Gwen knew I was there. I sat looking at the exposed bit of her face, its familiar lines now strange with bruises and swellings. It was the first time I had ever seen her looking pitifully old. Her hair was scraped back so that I could see a patch of white hair, which I'd never seen before, behind her ear. I hated being privy to this: discovering a secret while she was helpless. I went on rubbing her knuckles with my thumb, and occasionally murmuring things.

There were few lights on in the ward and a kind of semi-silence smeary with the noises of illness: a groan here, the creaking of a bed there that spoke of the pain with which some turn was made. A single nurse floated by from time to time, apparently not looking at her patients, but then stopping, surprisingly, by a bed. It was intolerably hot, airless. There was a smell of strong tea and disinfectant against the deeper scent of sweating bodies that had lain too long in rumpled sheets.

I'd no idea how long I sat there, or what the time was. Dan arrived. He stood beside me, looking down on Gwen, a muscle in his jaw clenching and unclenching. He asked no questions. Then the floating nurse stopped by us, said she wanted to settle Gwen for the night. As I stood up, Gwen opened her visible eye. The small twitch of her mouth perhaps meant she knew we were there.

We left the nurse to give Gwen her pills and said we'd be back in the morning. Dan had come to the hospital by taxi so that he could drive me home. I was glad of that. I was glad to be in the passenger seat beside him, safe.

At home we found Bert sitting by the kitchen window, anxious. Dan poured glasses of brandy. We sat up for a long time. Through our desultory talk, only of how best we could help Gwen, I looked at Bert and found it hard to believe that anything untoward had happened between us. Never again, I now knew, would there be another flaring of whatever it was I had felt for him in that moment on the stairs. Whatever it had been was totally – mercifully – obscured by the vital matter now confronting us all: Gwen.

BERT

Carlotta calmed down a little after the gabbling in the bathroom. By the time we got to the kitchen her descriptions of what she envisaged in place of all the old stuff were painstakingly detailed and slow. Back among the dustsheets of the sitting room at last, I suggested we had something to eat. We could walk to the nearest place, an Italian trattoria, in the King's Road.

Carlotta pondered this idea for a long time in silence. Then she agreed – with some reluctance, I thought. I was relieved to leave the house … and all thoughts of interior decoration.

Over *ravioli alle vongole* we shared a bottle of mineral water – she didn't want any wine, and suddenly I didn't either. I told her she was doing an excellent job and I was very grateful. I approved her budget and wrote her a large cheque so she could keep paying the builders and so on. Then I suggested it would be best if I didn't come again till it was all finished. 'Very well,' she said. 'You'll have to leave the green to me. It'll all be about another three weeks.' I could move back then, though there would still be details to complete.

'You show great trust in me,' she added, with a smile.

'I do,' I said.

It was a low-key occasion: no awkwardness, but no electric current, either. Her strange strip act was not mentioned: it might never have happened. She didn't ask how I was doing with the Grants, nor did she enquire about my future plans. We talked about the mime scene in *Giselle*, which she'd been to see the night before. She said that the great majority of audiences had no idea of what was going on. But, she added, she was lucky enough to be one of those who did. She's full of arcane scraps of knowledge, Carlotta. I like it when she comes up with such surprises.

I had the feeling she was controlling herself, determined to deny me any signals. It was impossible to guess what was going on in her mind, and I didn't much care. Dinner was passing easily enough.

It wasn't till our second espressos she apologised for her strange behaviour in the bedroom.

'*So* stupid of me,' she said. 'Very poor joke, very poor taste.' She didn't know what had overcome her. But she was always making mistakes. I assured her I was too, though not quite of the same order. We both laughed. I urged her not to give the matter another thought. It was forgotten.

It wasn't entirely, of course. Back at her car I wondered if she might ask me to her flat for a drink. Unclouded by wine, I was feeling wakeful. I wouldn't have minded seeing her breasts again, closer. But had she invited me, I daresay we would have ended up predictably. I haven't slept with anyone for weeks now, and a man can only go for so long without a reminder from his loins. It would have been straight fucking with Carlotta: there would have been no pretence of love. How could there be? My love is reserved entirely for Isabel. Beside her car, I ran an index finger down the line of small buttons that crouched between Carlotta's breasts. She backed away. Said goodnight and thank you, without so much as a kiss on the cheek – my turn to be rejected, I suppose. I didn't much mind. Just needed a moment to re-adjust. Then, in the car, driving back to Dan and Isabel, I thought why am I even *thinking* of fucking Carlotta when I feel as I do about Isabel?

Thank God, though, it didn't happen. I arrived back soon after ten to find Dan alone, apparently waiting for me. He briefly explained about Gwen and said now I was there to baby-sit, he had to rush to join Isabel at the hospital.

When he'd gone, I poured myself a glass of brandy. Gwen, mugged? I hardly knew Gwen, scarcely saw her, though she'd been delighted by the £20 I slipped her yesterday. How absolutely bloody awful for her.

London, these days... worse than New York. I needed music.

I put on Borodin's D major quartet. In its melancholy nocturne I always find an antidote to my own low spirits. Then I sat in the chair by the window, looking out at the garden. The trees were roughly-shaped gatherings of intense darkness against the semi-darkness of the London summer sky. There was a smell of jasmine that I knew would always remind me of Isabel.

'What now?' I thought.

Perhaps this dreadful event would shift things in a way I could not guess at. Perhaps it would provide a pointer, a direction. But what that would be, for all my reflection, I still did not know and could not guess. I sat there with the music until Isabel and Dan returned. Isabel was very pale, very quiet. I knew that whatever the changes turned out to be, they would not shift my love for her. Gwen's brutal mugging, and its consequences, could make no difference for my – yes – deepening love for Isabel.

I poured glasses of brandy for her and Dan. They were plainly shaken. We sat up very late, conjecturing in the hopeless way that people do after an event that has no explanation. Was Gwen a random choice, or was it a planned attack for some reason we could not guess at? We could not answer our own questions.

In my room, still very awake after the turbulent evening, I sat at the desk looking onto the same view as the one downstairs: wondering, wondering. The sky paled. The trees lightened. I could see their leaves again. Without bothering to undress, I lay on the bed.

SYLVIE

I went with Mama after school to see poor Gwen in hospital. It was her second or third day there I think, and only the second time I've ever been in a hospital. It was absolutely horrible – the smell, a sort of sick-making sweet smell seeping out under a disguise of disinfectant. Mama didn't seem to notice it so I didn't say anything.

Gwen was at the end of a very big ward. As we walked down it I didn't look too hard at the people in the other beds. I didn't want to see a lot of blood and stuff, or people groaning in pain. Gwen was sitting up, most of her face covered in dressings, and her arm bandaged. The bit of her face I could see was the colour of a thunderstorm, all green and yellow, the skin. And her eye was bright red as if it was filled with blood which couldn't get out. But she smiled at us and said how good it was of us to come. She said she was much better, feeling brighter. I remembered how whenever I was recovering from a cold or something she would ask me if I was feeling brighter. We sat by her bed on nasty plastic chairs. The old woman in the next bed coughed all the time.

While she and Mama were talking I looked at the bedside table. There were two very big bunches of flowers with small white cards beside them – Mama's writing on one, and Bert's on the other. There was also a vase of marigolds, the orangest orange I'd ever seen. Beside it was a big card with a picture of a cartoon lion which wasn't very funny. I don't suppose I should have, but I picked it up and looked inside. There was a message written in smudgy biro. It was from someone called Gary who said he'd heard about Gwen's troubles from the lady who lived in the flat beneath her, and had guessed she must have gone to this hospital and hoped the card would reach her. He said he was so sorry, and wished her a speedy recovery, and he would be in touch again one day but for the moment he had business in Yarmouth. When I put the card back Gwen smiled and said it was from a friend. Then she handed me the only other card with a picture, a boring pot of geraniums, and said it was from her son up north. She still hadn't heard from her daughter, though the hospital had rung her yesterday and left a message. Mama said something like I expect she'll call soon. But I've never ever heard Gwen even mention her daughter, so there's probably some trouble there and she'll be jolly lucky if she ever hears from her.

I gave Gwen the piece of Chanel soap Mama had bought for me and she was really pleased. She said it was very extravagant but it was just what she wanted as the hospital didn't run to nice soap, and the towels were like sackcloth, whatever that is.

We didn't stay long. Mama said we shouldn't tire Gwen. She leant over and said something I couldn't hear because the old woman was coughing so much. But Gwen seemed to be disagreeing with Mama, and wagged her unbandaged finger. Then I bent over Gwen to kiss her goodbye. I've only ever kissed her on Christmas Eve, before, to thank her for a present, and I found it quite hard, putting my mouth on those horrible coloured bruises. I shut my eyes and managed it quickly – I mean, I had to do it. I sort of love Gwen. I don't know what we'd do without her. She smelt strongly of tea. When I stood up again I think I saw a tear in her red eye.

I have to admit I was mega glad, like, to leave the hospital. I asked Mama what would happen to Gwen when she came out. Surely she wouldn't be able to manage on her own? Mama said she had been thinking hard about all that, and had come up with a plan. I said she ought really to come to us, but where would she go? With Bert in the spare room...

She didn't answer, so I asked if we could stop off for a video for after tea, and for once she said we could.

BERT

I'd been to an interview in Soho – some film company wanting a financial adviser. Of course I said no. The idea of going to their grey offices every day... nothing would induce me. On the way back I stopped in the market and bought a huge quantity of cherries. I was putting these in a bowl on the table when Isabel and Sylvie came back from the hospital.

Sylvie gave instant news: Gwen was better though looked pretty terrifying, she said, and the smell in the hospital had made her feel sick. Then she went off to do her homework.

Isabel bent over the table, picked up a cherry. I noticed that when her head was at a certain angle a couple of lines appeared on her neck. She was silent while she ate the cherry and spat out the pip. Then she said Gwen was to be released from the hospital at the end of the week. Of course, she shouldn't be, she said, but they needed the bed. When Isabel looks concerned I swear her eyes turn a deeper blue.

Quickly, before she could voice the suggestion I knew she would find hard to make, I said that Gwen must come here, have the spare room. She looked at me, incredulous, but I could see she had no heart to disagree. 'You could have the sofa bed in Dan's study,' she said – but no, I answered, not for anything. I'd be fine. I'd either go to a hotel – it would only be for a couple of weeks, or I could take up Carlotta's invitation. At this idea, produced in jest, she looked doubly anxious for a moment: then we both laughed.

In that moment of laughter, an idea came to me. I've no notion from where. It wasn't anything I'd thought about. It was one of those inspirations that sometimes come to the rescue at a crucial moment. Even before I put it to Isabel it excited me. I picked up several of the yellow cherries and was filled with a kind of amorphous relief: Gwen's accident had provided a solution. Here was a valid reason to distance myself from Isabel, much though that was the last thing I wanted to do.

I would go to Norfolk.

I explained to Isabel that this was something I'd been

contemplating. She didn't seem to think I was lying. I'd been thinking of no such thing, but now the idea had come to me it seemed a reasonable one. It was easy enough to persuade her I'd be happy to get out of London – much though I loved staying here – and re-visit the place of my birth. She said of course she could understand that. She mumbled on that if I really didn't mind, and obviously Gwen wasn't fit to look after herself for a while, and there was nowhere else for her to go… Her children were scarcely in touch, she said. They certainly wouldn't do anything for her and…

'I need a drink, Bert,' she said.

I fetched an open bottle of white wine from the fridge, and glasses. We both sat at the kitchen table. Isabel's shoulders were hunched, her arms folded under her breasts. I could see – I *think* I could see – what was going through her head: the difficulties of both looking after Gwen and trying to continue her work.

'It'll be tough for you,' I said, 'but I daresay it won't be for long.'

'I'll manage' she said, with a wry little smile.

We sipped at the cold wine in silence. I was aware of a guilty longing to put my arm round her shoulder – and of course if it hadn't been for my feelings for her there would have been no guilt – but we were sitting close to each other and I watched, like some surprised spectator, my own arm go round her. She dipped her head, did not try to remove it. Perhaps this was because the gesture meant nothing to her. I realised that. I could see it in her face. Whatever flame there had been, on the stairs, had died completely. I was back to being what I had always been in her eyes: Dan's friend, a comforter in a sad situation.

I removed my arm. She thanked me for everything. I said there was nothing to thank me for. I was conscious there was something in my voice that might betray my intense feelings at that moment. But, pre-occupied, she didn't seem to notice. I wanted to go on sitting there for ever, looking at the bowl of cherries, Isabel so damnably close.

But the front door banged. Isabel gave a quick sigh and stood up. She moved towards Dan. They kissed: he briefly put both arms round her. When she stepped back it seemed as if their touching had relieved her of her present anxiety, whereas my arm round her had had no such effect. Oh God to have been Dan, to have been able to do that for her.

'How's Gwen?,' he wanted to know, 'what's the plan?'

I handed him a glass of wine. Isabel should be the one to tell him, I thought. She filtered away to the far end of the room, her silk skirt doing its usual silent swish behind her, catching lights so fast its solid blue appeared entirely speckled. Dan and I were left facing one another, eye to eye.

From the far end of the room Isabel broke the news.

DAN

Obviously, that's what had to be done. There was no other solution. Gwen could not possibly go home, be on her own.

'Of course, of course,' I kept saying.

It was hard not to mind about the plan – Bert having to go after only just over a week. We'd got used to him. We enjoyed his company. He was the most discreet and tactful of guests. Isabel, I think, who hadn't known him well before, had grown fond of him. Sylvie certainly had. And he was a great comfort to me, letting me bang on about the play. Another two weeks of him would have been wonderful.

But there's no alternative, I see that. Bert seems genuinely happy with his idea of a holiday in Norfolk. If he's trying to escape Carlotta – and I can't be sure of what he really feels – it will be an easy way out.

I'm a bit worried about what it'll be like for Isabel: she's no natural Florence Nightingale. Carrying trays and so on will mean her precious mornings are interrupted: and then she'll have to do a certain amount of housework, which she loathes. So I hope for everyone's sake Gwen's recovery won't take long.

It's odd how, when a crisis disturbs the norm, irritation can lie within sympathy – not the sort of thing one wants to admit, of course. But a fact.

Chapter Nine

GWEN

I sit here. I sit in the armchair by the window looking into the garden. It doesn't feel right, somehow. I don't feel I should be here. And yet it's wonderful, too.

I did my best to persuade Mr. and Mrs. G that I was all right to go home. But they weren't having any of it. They insisted I should come here, just for a while. Just till I've got my strength back. They said Mr. Bailey was going off to Norfolk. Apparently he was longing to get out of London. Can't say I blame him. They came to fetch me from the hospital in Mr. G's big car. I felt a little shaky walking down all the corridors, but once I was in the car the comfort and luxury made me feel so much better. It occurred to me how rarely in my life I'd been in a car since Bill had gone, let alone such a grand one as that.

Mrs. G must have taken a long time preparing the room – doing my job, as it were. Everything dusted and shining, a jug of sweet peas on the dressing table, a bottle of mineral water by the bed – bed made up with linen sheets and turned down for me. My! It's like a dream. I slept so well – the silence. It made me realise how noisy my flat is. I hadn't slept like that for a very long time. It was impossible in the hospital. When we arrived, it was quite late after their evening meal, Mrs. G unpacked my few things, put my old sponge bag in the lovely cosy visitors' bathroom – I can't think how often I've shined the brass taps, and there they were just as sparkling and I hadn't touched them for a week. I don't like to think of Mrs. G spending so much time on things for me. I didn't know what to say. I felt close to tears.

I put the big bunches of flowers that they'd sent to the hospital on the dressing table, then I braced myself for a peep in the mirror. A horrible sight, as I knew it would be. Bandages off my head now – just those transparent bits of dressing over the wound that runs from hairline to cheek. There must have been two bashes because it's the opposite eye that's bad: still filled with blood and the skin puffy and purple underneath it. The bruises on that cheek have turned a yellow green, but there's no wound. And my left hand is no longer in a bandage. There's just a light dressing. I haven't liked to ask what the damage is beneath it.

I stood looking at this picture of myself, unrecognisable, shocked. How long will all this take to clear up? They couldn't say at the hospital. Bruises take longer once you're older. They were more concerned about my mental state. Would I like to see a counsellor? 'Not on your life,' I said, 'Counsellors aren't for me.' But I think I gave a good interview to the two nice young policemen who came to my bedside. The old girl in the next bed was so intrigued she stopped her coughing. I could see she was trying to hear what they were saying. In all honesty I think they only bothered to come and see me because mine was the sixth snatch and hit incident within two weeks, in the same small area of Shepherd's Bush. They had a feeling it might all be the same man, acting on his own. Obviously they were keen to catch him. I agreed to go to an identity parade when I was up to it, and told them all I could remember. They said, 'Gwen, you've been very helpful.'

This morning Mrs. G came in with a tray of breakfast. Breakfast in bed! Me? I couldn't believe it. Again, I couldn't find the words to thank her. She pulled back the curtains and the sun came in. She puffed up my pillows and put the tray on the bed: so beautifully done – the china with the cornflowers that she keeps for visitors, the lace tray cloth that I have to be so careful ironing, not that it's used very much. There was a brown boiled egg, triangles of toast, a small silver pot of tea, and a single rose from the garden. She said she'd get me a paper later. Talk about spoiling.

I ate my breakfast slowly, knowing full well that this sort of thing, which would last for a few days, would never, ever happen to me again. It was only recently, getting the room ready for Mr Bailey, I remember thinking my dream would be to spend a night here, little knowing.. So I eked out the pleasure of the wonderful breakfast, and thought about what an odd thing happiness is. So often you can think back on a time which you remember was happy, like those days with Barry. But so rarely can you think to yourself I am happy *now*.

Sitting in the bed I think I did get pretty close to that, although there was the niggling feeling that this was all wrong. I wasn't a visitor in the house, I was an employee. Besides which I knew what time and trouble it would cost Mrs. G, seeing to me, keeping her from her work. Well, I shall go as soon as I can. As soon as I'm able. But it's quite true – I don't think I could have managed alone at home. Not just for a while.

I put aside my tray and picked up the cards I'd brought with me. There was an ordinary postcard – looked as if it had been in a drawer for years – from Jan. Well, she wouldn't be one to run to a greetings card to her mother. I only sometimes get a phone call on my birthday. There was Ernie's card, too, a cartoon of a woman with a feather duster – very appropriate, I suppose he thought. He'd written quite a long message about how sorry he was, and added for good measure how Lynn sent her love and best wishes. Expect me to believe that! Lynn's never given me a thought. – Then there was the one from Gary. A cartoon lion. I wonder what was going through his mind when he chose that.

And of course I wonder so hard – it's what gives me the headaches, I reckon, rather than the bruises themselves – whether it was Gary did this. I try with all my might to picture a face, and the face that comes to me is sometimes him, sometimes isn't. Perhaps I'll never know. Perhaps I'll only be sure if I can recognise a face at the identity parade. There's no point in worrying over it. What's done is done. But what puzzles me is Gary's behaviour. He must have gone round to my flat – to apologise for his menacing ways, who knows? – and, on finding me out, went to Edie downstairs who gave him the news. So then this card: perhaps a sign of remorse either for all his horrible stalking, or just feeling sorry for what had happened to me, or for feeling sorry for what he had finally done to me. In any event, it shows he has some feelings. Perhaps he thought of me as a friend and I let him down in some way. Anyway, I surprised myself by not throwing the card out, and going back to thinking that Gary can't be that bad. – Well, I was a bit dozy with all the painkillers, wasn't I? But to my way of thinking Gary was a friend for a while. I haven't enough friends to lose one, so it's a pity he's going to Yarmouth, if he really is. Perhaps we could have got everything straightened out.

So here I sit. Most peculiar, being here in quite a different situation from normal. My instinct is to go and find a duster. But Mrs. G has made me promise not to move. And it's true, my head does ache quite badly still. But I'm not shaky on my feet any more. I'm on the road to recovery. It's hard not to feel guilty, a little uneasy, switching from daily lady to guest, and I know it means not only extra work for Mrs. G, but also upsetting her normal routine. Still, she has managed to convince me she really wants me here, and I'm no trouble. I must make sure I'm as little nuisance as possible, and I might as well make the best of this recuperation time. I know I'm the luckiest person in the world, benefiting from the kindness of the Grants.

I shall get up, now. Go and chose a book from the shelves: it's like a library, there are so many. And I shan't think about going home. That's something I don't want to think about at all. I dread it, what with Gary being so unreliable with the truth. It's my guess he hasn't gone to Yarmouth, just wants to calm me down for a while.

ISABEL

I hope very much I've managed to convince Gwen how pleased we are to have her here, how she's no trouble at all, and how she's got to stay until she's completely better. The truth is, and I wouldn't admit this to anyone in the world, it's a bloody nightmare.

This is for several mean, uncharitable ... despicable reasons.

It means I have now to do a certain amount of housework, which I loathe more than anything in the world and am very bad at. I ironed one of Dan's shirts yesterday. The result had me crying with rage at my own incompetence. I have to spend more time on petty journeys out – going to the laundry and the cleaners – to relieve myself of such chores. I have to cook Gwen a simple but proper lunch: she needs feeding for the return of her strength. I have to lay trays. I have to spend at least an hour a day talking to her. I have to keep making sure she has everything she wants and is generally all right — which she always declares she is.

I'm deeply fond of Gwen. I respect her, admire her. I rely on her totally for relieving me of the burden of domestic life so that I can get on with my work. Her capacity for hard work, her constancy, her understanding of my need for time each day to be alone, are extraordinary. I know she loves the family, feels part of it. She joins in celebrating our small successes, and sympathises — but not overly — with our failures. She never grumbles — even about her hard hearted children — and she neither questions my life, nor regales me with stories of her own. She's one of the old stiff-upper lip brigade whose self-containment and ability to glean the best from her quiet existence are extraordinary. The idea of her not being a part of our life is too awful to contemplate. Dan and I would never not have insisted she came here. We wanted her. We want her.

So it's not Gwen that's driving me mad: you could not hope for a more perfect invalid, and her gratitude for my feeble attempts at Florence Nightingale is touching. No: it's simply that having another person in the house, by day, means goodbye to the routine I so rely upon. Bert was different. He left early each morning, never appeared till the evening. Gwen is a presence. I can never be unaware of her, quiet though she is in her room. In the most vile depths of my heart I resent that presence: it casts a shadow over normality. I sit down, an hour late by the time I've got things organised after breakfast, and start on one of the orders that's already overdue. Two hours fly by and I'm interrupted by the maddening thought of what I should be doing in order to have a cottage pie by one o clock. I'm enraged by something that's no one fault.

Bad temper rises. I can feel it, a physical wave, engulfing. I sweep aside threads and glue and the pile of beads I haven't had time to stick on the be-ribbonned mould, and stomp downstairs. I bash my fury into the mince. The scraper snarls over the potatoes. What am I bloody well doing, here in the kitchen in the midday sun, when I could be upstairs at my masks?

I hate myself for such thoughts, such uncharitable rages. I tell myself this is all just a temporary thing, not long. The sooner Gwen recovers the sooner we can all get back to normal. And meantime her delight in the spare room is touching. Yesterday she asked if I could find her a few yards of the *toile de jouille*. She wants to make curtains for her own bedroom.

She's much better – suddenly in the last two days. Her dressings are off, though one eye is still a terrifying red, and her bruises have moved into the lurid stage of ghastly greens and yellows. Today she insisted on coming down for lunch (relief!) though that meant I had to share the cottage pie: I couldn't sit there watching her while she admonished me for only eating half an avocado. She said she'd like to clean the silver this afternoon: she'd feel better back at the kitchen table doing something useful. She didn't have to press me very hard to agree. She also said she'd be fine to go home on Friday – two more days. I insisted she stay the weekend. The argument wasn't resolved.

My loathsome seething left me drained and weary. After lunch I came up here to the studio, but there was no hope of work. I turned on Radio 3 and listened to a Haydn string quartet, and thought about Bert. What on earth can he be doing in Norfolk? He left in his teens: can't be many friends still around. I rather miss him. I liked him coming back every evening, sometimes before Dan, pouring me a glass of wine, standing talking while I chopped things. And he's so good with Sylvie. He bought her a really expensive notebook for her collection of words: she was so pleased, especially when she opened it to find he'd filled the first page with suggestions, none of which she knew. And it was lovely to hear him and Dan banging on about their usual things, scoring off each other, laughing. Yes, I definitely miss him.

I then thought of Carlotta. I hadn't rung her for ages: she didn't know about the whole Gwen saga. As usual, when I'm not in touch with her for a while, l feel guilty. I don't know why. It's unreasonable to feel guilty about not much communication between friends – we all understand about the busyness of each others' lives. But for all Carlotta's bravado I know she's ultimately a bit sad, and sometimes lonely, and likes to speak, if not to come round, at least twice a week. I must overcome my reluctance and telephone her.

I must. I will.

But right now I'm going to ring Bert. Not a word from him. I want to know what he's up to, how he is, what he's doing.

SYLVIE

This afternoon I took a tray of tea up to Gwen with four ginger biscuits which I know she likes. Mama had taken lots of trouble making it look nice, with the best china and everything. I don't know why she takes *quite* so much trouble when she's got so many other things to do. I wouldn't.

Anyway, Gwen was sitting in the armchair by the window looking much better now the bandages are off, though she's still a horrible colour and her red eye is really spooky. She seemed pleased to see me and said she wasn't used to being waited on like this, and it was all very strange. I asked her if she'd had any nightmares about the mugging. She said she hadn't, yet, but wouldn't be surprised if they attacked her soon.

I sat on the floor and ate two of the biscuits, and we got to talking. I don't know why – it just came into my head – I asked her if she'd had any boyfriends when she was young. She said just the one, Barry, in Blackpool on holiday. When I asked what they used to do, she said they mostly sat on a bench eating fish and chips or ice cream, looking at the sea. They specially liked it in the evening when the sun was going down. I expect it was very nosey of me, but I asked her if she was in love with Barry (Elli says she's in love with a boy called Rick who she met skating but she didn't tell me exactly how it felt. Elli says she thinks her mother is in love all the time, with different men). I thought Gwen might be able to tell me exactly what 'in love' was, if she could remember. She said she could remember all right, and she turned her spooky eye to look out of the window, though I had the impression she wasn't seeing the garden, but

Barry in Blackpool. She said it made the whole world unrecognisable. Ordinary things glittered, she said. One morning after she'd come home she went to fetch in the milk bottles and the dew on them had turned to diamonds because Barry existed. I didn't think that sounded very exciting – I mean, dew melts – but I didn't say anything. She said when his letters arrived her heart beat so fast and her eyes were so blurry that she was hard put to read what he said. And when she did – here she gave a small sigh – they weren't quite the letters she was hoping for. Letter writing was not one of Barry's strong points, but between the rather disappointing lines she could tell that he loved her and felt the same as her. He always finished up by saying *all the love in the world to you, my dearest Gwen.*

So why didn't you and Barry get married? I asked then, because she didn't seem to mind talking about him, even though she was no good at explaining 'in love'. She gave a bigger sigh than the last one and said it all came to an end when he went to Canada.

I decided she wouldn't mind just one more question. So why didn't she marry someone else?

It's all a question, young lady, of finding the right man, she said. I found no others, she added, after ages. Barry was the only right man for me. But I did find a second best, and married him mostly for security and children. We got on all right, but no one would say it was a love match. As for the children…well. They haven't turned out quite as I imagined. But still, I count myself lucky, she said, in many ways.

She seemed a bit tired, then, or down or something. I took her tray and said I was very sorry about Barry. I don't know if she heard me.

What I can't imagine is what her life is like when she's not here in our house. But I'd never dare ask her that.

CARLOTTA

Zero spirits at the moment. I've been going out a lot with friends who are friends but not great friends: all rather pointless and I'm suffering too many late nights. It's been hell at work. Everyone complaining, Susan announcing she's pregnant and has to leave shortly – I'll never find such a good secretary again. Long meetings have lost their charm and the whole hassle of actually getting to the office every day has become almost unbearable. 'Why do I do it?' I ask myself. I suppose, if I didn't, I'd be bored out of my mind. At least I know that I'm making some considerable contribution to a very large firm, and the money's nice. My bonus last year was fantastic. But I think I'm becoming disillusioned. I'm no longer spurred by intense ambition. I often think I wish I'd never got caught up in this whole career business.

The only thing I'm enjoying at the moment is doing Bert's house. I think it's really pretty good. He should be pleased. I haven't bothered him at all with problems. I've taken various rather serious decisions myself. But there's one thing I really must speak to him about – that is, his vile old chair. I long to throw it out, it'd be ridiculous in the new rather minimalist look I've gone for. But he has some daft sentimental attachment to it, and I know that to abandon it without consulting him could be disastrous. So … I must ring him, reluctant though I am.

The answerphone was on at the Grants. I decided to try Dan at the office. His secretary, perhaps, could give me Bert's mobile number … though I wouldn't mind a word with Dan. I haven't spoken to him or Isabel for over a week. What's up with them?

I picked up the telephone. The thought crossed my mind that if Dan and I hadn't experienced two minutes of nefarious passionate kissing, then such a call would mean absolutely nothing and I'd have no feelings of trepidation or anything else. As it is, I feel guilt. It feels very odd, knowing he and I are bound by a secret moment. I still sometimes wish...we'd...

I was put straight through to Dan. He apologised on Isabel's behalf and his own for not having rung for so long, but explained about poor Gwen. And said Bert had gone off to Norfolk in search of his past, and no one had heard a word from him. 'Bugger Bert,' I thought. 'He could have left his number with his interior decorator. Men just don't *think*.'

Dan chatted on for a while – plainly it wasn't a very busy morning at the office. Then he suddenly said he was still worrying about my powers of secrecy, and was I absolutely trustworthy? That made me pretty cross. I reminded him I'd given my word and we should leave it at that. He was slightly contrite, then. Said he didn't doubt me, but he supposed that due to his conscience he couldn't resist checking up. Then he said the best thing would be if we both forgot about that evening completely, as soon as possible.

I agreed.

Actually, I added that I *had* forgotten (not true). It was he who had reminded me, I said.

He ended by suggesting I came round at the weekend. I said I'd think about it. There's something of an old woman in Dan. I'm not sure starry-eyed Isabel has ever noticed.

Having got the news from him, there was no need to ring her. Oddly, I didn't feel like it anyway, though in my heart I missed her.

Instead, I rang Bert. It was nine thirty. It hadn't occurred to me he wouldn't be up. But, sleepily, he explained he was in a four poster bed. Alone. Scarcely awake.

'What on earth are you doing in a four poster bed in Norfolk?' I asked.

As I did so I felt a surge of unease. People aren't usually in four poster double beds by themselves. He was as capable of lying as the rest of us. God knows why, but I didn't fancy his being with anyone else.

He laughed, more wakeful.

'All alone, I can assure you,' he said, and I believed him.

Evidently he was staying in some very expensive hotel, eating well, re-visiting scenes of his childhood, having 'various thoughts.' About what, he wouldn't say. So I asked him about the chair. He said at all costs it must not be thrown out as it would come in useful one day.

'What day?' I snapped.

By now his air of mystery was unnerving me further.

'Well, I'm making possible plans, coming to various conclusions,' he said. But, again, he wouldn't be drawn.

Then just as I thought the rather edgy conversation would come to an end, it changed key. I can't quite remember how, or exactly what we said, but it was all rather silly. He made me laugh describing some London woman he'd met in the baker: her braying voice and Gucci shoes.

'Didn't used to have those sort of people in the village,' he said.

I forced myself not to ask him when he was coming back to London, and he didn't enlighten me. So – thinking I should be the one to finish the conversation – I said I'd let him know when the house was absolutely finished, and if ever he came back from Norfolk I could show him round. He laughed.

'I look forward to that,' he said. 'I must say I do rather look forward to another view…'

In the crystalline pause between us I knew just what he meant.

And to my huge surprise the sensation that now overwhelmed me was one of sheer lust. Also, I suddenly *liked* Bert very much. His odd charm had come zooming over the telephone. It occurred to me I no longer wanted him *just* as a friend, as a useful man. His admitting he'd obviously liked 'the view' caused some odd and unexpected change. It made me realise I fancied him like anything – or at least I did in this brief long-distance moment. Our goodbye was rather smudged with laughter. Perhaps he felt the same way. I'd have to go carefully...

Mind filled with possibilities, the day improved.

DAN

Isabel's being marvellous with Gwen. I think and hope it isn't interrupting her work too much. She says it's all fine, but she seems a bit *distrait*. Still, it won't be for much longer.

As for my work ... I've suddenly almost given up – on *Rejection,* at least. For a while I tried to convince myself it was because I couldn't find the right title. Not usually a problem. But now I know it's not that. The fact is, it's simply not working and there's not much point in struggling on with Act Two, because the play is never going to be produced. That's a tough thing to tell oneself, but I know it's the truth. I keep assuring Isabel it's under way, now, and I'm happy. But I'm miserable. It'll be the first time I've ever given up before the end.

So ... I sit here. In my study. At my desk. Swing from right to left, left to right, in my comfortable old swinging chair. I know every note of the groaning song it sings when I move. I look out of the window. The pattern of leaves that straggles across it is just beginning to turn. Evenings are getting cooler. My best time to write, September till Christmas.

And I've nothing to write.

'Why,' I ask myself, 'do I keep writing?'

It would be so much easier to give up, acknowledge that though it was a compulsion, I was no good at it. Well, perhaps that's going too far. In all honesty I'm quite good, but just not good enough. My Oxford play was an inspired moment and, after all, undergraduate stuff: easier, among friends, especially those who want parts, to win praise. Pity it made me so vain. Pity its success encouraged me to keep trying. In a way I can laugh at myself. I'm simply one of those millions of people who fancy the idea of being a writer, and spend a great deal of their time and energy producing stuff that's no good. Perhaps the hardest thing is to realise one's own limited talent, the fact that however hard you try you're never going to achieve whatever it is that's suddenly recognisable, desirable. And just like those other writers and painters who put *painter* or *writer* on their passports,

I'm reluctant to be defeated. I'll go on hiding from myself the fact that I haven't actually got what it takes. Is this masochism? No: because I enjoy the whole process so much. So maybe it doesn't matter that none of the huge amount of work piled in my cupboard will ever be produced.

Except, it does. It's a constant sadness.

The act of writing, I think I believe, is when you push aside the kind of daily thought we all have to live with, and allow something else to happen. There's no denying that's a process of extreme excitement. The idea that you're trying to produce something that, as Conrad said, will make people hear, make them feel, above all make them see – is satisfying like nothing else. The fact that you're not capable of achieving that doesn't make any difference to the pleasure of trying.

I open the desk drawer and take out a cutting I've read so many times it's close to falling to pieces. Balzac's words, written in despair while struggling with *Cousin Bette*. 'Great artists, true poets, do not wait for either commissions or clients, they create to-day, tomorrow, ceaselessly. And there results a habit of toil, a perpetual consciousness of the difficulties, that keeps them in a state of marriage with the muse, and her creative forces.' As one who's far from a great writer, I must suppose myself also bound in a habit of toil – a habit from which I don't want to be free.

Goodbye to *Rejection*, but if and when a new idea comes, I shall start a new play.

I pick up the manuscript, add it to the piles of other rejections in the cupboard. No point hanging around here any longer: I'll go down now and talk to Isabel. But I shan't tell her what's happened.

Not till I start again.

BERT

This was the best decision I could possibly have made. I lie in a bloody great four poster, cup of coffee by my side, bit of the huge Norfolk sky pale through the window. Slept like a baby, every night. What with all the walking, I suppose, and the breathing in of the famously soporific air.

When Carlotta rang a few minutes ago, I have to admit it was the first time I'd thought of London, her, Dan – though Isabel, of course, has flared constantly in my mind – fantasies, fantasies, superimposed over reeds, marsh, sand, sea.

Soon as I got here I became immersed in the place that I once knew and loved so well, but hadn't re-visited for years. I didn't give a damn about all I'd left: I just wanted to fade far away, dissolve and quite forget all the unease of returning to England, a changed London. I wanted simply to remember and remind.

Carlotta snapped my dreaming. She sounded quite cross with me at first. Well, I suppose I have been a bit thoughtless. Forgot to tell her I was off, didn't ring. But in the end she was jolly, friendly. We went in for a bit of banter. I remembered her breasts. I suppose, given such a long period of abstinence, we could get it together. But there'd never be any pretence of loving Carlotta. All my love is for Isabel.

I finish my coffee, lie back. I want to re-think things before I get up. Be quite sure. Because I seem to have made a wild, mammoth, life-changing decision. I just want an hour or so more to re-affirm it isn't a mistake. I don't mind rash acts, but I like to be sure they are going to result in something good. Last night, convinced I'd done the right thing, alone I drank a lot of the kind of claret Dan would have enjoyed to celebrate my plan. So my rationalising was cloudy. The businessman within me says 'Give yourself an hour or so longer, Bert old man, before you get up and set about signing things.'

First two days here were extraordinary. The village in which I was born, always a pretty place of Georgian houses round the green, seemed to have become a Mecca for the loud voiced Londoners in uniform clothes, their huge cars parked everywhere. To accommodate their tastes, the locals had provided what they wanted: gift shops, estate agents, shops selling over-priced clothes and tat, boutiques stuffed with ceramics and tiles, and Indian rugs (how Carlotta would sneer).

When I was a child you could buy rope, saddles, fishing gear, buckets, soap not fashioned into the shape of a Beatrix Potter character. It was an ordinary village scarcely frequented, out of season, by visitors. There was a butcher, a baker, a greengrocer, but no fancy shops and I don't recall an estate agent. The simple pub had been transformed into the very expensive hotel I'm now staying in – good food, disgusting coffee. It all took some getting used to. I went through the turmoil of thinking well at least the local shopkeepers are making a good living, and how sad that so undiscovered a place had been ruined by crowds of rich people. I wandered about, amazed at all the shops that had disappeared, but re-appeared in some fancy guise. The only pleasure was a bookshop – the village had always been sadly lacking in books, so this calm new shop was an improvement. I saw no one I knew. Hardly surprising.

Then I drove off to the beach – various beaches, observed how the dunes had been eaten away, some beach huts were almost buried in the sand, a car park near the golf course was full as a supermarket car park. Still, I walked away from the crowds. I walked miles along the dyke, and out to the island, the north shore. The skeins of birds were the same: and the distances made miniature by the vast arc of sky. The wind, the faint smell of gorse. And I went to the staithe, down on to the hard where Tom and I used to go crabbing as children. Bits of bacon on lengths of string: foolish crabs whizzing towards them to meet their end in a small red bucket. God, the stink, a few hours later. There were boys, there, still crabbing. I turned back, looked at the Sailing Club – much enlarged now, with a bar and providing sophisticated sandwiches. I remembered so many summer nights when we'd go down to the sea's edge to jump in the phosphorescent sea – girls holding up their skirts, boys soaking their jeans. Those millions of sparks of light riding on the small waves, frothing up at us when the waves broke with their small watery chords, a mystery to those of us who were no good at science, so weird and beautiful there was no room to think of holding a girl's hand.

And the teenage dances – I remembered those. Being

sick somewhere among the boats. Snogging some girl on the marsh path, I think in view of everyone – we couldn't wait to walk a few yards till we were out of sight. When at last – we must have been clamped together for half an hour – we pulled apart, I saw she was holding, in her free hand, a pair of glasses. Tried to hide them. I also saw – now that the moon had appeared from behind a cloud – that she was far from pretty. One of my first conscious shaming acts, then: I ran away from her, never spoke to her again. I thought nothing of this bad behaviour. What a brat I must have been.

Yesterday morning I went back along the marsh path. Horses were tethered, swifts traced the grey sky, but I was alone. And a strange sense of being back, being home, overcame me. I had resisted returning to the house where I'd spent my childhood for fear of seeing change there: I didn't want to see the flowerbed, where my mother had dropped dead among the lupins, re-planted. But I didn't have to visit the old house to feel I'd come home. It occurred to me, in that strange and misty way that ideas come to one, that during the afternoon I would make use of the many estate agencies. See if they had anything on their books that might be appealing.

But I continued on my walk towards Brancaster: I'd decided to spend the whole morning walking. The small

path runs close to a wall that divides the marsh from
the few old houses that have been there for ages – no
visible new buildings there, thank goodness. Doubtless
not many people want to face the marsh in winter.

I came to the small flint and brick house I remembered
well: a friend of Tom's lived there. I looked over the wall.
The gate to the garden – much improved – was open.
An old woman, in bright yellow oilskins, was talking
to a young couple. They didn't look like locals. They
followed her round the corner out of sight.

I stayed where I was, marvelling at the planting of the
borders. A yellowhammer sat on a branch of buddleia,
frightening away a goldfinch. It was obviously a garden
full of birds: I've no recollection of its popularity with
birds when I knew it as a child. My only real memories
are of making camps in the apple trees. They were still
there, heavy with fruit.

The old woman returned, alone. She waved at me.
Shouted that she knew all along such people wouldn't
want it – she wouldn't have let them have it anyway.
Waste of time. She came right up to me. From her side
of the wall that divided us, she looked out over the
marsh with forget-me-not blue eyes. I knew she'd taken
in the view so many times that her glance was no more
than a confirmation of a picture that lived deep within

her. Then she turned to me. Her scant white hair stood upright like a flag in wind. Her skin was battered and bronzed, but beneath her cheek bones were hollows so shallow they could have been pressed by the delicate thumbs of a potter. I could see that years ago she must have been beautiful.

'Years ago,' I said, 'I used to play in your garden. The house belonged to the parents of my brother's friend.'

At once her irritation, disappointment, whatever it was the young couple had caused her, disappeared. She looked interested.

'Come and have a look round, you must,' she said, 'see what I've done over the years.' Her accent was gently lilting, Irish.

I passed through the open gate and went in. We walked slowly along the main border while she explained how difficult it was to grow shrubs and flowers with any success in so unprotected a position: the word unprotected did something to my heart. I felt a kind of strange excitement – anticipation, perhaps – that was even stronger than the pleasure of so unexpected an encounter. Then I was invited in for a cup of coffee and a slice of carrot cake. She said she more or less lived on carrot cake, it was the only kind she could make. As we walked towards the house we introduced ourselves.

Her name was Rosie Cotterman. She had to leave, now, she said, and move to a wing of her married son's house in Oxfordshire. Health reasons, she added. I noticed she limped. Old age, bugger it. Leaving was the last thing she wanted to do.

'I don't want comfort,' she said. 'I want sea and sky.'

She reckoned she'd die pretty quickly once she'd left the marsh.

She mentioned this with no trace of self-pity or fear: it was, as she saw it, a simple fact. She herself would rather have died in her sleep during one of the harsh winters that can assail this coast, but her son had insisted she be in a more *comfortable* place – she delivered the word with a sneer – and was *overseen*. That word, too, came out as a sneer.

She flung off her yellow oilskin and made her way through the detritus of the kitchen to the kettle. The place was a shambles: stained cracked walls, rust, dust, stalagmites of books and boxes and, everywhere, water colours. They hung tilted on the dun walls, they were stacked up on the floor. A pile of sketchbooks occupied a chair. At one end of the room was an easel, on which was propped a half completed painting of the marsh, and a table which bore a rubble of paints and brushes. Rosie Cotterman was an artist. I asked her if she made her living from her paintings. She turned from the stove, gave me a long, long, silent, stare.

'There used to be a very constant buyer,' she said at last. 'That source of income has dried up now – but, yes, well, I sell the odd picture from time to time.'

I was pacing about, hoping not to appear either intrusive or too eager, eyes flitting along the quiet landscapes. She seemed to have inherited something of the understatements of the Norwich School: a kind of fierce delicacy that, to me, is the essence of Norfolk.

'Could I be a buyer?' I asked.

I pointed to three pictures that particularly appealed to me, but I would have been happy with any of them.

Rosie Cotterman staggered for a moment – hand searching for a stick she had mislaid, so she leant against the stove.

'Is this possible?' she asked at last. 'Why now, which ones would you like? ... But first,' she said, and I could see she was barely able to contain herself, 'we must have some refreshment.'

We sat in armchairs that might have been storm-tossed, so battered were their covers and exposed their springs. Old cushions with crocheted covers made no contribution to comfort. But there was a faint, summery warmth from the fire: the coffee was marvellously strong, and the carrot cake, which she sliced onto chipped and faded plates, was sublime. On a small table by Rosie's chair were a pile of unopened brown envelopes, a pile of Agatha Christie paperbacks, and a new looking copy of Ovid's *Metamorphosis.* She saw me looking at it.

'I do enjoy reading the *Calydonian Boar Hunt,*' she said. I sensed she was trying to contain herself, put off for a moment longer the overwhelming fact that I wanted to make a purchase.

'I read it over and over again,' she said. Was I acquainted with it?

I said I'd read Classics at Oxford, and, yes, indeed, had much enjoyed the Boar Hunt, though I'd not read it for many years. From there we progressed to the past, her life here – never lonely for a single second. 'Solitude is an art worth learning,' she assured me. I understood her once eager buyer of pictures to be a married man, but she did not go into any detail. We discovered we had a few Norfolk friends in common, though two of them were now dead. She explained that these days her work was much interrupted by completely unsuitable people the estate agent sent to 'view' (another of her sneers) the house. Some of them were so appalled they didn't even bother to look round, drove away fast.

'People fancy they'd like remoteness,' she said, 'but faced with the reality they soon change their minds.'

A lot of London people had been moving to the east coast in recent years, but couldn't take the harshness and – thank God – moved away again. She smiled, laughed – a soft, cooing laugh like a mourning dove.

We sat talking through the afternoon. She produced fish pâté and homemade bread, more carrot cake, and damsons from the garden. A bottle of claret was opened. I fetched logs from a pile outside and put them on the fire.

Eventually, she thought it time to wrap my pictures, and in the intense muddle of the room managed to find paper and old plastic bags. They came to a very large amount, she said: I said I didn't mind, and wrote her a cheque for what seemed to me a rather modest sum.

And then – I don't know how it happened. It certainly wasn't a premeditated thought. But as I walked towards the door, mellow with food and wine, pictures under my arm, I asked if I might buy the house as well. It'd save you any more bother with estate agents and unsuitable viewers: we could negotiate between us, I said, to break a long silence. Rosie stood bemused, pink cheeked, incredulous.

'The house is yours,' she said quietly.

'I'll come back tomorrow,' I promised, and kissed her on the cheek. It was the happiest afternoon I'd spent for years.

And, yes, now, reflecting on it all, I'm convinced I've done the right thing. Living here is a thrilling prospect. What I shall do, exactly, I'm not sure: what I would like to do is put a large part of my fortune to good use. I can consult Rosie about that. She'll know exactly how best I can help around here – the preservation of Norfolk churches, perhaps. She'll have lots of ideas. And when I'm not working at whatever it is, I'll read all the books I've been meaning to read for years, when there was no time. I'll walk, I'll sail. Like Rosie I'll learn the art of solitude. Isabel will slowly fade.

But for now I must get up, return to Rosie to make arrangements, which should be very simple.

The telephone rings. *Isabel.* Isabel!

She wants to know how I am, what I'm up to, when I'm coming back to London. In my internal struggle about whether to tell her what has happened, I become hopelessly inarticulate. She's annoyed by my reticence. 'Something's up, I can tell,' she says.

So I tell her. I tell her of my change of life plan, and the story of how I bought – well, am about to buy – a house. There's a long silence.

Then Isabel asks if I'm *sure*. I tell her I am: I'm sure, I'm thrilled, this is the answer I've been waiting for. Then I swear her to secrecy. I confess I would not have told anyone, just yet. But I was in a state of such excited anticipation that it would have been hard to keep it entirely to myself. Darling Isabel said she quite understood and swore not to tell anyone, even Dan. I have a feeling – though I could be wrong, I'm so happy my antennae could be muddled – she sounded a touch sad. But I assured her I'd be back in a week or so, and would come round immediately.

She said: 'Do. We miss you. I miss you.'

Isabel misses me...

A few moments later, putting on my socks, tiresome practical thoughts zoomed in: the house is in a terrible state, needs a lot of work. How should I set about all that?

I tie the laces of boots suitable for the marsh path.

Carlotta comes to mind.

Chapter Ten

GWEN

In the end, I stayed till the Sunday afternoon. Mr. G had taken Sylvie off to see her grandmother, so Mrs. G and I had an omelette and salad, then Mrs. G drove me home. She gave me a basket of provisions – everything I could possibly need, for the next few days, and a lovely pot of jasmine besides. 'A real Red Riding Hood,' I said. She's kindness itself, is Mrs. G. The arrangement is that I go back to work at the end of the week if I'm feeling up to it. Which I'm sure I will. Besides, I'd be bored stiff sitting at home all day, nothing to do. I can't wait to get back to normal.

I'm definitely well on the way to recovery. My cheek is still various nasty colours, but fading, and the swelling has gone down. Even the red eye is better. Well, I suppose I'm a tough old thing, I told myself, as I took a long hard look in the bathroom mirror. I do look more like a pensioner than I did before the fall, but it would take more than a punch or two to knock me completely off my feet ... thinking of which, my legs for some reason are still a bit wobbly. My knees were shaky coming downstairs at Number 18, but then the doctor said shock takes us all in different ways. Perhaps the shock still isn't out of my system, though the mercy is I haven't had any nightmares.

Home! My...! Needs a good dust and a breath of fresh air. I opened the windows and put on the kettle. The past week, the comfort, the kindness, it's been like a dream. Whatever would I have done without the Grants? I put on the kettle and sat down at the table. The chair was very hard beneath my legs. I wondered if I'd ever noticed that before, or has it just come to me now I'm used to the Grants' lovely furniture? I moved to the armchair, and there again I was surprised. The springs in its seat, pushing up at me. I don't recall them, either. It came to me what I should do is save for a new armchair, and few yards of the pretty cotton stuff with the pictures in the spare room at Number 18. I'd grown so fond of it. I knew those shepherds. Yes: that was my plan. Save for a few nice things. Life isn't worth living if you've nothing to look forward to. I'd look forward to a few improvements here, very much. Only wish it wasn't so noisy, and there was a nice view over a garden. Still, you can't have everything and compared with some, I'm pretty well off.

I went back to the kitchen table with a cup of tea and began to open my post. Nothing interesting. I was half hoping for a word from the children – but no. Only circulars, the gas bill and an official looking communication from the police. Seems they want me to go along to an identity parade at my convenience. I'll have to let them know that my convenience won't be for a while.

I decided that when I'd finished my tea – and Mrs G, bless her, had put in a box of very top of the range ginger biscuits – I'd unpack my bag, get out the hoover, take things slowly. I looked through the envelopes again to make sure I'd missed nothing before throwing them away. I suppose I'd been hoping for some word from Yarmouth: but that was a foolish hope.

'You're very lucky, Gwen,' I said to myself. 'You could have been really badly injured, or even dead. So count your blessings, take a grip. Next week, perhaps, think about getting out a bit. Ring your old friend Sheila, start going to Bingo again. Maybe the mugging was a message from above to say live a little, Gwen: don't get stuck in a rut.'

Maybe, I thought, I would sum up the courage to go

to the pub one evening, just have a quiet gin and orange, look at the people, come home. Maybe I'll do that once the identity parade is over.

Maybe I will.

CARLOTTA

Yesterday afternoon I went round to number 18. I was fed up with being so out of touch with Dan and Isabel.

'Oh yes, Dan told me you'd rung and would probably come round,' Isabel said.

With a funny sort of look, I thought. As if she wasn't entirely *au fait* with the idea of my ringing her husband. But maybe, in my rather odd current state, I was imagining that.

Dan had taken Sylvie off to see her grandmother – relief! So it was just Isabel and me. She'd just come from taking Gwen back to her flat. Gwen'd been in the house for over a week – pretty noble of the Grants, that. Not a word of grumbling from the saintly Isabel, of course, but I bet it drove her barmy, having to do the housework before getting down to work. She made us tea and talked for a very long time about Gwen. Described her flat in minute detail – I could *imagine*, for heaven's sake. She didn't seem to notice my lack of interest. On and on she went. I fear Isabel has a tremendous *penchant* for those less fortunate than herself, but God she can bore on about them. I sat at my usual place at the kitchen table listening. I wanted to scream at her to shut up. But I just went on listening. I could feel the mock interest setting hard across my face.

When at last – at last – she stopped droning on about Gwen, she turned to Bert. What on earth did I think he was doing in Norfolk? She said she'd had a long talk to him on the telephone – this piece of information she delivered, I thought, with an air of gleeful superiority. *She* had been in touch with him, was her triumph. Not for anything would I have told her I'd had a long talk, too. Did he ring you, then? I asked. I couldn't resist that. There was a long pause. Then Isabel – as if she'd been undecided how to play the truth – admitted that it had been her who had rung. I gave her a huge smile and said how lucky she was to have Bert as such a close friend. She blushed a little, I swear. Perhaps she has a secret fancy – but no. Never. She's dottily, quite boringly in love with Dan. She went on to ask how Bert's house was getting on. It was my turn to bore her.

I wished like anything that Dan and Sylvie – yes, for once, Sylvie – would come back. But they didn't. Isabel and I eked out conversation, oddly, awkwardly.

It was as if there was suddenly no longer anything to talk about. All the old ease had gone. A kind of mistrust, or suspicion, had risen between us. Why? How? Surely, surely Dan hadn't said anything, despite his stupid belief that you should tell a spouse *everything*. But I don't think it could have been that: he was so agitated about *my* not saying a word – hardly likely he'd do so himself. So I don't know what's happened. A sort of horrible gap has opened up between Isabel and me, after so many years of easy friendship. Perhaps our lives and interests have diverged so far there's nothing but the past left to bind us anymore.

Isabel pressed me to wait till the others got back, stay for supper. But I said no. I was really depressed by the hour we had together, and longed to get out of the house – the house in which I'd had so many good times, knew as well as my own. But I didn't want to go home for a Sunday evening on my own, yoghurt in front of the television. So I decided to go round to Bert's, see how things were progressing.

There, I cheered up. The builders had done brilliantly. They must be the only builders in London who actually get ahead of their schedule. I wandered from room to room, marvelling at the transformation. Surely Bert would be pleased. What's more, though there were still a few minor things to do, and curtains to be put up, any time he wanted to come back from Norfolk he could move in. I'd ring him tomorrow, let him know.

In the sitting room I threw back a dustsheet from the sofa and sat down. I calculated I'd only need to take one whole day off work to get everything finalised for Bert, then there'd be all the fun of seeing his amazed face. I rather look forward to that. I'll make sure there's a bottle of Veuve Cliquot – I think that's his favourite – in the fridge.

I sat back in the sofa and found myself thinking how nice it would be to live *here*, rather than my flat. How nice it would be, actually, to live here with Bert. I don't know how I've come round to thinking any such thing, having been so determined I wanted him only as a friend, but I have. Necessity, perhaps. There's not much choice around. But no, it's not that. I'm intrigued by Bert's capriciousness, his odd charm, his determination to keep his distance, his *strength*. God, there aren't many men who could have resisted, with such dignity, my foolish strip tease, and then had the charity not to berate me. So, yes, in an ideal world Bert and I...

But I'm not blind. I know damn well when something isn't reciprocated. To him I'm nothing more than a friend and useful decorator. He needs me only for getting his house done. Once he's seen it, and said thank you, that will be that. Oh, he might ask me out occasionally. We might do a few things *à quatre* with Dan and Isabel. But I know I'm not in his calculations, and never will be.

I also know I'm suddenly fed up with London, my job here, my life. The feeling that's been creeping up on me exploded, surprisingly, in Bert's half-done sitting-room. I'm nearly thirty-seven.. I want something to happen. So: I'm going to make it. I'm going to leave London, go to New York. I've lots of friends there. With my qualifications I'll have no trouble finding a job. I'll get an apartment in the Village, go and stay with the Haileys at their house in the Hamptons. Suddenly, I can see it all.

The gloom of two hours ago vanished. I'd hand in my notice in the next few days – they'll let me go in three months, I reckon. Then, a new life.

The excitement was immense. I decided not to tell Isabel, Dan or Bert. Or anyone, just yet.

DAN

Dejection – utter dejection, these last few days. Nothing to write, no ideas. A feeling of hopelessness, of loss, of wandering in a wilderness in which there are no signs.

When you're not working at something you love doing, there's a pointlessness in life. I didn't tell anyone – not even Isabel. I went to my study each evening as usual, read other peoples' plays – *Tartuffe, Betrayal, Cymbeline, Jumpers.* They were meant to inspire, but they just depressed me. Perhaps I should recognise the fact that writing a play is out of my reach: but I can't. I can't stop believing in possibility.

One morning a few days after Gwen had left, after I'd dropped Sylvie at school, I drove to Holland Park and went for a walk. My rather dotty old father-in-law was always on about walks being a cure for almost everything. In his case, except for moments of acute vagueness combined with some rum ideas, that did indeed seem to be so. I fell to thinking about him as I hurried along the paths, still empty at this time of the morning. He was a man of great tenacity. I remember the instance of the fountain. He was determined he should build it with no help, though he knew nothing of drainage or water design, or even how to stick stones together. But he stuck at it. Over two years of work, it took him, making mistakes and then having to re-build. I think all of us gently scoffed at him at the time. But he took no notice, kept at it for hours every day. And in the end he achieved it – an amazingly handsome fountain admired by all. He was so pleased with himself, the evening of its 'opening' as he called it. We all stood around drinking pink champagne, congratulating him. I've never seen him so happy. It's a good feeling when you overcome difficulties, I remember him saying in his very long launching speech. He hadn't had the opportunity to make a speech for years, and was making the most of it, though his voice was barely audible against the tinkling jets of water he had so painstakingly designed to arch before they fell. But then, later, I saw doubts rush in. The long job accomplished, what now? What now? he whispered to me. I know how he felt, though I'm still waiting for something equivalent to his fountain.

It was a cool morning in Holland Park: leaves beginning to turn, intimations of autumn, my favourite season. Having walked so fast I was out of breath. I sat on a bench to watch the peacocks strutting on the grass, trailing their trains of iridescent greens and blues and aquamarines, the colours of Turkish seas, and the shot silks I once bought Isabel in China. They had a snobbish, proprietorial look that made me smile. Should I deign to approach their territory, I felt, they would make known their disapproval in some alarming way. Already they were squawking their warning in horrible voices, ill-matched to their magnificent feathers that seemed to come from wooden throats. One of them raised its tail. Through half closed eyes I saw that a giant fan appeared to be approaching me with some speed. I was determined not to be intimidated, and kept my seat. The peacock came to a halt at the edge of the grass, considered me for a few moments, head on one side. Having summed up the very small potential of my threat, it turned back to join its companions.

'What the hell am I doing, sitting in the park watching peacocks?' I thought. I wished Bert was in London. Had he been here, I might have talked to him. He was always so patient with my glooms, so wise in his advice and encouragement.

Then, from nowhere, something appeared. Where do ideas come from? That is the question writers are so persistently asked, and find hard, if not impossible, to answer. In my own case, a scrap of reality – an incident, or an overheard sentence – sometimes spark an idea. That wasn't so this morning. There I was sitting, despairing, watching peacocks in the park when suddenly I knew without doubt what should be the subject of my next attempt. It would be something that was becoming familiar to me, and must be familiar to many others.

I stood up, a chill down my spine and more ordinary cold across my shoulders and chest. Wished I'd worn a jumper. I hurried back to the car and was glad of its warmth.

I knew this rising of hope, this foolish excitement, so well. I would surf the wave, buy quires of new paper, spend God knows how many hours trying – and this time, I would tell myself yet again, I really believe it could work.

I longed to tell Isabel. But I decided not to just yet. The right moment would reveal itself. I stopped on a double yellow line to buy stacks of paper – prematurely, I know, nothing to print out just yet – But it was a positive step. I came out to find a parking ticket, and didn't care. The stationer's plastic bag sat beside me on the passenger seat, symbol of my new and thrilling plan.

I was on my way, again. On my way.

ISABEL

Gwen gone! Huge, secret relief. Life won't be quite back to normal till she returns to work in a day or two. But oh, to have the house to myself again. She was the most perfect, undemanding and appreciative guest, but the fact is I don't much like visitors of any kind. On Monday morning I was up in my studio even before Dan and Sylvie had left, and began on an order for six masks which will be very late unless I go back to work in the evenings for a while, too. Well, that's fine. Dan always disappears into his study – this play seems to be taking a particularly long time to finish. From time to time I rather like working at night, then meeting Dan for a glass of whisky and the ten o clock news. I can see that some people might think our life very dull.

I suppose it might have been the whole thing of having Gwen here, upsetting my routine, that made me so irritable, and then so awful to Carlotta when she came round on Sunday. She will do that, appear without warning, and I hate it. I'd planned to collapse for a few hours with my book, while Dan and Sylvie were out. Her arrival put paid to that idea.

I fear I was not just unfriendly, but sort of scoring over her, too, and getting some pleasure from it. The Bert thing: letting her know I'd had a long talk to him. She, obviously, wouldn't ring him unless it was some work thing to do with his house. They're not that sort of friends. I think he's bored stiff by her pushiness.

Anyhow, I watched her face carefully. She put up a very good show of slight interest and not caring. But I could read her: she was jealous. Why? I think I know. For all her protestations, she wouldn't be averse to some interest or admiration from Bert. I mean, anyone can see his attraction, and she's become used to money. So it was mean of me to goad her a bit, but in an uncharitable way I enjoyed it at the time. She was in an odd mood, anyway: huffy, edgy. Said she'd been going out a lot, was lacking sleep. God I'd hate her life. I felt bound to ask her to stay to supper, though perhaps my invitation was lacking in enthusiasm. Luckily she said no, she had a date with 'someone.' I didn't give her the pleasure of asking who.

Then, of course, when she'd gone I felt awful. I'd been mean, bitchy, behaved shamefully. After supper, when Dan was safely in his study, I rang her. Rather unsurprisingly, she was in – some quick story about the date's airplane being held up in Paris. I know her face-saving lies, and offered sympathy. She must have known I guessed the truth.

Anyhow, I apologised. I mean I really was sorry for being such a cow. Carlotta is dementing at times, but she has a vivacity which is infectious. Loving her is an old habit. She took all this very nicely: said she quite understood what a trial it must have been having Gwen, and how lovely for me to get back to normal. Then, after a small friendly pause, she said that, actually, she had talked to Bert in Norfolk, too.

Yes, she, too, had rung him, but only to ask whether

she could throw out his old chair. We both laughed, recognised we were quits, somehow. Carlotta's not one to bear a grudge or maintain even the slightest hostility after a dispute: it's one of her many qualities. I ended by saying that once Bert was back – and, as neither of us knew when that would be, we were doubly bound in ignorance – we should all have a get together here.

'I'd like that,' she said, and I knew from her voice she meant it.

SYLVIE

Honestly. Grownups talk about children being moody. But what about them? Ma and Pa have been so weird lately. I'm sure they think whatever it is that's bugging them doesn't show, but it does. Mama's been vaguer than ever, hardly seems to hear my questions. She's sort of on automatic pilot. She's not bad tempered, exactly, but just distracted. I asked her what was the matter and she gave that boring old reply about there weren't enough hours in the day. I think that secretly she found having poor Gwen to stay was a bit difficult. I mean looking after her, and the housework and everything on top of her masks. I see that was difficult, but not *that* difficult.

As for Papa, I don't know. I suppose it's something to

do with his play, which he seems to have been at forever. But he never talks about it and I don't like to ask. I just wait for the day when it will all work for him and we'll all be going off in a limo to the first night and everything. No one's come round for ages. Every evening it's the same: just the three of us for supper, subdued, each of us caught up in our own thoughts, I suppose, and not bothering to make much of an effort. Boring.

What I actually think is that perhaps the rentals are having a mid-life crisis. Elli says that's what's happening to her parents, especially her father. She heard him saying to someone he thought his pulling power was on the wane – I mean, like, who could bear to be pulled by Elli's father? Fat and bald. Horror. Anyhow he's taken up jogging. We saw him once on the way to school. In shorts – *shorts!* Even Papa, who never says anything mean about anyone, thought it was a pretty gross sight. I didn't tell Elli we saw him. She would have died.

As for her mother, her mid-life crisis apparently means she spends even more money on facials and Pilates and having her hair blonded and aromatherapy and all that rubbish. Elli says it's embarrassing how much time and money she spends on herself these days. She now only actually works in the mornings but is still on the telephone all the time. And what *for?* That's what we both wonder. We had a long talk about it all the other day – Elli was in tears because her mother had mentioned having a face-lift, which Elli thought would be completely awful. I tried to cheer her up. We got pretty serious about what it must be like being grown-up: we tried to imagine being forty something, and we ended up saying what we really hoped was that we wouldn't be so vain. We made a promise that if ever one of us saw the other starting to do daft vain things, we'd say something. We're determined to keep that promise. Though I do sometimes wonder if Elli and I will still *be* friends in thirty years' time.

GWEN

Back to work, thank the Lord, and pretty much my old self. I feel much better. My face is almost its normal colour and I'm full of modest plans. I think the whole incident must have given me a jolt.

Mrs. G had done her best but she's not a natural housewife. I had to give a thorough turn out to most of the rooms, and plainly the stairs hadn't been hoovered for a week or so. There were six or seven of Mr. G's shirts to iron – Mrs. G says she ruins anything she tries to iron, so I took some home with me. I didn't say anything, of course. In fact I congratulated her on how well she'd done, and she was very pleased. I went on to make a little joke. I said you don't really need me, Mrs. Grant. You can manage on your own. She looked horrified, I have to say. It's nice to know you're appreciated.

I was rather dreading doing the spare-room. It had come to feel like my room, and I'd hated leaving it after my lovely week there which I shall always look back on as if it was a dream. But in a funny way, once I'd left it, it had just become the spare-room again, nothing to do with me, so I didn't mind. It even looked different. Well, I suppose I was sat so long in the arm chair looking out of the window, the visitor. And now back in my job I was busy getting the tops done and everything. No wonder it looked different. 'You're a daft one, sometimes, Gwen,' I told myself.

There's a date set now for the identity parade. I had ever such a nice letter from the police. I'm a bit nervous, of course – I've never had occasion to be in a police station – but they assured me it would all be over very quickly and there was nothing to worry about. Mrs. G said the same: nothing to worry about. She was pleased they were going to some trouble to try to track down the man who mugged me, and all the others. So was I. I was pleased to be able to help their efforts.

What I did think was, it was time to buy a new coat. I hadn't had a single piece of new clothing for as long as I could remember, and this was just the occasion. I wanted to look smart for our Metropolitan Police. I wanted to look like a responsible person who could rise above adversity, and my old coat wouldn't be much use at that. So I decided that I'd spend a nice quiet hour or so in Marks: treat myself to a new bag – the one the man got away with was on its last legs and there were only a few pounds in the purse – and a coat or jacket that would suit all weathers. I'd not shopped for clothes for ages. I set off quite excited.

BERT

In the week that followed my meeting with Rosie, a great deal happened very quickly. I didn't change my mind about buying her house. I remained convinced it was the best idea I'd had for years – one of those fallen from the sky, coincidence things. Or fate, perhaps: my arriving over the garden wall just as potential buyers, not wanting the house, were leaving. Such happenings, I like to believe, are kindly arranged by the Gods.

Rosie and I got down to things the day after we met. I agreed to pay the price that the agent had suggested.

And it was amazing to find how quickly the negotiations for buying a house can be accomplished if two decent lawyers work keenly towards the same purpose. By the end of the week the contract was signed, the deposit paid. I spurned the idea of a surveyor: I was aware a lot of structural work needed doing, and had no interest in knowing exactly how much it would cost me before the place was mine. My London house, which I would sell as soon as possible, would be worth at least three times what I was to pay Rosie.

I spent part of every day with her, and bought three more of her paintings. She was pleased to think they would stay on the walls.

We went through the house very carefully, room by room. She pointed out the copious work that would have to be done. The garden that I would inherit, though, was perfection. I'd always fancied myself as something of a gardener. I'd have the time, now, and would enjoy learning.

Rosie supplied me with constant carrot cake: I took her bottles of claret, which she loved. One night I drove her to the hotel for dinner. She had dressed herself up in an old velvet dress, and several scarves that shimmered and glittered, gipsy-like. She looked marvellous. Must have been quite something when she was young, I thought again. What a dinner, what a companion! We had already discovered she had known several of my parents' Norfolk friends, but she was always vague about her own past and I did not press her. No: we talked about local poets, and the crisis of the eroding dunes, and job possibilities for my new life. She suggested several causes – mostly environmental – that would benefit from both my money and my business experience. I said I would look into all of them as soon as I returned. She then questioned me, a look of concern in her merry eyes, about how I thought I'd manage living alone on the marsh?

This was something I had not thought of much, knowing it would be fine. I'd never shunned solitude. I'd always been attracted by the idea: far better to be on your own than to be with the wrong person, I said. At this she pursed her lips, questioned my belief that I'd be happy. It was one thing to live alone when you had a great passion in life which you could pursue without interruption – painting, writing, composing, whatever – quite another if you had nothing specific to do. Then, the days could be long ... and lonely. I assured her I was pretty good at regimenting my days, and once I'd offered my services to various local organisations, I'd be off to work every day, as in London or New York.

The joy would be coming back to the marsh. Rosie still looked doubtful.

By the time we were drinking brandy with our coffee she had become emboldened enough to express slight curiosity about the romantic part of my life. I felt it safe – and rather agreeable – to be able to tell her that I was in love with a married woman, my best friend's wife, which made it hard to contemplate anyone else. She smiled: said she could imagine that. For over forty years I'd been on my own, I said, and quite happy, and it might be too late to change. I'd probably become stuck in my ways and no woman would be prepared to put up with them. – Besides, where was I going to find a wife on the marsh?

Rosie laughed. By now there were two vivid patches on her cheeks that matched one of the scarves. She suggested I keep a tiny *pied à terre* in London, so as not to cut myself off completely, and so that I could still indulge in some cultural life. I agreed. I was no hermit, I said.

We were the last to leave the dining room. Rosie claimed she hadn't enjoyed herself so much for ages and nor, I realised, had I. I drove her home and told her that I hoped that in the event of finding a wife, my dearest wish would be that she would become as enchanting as she, Rosie, in forty years time. When I kissed her on the cheek there was a faint scent of my mother's powder – or was that a nostalgic illusion, such as I'd been struck with when I smelt it on Carlotta? My mother's laugh, too, had something in common with Rosie's – soft and cooing, a kind of burbling stream-like laugh that made you think that some people were blessed with the art of always finding things to amuse.

On the way back to London, I drove slowly, thinking of all the strange and unexpected things that had happened during the week. I kept procrastinating about contemplating the immediate future. Carlotta had rung me to say the house was ready for me: have to say she's done well. It was going to be very hard indeed telling her I no longer wanted it. We had made a plan that I should go straight there, and she would drop by in the evening to 'explain things,' and hear my reaction. God, I dreaded all that.

And there was another thing: Dan had asked me round to supper the following night, plus Carlotta. So what was I to do about breaking the Norfolk news to him and Isabel? Say nothing, yet? Waffle on about how well Carlotta had done, and at some future date explain to all of them that in fact I was leaving London?

Or should I, at this dinner for the four of us, make my announcement?

Perhaps that would be the best thing. Hard to decide.

I let myself through the front door mid-afternoon and found the place unrecognisable. Carlotta certainly had done a wonderful job, if a spanking new look with pale colours and muslin curtains and vivid cushions are what you fancy: it was nothing to do with me. My house no longer. Even my chair, newly upholstered and covered in taupe linen, was a stranger. Carlotta had certainly thought of everything. There were flowers and pot plants everywhere. The − new, huge − fridge was full of delicious expensive foods, and Veuve Cliquot champagne. She must have remembered it was my favourite. Top marks, I thought: top marks, but I didn't like any of it. I couldn't wait to leave.

In the two hours before Carlotta was due to arrive I did my best to make the place look a little lived-in: I hoped she would take this to be something of a compliment. I flung down the papers and put files on the desk. I hung two jackets in the hall, made a cup of tea and didn't wash up the mug. I put on some Schubert and tried out the face-lifted chair: horrible. Thank God, I thought, there'll only be a very short time living with all this.

Carlotta arrived promptly at six, expectation coming off her like static. She was looking good, in modest scarlet and a wonderful necklace of faux rubies. 'Oh Lord,' I thought, 'I'd better jack up the invitation to dinner from the place round to the corner to somewhere a great deal grander.'

I'd opened one of the bottles, poured her a glass, explained I was overwhelmed by all she'd done. She looked a little uncertain, rather touching in her sudden lack of confidence.

'Do you *really* like it?' she asked.

'I do,' I said, and gave her a kiss on both cheeks.

To make her assurance double sure, I then sprayed on the adjectives: marvellous, subtle, wonderful, amazing – and all so fast and efficient. I could see her storing away every new exclamation of delight, and felt like a shit. She insisted I do a tour of every room with her: I'd already done one on my own, but of course agreed to this with a convincing show of eagerness. She gave me little histories of things – how she'd been so lucky to find the antique quilt now on my bed at a sale somewhere, and as for the Kelims…I listened, hoping I showed interest.

I thanked her for the flowers, food, drink, and above all her extreme kindness in doing all this. Then we returned to the sitting room and re-filled our glasses.

She asked perfunctory questions about Norfolk, and I assured her I'd had a good time. Then she looked at her watch: my cue to suggest dinner.

'Oh,' she said, 'that's very kind but I wasn't expecting to have dinner with you. I'm off to the Opera.'

'Some new admirer?' I asked.

'You could say that,' she answered, looking down.

I expressed my disappointment in a way that disguised the relief. It meant I could have an evening on my own: unpack, find my bearings in all this alien newness. Later, I'd ring Rosie, tell her about it. It would make her laugh.

Carlotta stayed for a little longer. I have to admit she looked awfully good in scarlet. What my mother would have called striking. We had a short business discussion about the bill – rather sweetly, she assured me she was in no hurry for the balance that I owed her. Then she put down her glass, came towards me and put her arms round my neck. She said she'd loved doing the house for me: it had been a good diversion in a rather low time. I kissed her forehead, then she stepped back from me, and I saw a moment of sadness cross her pretty eyes. But quickly she was all gaiety again: admitted she had been dreading my reaction to the house, but was over the moon I'd liked it. She hurried out with a wave, saying she was going to be late, but we'd meet again tomorrow night with Dan and Isabel.

Had I done all right? I wondered. I didn't know.

Much later, having enjoyed choosing things for dinner from the fridge, I returned to my chair and finished off the champagne. I felt a little drunk, a little muddled. Carlotta in her scarlet, and I don't even like red.

In an odd way I rather wished I'd been the man taking her to the opera.

Chapter Eleven

ISABEL

Gwen seemed to be both excited and nervous about the identity parade this afternoon. She told me she had bought a very smart new green coat, her first for fifteen years, and did I think she should wear a hat? I said I thought that wouldn't be necessary. But she's of the belief that a hat is synonymous with being dressed up. She said she was determined to show both the police and the men she was going to inspect that she was a woman undaunted by an attack. When she left, her mind was still not made up about the hat. I noticed that several times this morning, when she was in the kitchen, she glanced out of the window, almost as if she was expecting to see someone threatening out there. She would never admit to being badly shaken, but I imagine it will be a long time before she feels safe walking about the streets of Shepherd's Bush.

I was in such a dither this morning that, very unlike me, I abandoned the whole idea of work. All because of dinner tonight: Bert coming from Norfolk. And Carlotta.

It will be the first time we've all been together since Bert arrived back from New York — not all that long, but it seems ages. It will assuage my guilt a little about Carlotta — being so unfriendly last time she was here. I have a faint feeling that she rather warms towards Bert, for all her protestations, and she's not going to get anywhere with him. He'll be delighted she's relieved him of employing strangers to do his house, but he's not going to ask Carlotta to share it. He may not even be in touch with her very frequently. I would guess he wants to start an entirely new life, meet new people, only keep on with his really old friends, like Dan and me. There's absolutely no point in his encouraging him towards Carlotta because he plainly isn't interested.

Gilbert…Bert. I suppose I've come to think of him as Bert by now, like everybody else. I've missed him. It was lovely having him here. That sort of ebullience he brings into a room, his laughter, his looks of such kindness and interest, so different from the sort of professional enquiry Carlotta sometimes goes in for. I do wish he'd get a job. Something he'd love doing. He doesn't need to earn much money, having made a fortune in America. If he roves about, aimless, I know he'll be unhappy. He should direct his energy into some beneficial pursuit. But what? I must try to think, help him find some work idea that will inspire him.

Bert...

Sometimes there's a small corner of my mind that goes back to that moment — that single moment, not more than a second or two — of confusion in the cellar. What was it? I try to work it out. Nothing more than a small quickening, really. A recognition. A glimpse of a possibility that could never come about, but in a funny way you're grateful it's acknowledged. Just to show — vain thought — that you're still appealing. And then there was that moment on the stairs — what was that? Nothing? Or further acknowledgement? And was it mutual, or my imagination? How can you tell, how can you ever know when you can't discuss it. Don't want to discuss it? Words from that old song ... *It's the wrong time, it's the wrong place...* In another life, perhaps Bert and I would have found — but no, what am I saying? Dan is the love of my life.

I'll never know the truth of the cellar moment or the stair moment, and perhaps that doesn't matter and the questions will fade away. What is left, though, is another question: does the recognition of a possibility, outside the marriage one loves, threaten or change the firm base of that marriage? I mean, why do I feel a small frisson of restlessness this morning just because Bert is coming to dinner? Why this inadmissible thread of excitement?

It spurs me to try very hard with dinner. I bought new candles yesterday, and an extravagant amount of flowers from the Portobello Road. I spent an hour going through cookery books, and in the end chose all Dan's favourite things.

And the really good thing is that Dan seems happy again. Whatever caused his gloom, and I imagine it was some new problem with the play, has gone. He's in extraordinarily good spirits. He woke me up at five this morning to tell me – not in so many words – that he was full of hope and optimism again. The block seemed to have passed. I long for *Rejection* not to be added to his rejections. May he succeed this time. That's one of the things I pray for.

SYLVIE

Goodness knows what happened but everything seems to be cool again. The rentals back to normal. They were acting so oddly. Mama a thousand miles away – friendly as always, but her mind just not *there* all the time Gwen was here. She was in such a dither, faffing about the ironing and the hoovering and how much she had to do and how was she going to complete her mask order if she never had a moment – boring. As for Papa, he just looked miserable. The fact was, though, I couldn't bring myself to ask him what was the matter. I absolutely didn't want to hear about his play, or any of his plays, ever. I think people should keep their feelings about their work to themselves. I don't drone on about my geography prep or whatever. When I'm grown up and a famous barrister or chairman of something I'm not going to bore my husband about my briefs (ha ha).

Elli told me a mega secret today. She said her mother had sent her upstairs to the study for supper extra early, saying 'someone' was coming round and they had to talk about business. But Elli went down an hour or so later and found a really fit looking man opening a bottle of champagne – years younger than her mother, who was in a floaty dress very low in front that Elli had never seen before. Elli said her mother tried to be nice, and introduced her to 'Charlie'. It was quite clear they didn't want her hanging around and underneath her mother's smiles it was obvious she was furious with Elli for interrupting. So Elli went back upstairs feeling sick with suspicion. Poor thing. My parents' odd ups and downs are nothing compared to what she has to go through. So I know I'm lucky.

When I got back from school Mama was in one of her cooking flurries. She gave me smoked salmon sandwiches for tea made from leftovers from their first course. I took them up to my room to eat while I was writing about the Wars of the Roses. I wanted to try very hard with this essay and didn't want interruptions like being asked if I'd mind laying the table.

Mama was in such a spin. Better to leave her to it, I thought.

GWEN

Well, my goodness. It's all over and not nearly so alarming as I'd thought.

In the end I didn't go for the hat. I only had my old one and I thought it would rather take away from my lovely new coat. So I pinned my little prancing horse brooch on the lapel instead. Bill gave me that brooch on our first wedding anniversary. It was the last present, if I remember rightly, he ever gave me.

I hadn't taken it out for as long as I could remember, and seeing it again turned my mind to Bill. I don't think of him very often, and when I do I always wonder the same thing – what in the Lord's name were we doing getting married? I suppose it was just youthful folly and he had rather a handsome face, though five minutes exposure to a weak sun and he was the colour of a beetroot. I discovered that on our honeymoon in Bournemouth, not a success in many respects. We had so little in common, little to talk about. He was all sport: football, the dogs, cricket – you name it, Bill was off of a Saturday watching something. He'd have a drink with the boys afterwards, though I have to say he wasn't a drinker. I could never hold that against him. He used to tell me a lot about his job in the post office, which I never found very interesting. But, true, he did well there. Several promotions. I suppose what we'd both wanted was the security of marriage, romance, children, a modest roof over our heads. It didn't turn out quite as we had imagined. Romance, for a start, is a talent like anything else, and Bill didn't have that talent. He wasn't an unkind man, or a mean man, he was just a very dull man, and that's something that clogs up the blood in your veins. Once I'd had the children I gave up my job as a receptionist up at the hospital – I'd enjoyed that, you met all sorts – and became the whole time mother. – Not much help from Bill. Saturdays he saw as his day at the track or the match, so I hardly had a moment to myself. But he did provide us with a little terrace house – very small, but no complaints. After about five years, I think it was, he took a sudden interest in pigeon racing and spent a lot of weekends with his brother in the north, a well known breeder. When I asked him about the pigeons he didn't seem very well informed, and I had my suspicions. Once I found a trace of lipstick on a collar. But I didn't say anything because I didn't really mind, and when the bed part of the marriage came to an end, about the lipstick time, I think we were both relieved.

Nine years of marriage to Bill. Then he passed away very suddenly – luckily not in the marital bed. I'm not one of those who'd fancy lying next to a corpse. No, he was apparently struggling to do up a button on his shirt – he'd put on a bit of weight – in his brother's house in Burnley. At least that was the story that I was given.

I was shocked, of course. The news of a sudden passing gives you a lurch even if you don't know the person well: so a husband dying unexpectedly, at a youngish age, is bound to shock. But in all honesty I can't say I was much affected. The children hardly took it in and didn't show any signs of disruptive behaviour that some nosey parker counsellor warned me they would. I just packed up Bill's clothes, gave them to a charity shop, and more or less forgot him. Bill was no more than a passing dull cloud in my life. Unlike Barry, who will always shine on in my mind.

Thinking these things on the way to the police station I quite forgot to be nervous. Then, in a funny way, I began to enjoy myself. The policemen were all so kind, and polite. I was asked to wait a while and one of them brought me a cup of tea. He was such a nice young man. I happened to mention my new coat, and he complimented me on my choice of green. Not many so smart come in here, he said.

Another very polite young officer took me along to a strange sort of room with a panel of one-way darkened glass. So I could see the line of men, but they couldn't see me. For a moment I thought what a waste of £59 on a coat – but it wasn't, really, because the police had been so appreciative.

Anyhow, I looked along the line of men brought in. Take your time, the officer said, and I did. I scrutinised the faces before me very carefully. They were black, white, one Asian. All the men were of similar height and build, none of them smartly dressed. There were good faces, bad faces, frightened eyes, guilty eyes, innocent eyes. Not one of them was remotely like Gary, or the face that I can scarcely recall that looked down on me. I'm sorry, I had to say. But none of these.

The officer seemed disappointed. He asked me to take one last look. This time, there was one particular face that struck me. I don't mean I thought he was the culprit – no: he stood out for me because of the goodness in his face.

He was quite a bit older than the others, in my opinion. A man well into his sixties, You're a mature woman in a late decade of life, not a young girl I should say. Fair hair, wavy. Blue eyes with crinkles all round as if he'd been smiling all his life. He had one of those faces that stand out in a crowd because…it's hard to describe to myself. But it's the kind of face that you can see is uncluttered, somehow, by any badness in his past. It would be inconceivable that he would mug or steal, that man. I know that. I was convinced of that. I couldn't imagine why he was in the line, but I suppose they have to scrape around and get anyone willing, for these sort of line-ups, who roughly fits the description of the person they're looking for. I wondered about him. – No, the man who attacked me is definitely not there, I told the officer. Perhaps, I added, to cheer him up, one of the other victims in a similar case to my own will recognise the offender. The officer gave what I'd call a very tired smile, and took me back to the front entrance. Bit of an anti-climax, I felt, walking home. I don't know what I'd been expecting, quite. But the whole prospect of the line-up had gingered me up for a few days, and now it was over I felt a little, I don't know...

But life is full of surprises, as they say. I got home to find a letter from the north, Ernie's writing. He said he was sure I'd be pleased to hear that his partner Eileen had given birth to a little girl, Gwyneth. He didn't mention when. – Well. My. A granddaughter. I sat down, coat still on. I hadn't heard anything about this Eileen – he's not one for letting me know the news, is Ernie. It was Lynne, last time I heard. But I was pleased, of course, to think I was a grandmother. I had a sudden longing to see the child.

But that didn't look as if would be possible for some time. For Ernie went on to explain that there was no chance for them to come south in the foreseeable future, and it would be difficult for me to stay over with them as the second bedroom was now given over to the baby. But perhaps in the New Year something could be arranged.

Perhaps it could, I thought. But the New Year was a long way off.

I sat for a long time at the kitchen table, didn't even bother with a cup of tea, thinking things through.

My mind turned to what was going on in number 18, the preparations for the dinner tonight. I looked forward so much to telling Mrs. G on Monday about my grandchild. She'd be so pleased.

And then I thought – I don't know why, I really don't know how it came into my head – I couldn't let the news of Gwyneth pass with no celebration. I had nothing but cheap sherry in the house – I use it for perking up a white sauce when I'm feeling down – and what I'd really like, though this was a very, very unusual feeling, was a strong alcoholic drink.

So soon after six, still in my new coat, I set out on a journey I'd never made in my life before. All of a tremble I headed off for my local pub. All I planned was just to have the one drink to my granddaughter Gwyneth's health, then return home very quickly.

DAN

I expect this high will turn into a low very soon. But for the moment everything is very, very good. I'm going to start the new play on Saturday morning. I've put the unfinished *Rejection* into the cupboard with all the others. I doubt I'll go back to it: no, I don't doubt it. I know I'll never go back to it. Because the new one is storming into my mind. In the office I scribble down a few lines on a pad, fill my pockets with odd scraps of paper, hide them all in my desk when I get home. But I know my ritual: choose a date and a time to begin, and keep to it. It's a sort of superstition. I wouldn't want to break it. So all this week I've been keeping myself in check – excited, happy. Saturday can't come quick enough.

Meantime there's this evening: Bert and Carlotta to supper. Isabel, who's been generally sunnier now normal routine's been re-established with Gwen's departure from the spare room and return to work, seems to be attacking preparations with especial gusto. I saw her starting on what I imagine will be a crème brulée. She only attempts this on special occasions, knowing it's my favourite pudding of all time. Can't say this evening's going to be a special occasion. But I'll love the pudding, and love Isabel for going to all that trouble.

Carlotta: oh, God, Carlotta. What I can't get out of my mind is that picture of the two of us locked together in an embrace that was soaring out of control, and then hearing Sylvie. It's a scene that haunts me, and won't go away. I know that had it not occurred I wouldn't have had a new play. But that isn't good enough. There's no way on earth I can justify such behaviour, and if my punishment is guilt for life, then that's what I deserve.

I stood for a while watching Isabel, watching my wife, beating things in a bowl, her cheeks an excited pink like fuchsia in a breeze, hair falling over one cheek. My own secret excitement was so great I only just managed to stop myself going to her, taking the whisk away from her and telling her my news. But then I thought, what a selfish idea. She'd be glad for me, of course. Interested. But timing's all, as Bert always says, and it was not the right moment. Her concern was preparing a wonderful dinner. It was not up to me to interrupt with irrelevant plans of my own. But when should I tell her? – Saturday afternoon, perhaps, once I'd started.

I went up to Sylvie's room. She was bent over her desk writing a history essay. She's been getting good marks in history of late. She even mentioned that she might like to be a historian, but her enthusiasms fluctuate. She said would I mind not interrupting her concentration, she'd speak to me at breakfast next morning. So I crept out.

I went down to our bedroom, changed my shirt, chose the latest tie that Isabel had given me. Then decided it would be ridiculous to wear a tie for supper in my own kitchen, and took it off. I know Bert doesn't approve of going without a tie. He sees supper with friends as a good enough excuse to strap himself into waistcoats and pinstripes and the sort of extravagant silk tie that inspires compliments. – Then I lay on the bed, hands behind my head, a faint sense of guilt because I wasn't downstairs helping Isabel. Try as I might to concentrate on the immediate future, all that came to mind were disinterested, unadorned thoughts: Bert, Carlotta, crème brulée, Chateau Margaux.

Then I swung my legs off the bed, urgently grabbed the pad on the table and wrote: *Philip: Whatever.*

Whatever was to be the first word spoken in Act One, Scene One of the new play. Oh, for Saturday.

CARLOTTA

I couldn't make up my mind – I'd been trying all day. Should I make my announcement this evening, say I was off to New York for an indefinite time? And if so, when and how should I put it? At the beginning? – No: everyone would want to be hearing about Bert's time in Norfolk. Perhaps I should wait till it was time to go. Say I didn't want to be late because tomorrow morning I'd planned to give in my notice.

How much would they all care? I wondered. Perhaps not that much. I mean, there's nothing more I can do for Bert. He's pleased with what I've done. He doesn't want me for anything else. Dan: well, to Dan I suppose I've become a subject of guilt which he can't shake off. He might be relieved to have me out of the way, though I believe he still likes me. Isabel? She might miss me sometimes, though she hasn't shown many signs of great friendship of late. – No, my scrap of news, if I produce it, isn't going to cause any great reaction. Ah well. The tides of friendship ebb and flow. Probably all three of them would feel pleased with my decision to move on, I thought, as I did my best to cover up the bags under my eyes caused last night by post-opera high jinks with some rich cad I never want to see again. Regret, regret. Living alone, the whirligig of hope causes one to make such stupid mistakes.

BERT

I can't get used to the new look of my house, and don't like it – Lucky I don't have to put up with it for long. My chair, in its impractical but no doubt fashionable linen dress, has lost all its charm. The only thing that really pleases me is the ice-maker in the fridge, from which pour more ice cubes than a single man on the brink of a new life could ever hope to use.

I left much sooner than necessary. Drove around a bit. It was one of those rather good autumn evenings in London: powdery sky over an undercoat of apricot, in Carlotta's interior decorators' language. Bronze fallen leaves cluttering the pavements of Isabel and Dan's street: those left on the trees mere skeletons, and the patched bark of the tree trunks, looking like army camouflage, now fully exposed to coming winter. – My heart gave a wild flutter as I turned off the engine, ran up the steps to the front door.

I doubt any man would not have fallen in love with the woman who opened it. Isabel was clearly not expecting me so early. She was an untidy pink with tousled hair and a dishcloth wrapped round her skirt. When she smiled, and opened her arms, and we clutched each other, the pathos of the moment was so keen I could not speak for a moment. Loving, and that love forced to be denied, is an agonising combination. When we drew apart, laughing – why laughing? – she asked why I hadn't let myself in, or had I lost my key? I admitted I had it on me and gave it back to her. I explained that in my hurry to see her – and Dan – I'd just automatically rung the bell. That was the extent of my message. She nodded. I followed her into the kitchen.

Dan was there, fussing about opening wine. It took

only an instant to see that he was in high spirits, happy. I assumed this was something to do with the play, and waited to hear. But as he was not forthcoming I began to tell them about my stay in Norfolk. I described Rosie, claimed I'd fallen in love with her – she was exactly my kind of woman, I said. Beautiful, funny, curious, talented, solitary, kind, gentle…I strung out the adjectives, all of which applied equally to Isabel, who eyed me with a brief quizzical flash, till Dan begged me to stop. And did you ask her to marry you? he said. It was only then I confessed she was not far off eighty. Isabel's back was turned, so I don't know how she took that news. Just enjoyed the joke, I suppose.

Isabel took off her dishcloth and we sat in the window, the three of us, with glasses of Pol Roger, while they questioned me closely about Norfolk – hadn't I been lonely, bored, eager to get back to London – all that sort of thing. With an almost perceptible effort they managed not to ask me about my future. Then I told them about Rosie's nephew, a theatrical impresario always on the lookout for new work. Rosie had assured me, I told Dan, he was one of those who really did read the manuscripts sent in, and was always polite enough to respond. I took out my wallet and handed the man's card to Dan. Immediately the old, familiar look of optimism – how well I know it – further brightened his face. Dan has an extraordinarily low threshold where hope is concerned: offer him the merest trace, and optimism floods through him. He's always been like that and I can't bear it for him that the only time he's been rewarded by his writing was so long ago at Oxford. – Could come in useful, he muttered. I could see he was trying to contain his childlike anticipation.

Carlotta arrived noisily at almost quarter to nine – she was of the belief, rampant among a generation surely younger than ours – that to arrive not less than an hour later than you are asked is the acceptable thing to do. – Though I know she does make an effort to be a mite more conventional when asked to married friends with children and early mornings. – Dan went to let her in. There was a moment's pause when, I suppose, they were embracing. I looked at Isabel who sat with eyes cast down, perhaps purposefully not looking at me. Then sounds of more laughter and mock berating came from the hall – why haven't we seen each other for such ages? – and Carlotta came in.

She came in with a dash, then suddenly stopped, like an actress who has made a false move. In the moment before Isabel and I got up to greet her, it occurred to me she had taken in the quiet tableaux of us and she guessed something of my feelings for Isabel. If this was so, and I think it's not over-vain to assume it meant something to her – she put a good face on it. She hugged Isabel, then me, and accepted Dan's glass of champagne all in one curiously flowing movement, as if an invisible ribbon linked her actions. I could not take my eyes off her due to the shock – the annoyance – I felt caused by her dress.

It was scarlet, the very one she was wearing last night. I knew it was meant to convey some perverse message: that she was bolder than Isabel? She knew I thought she looked good last night, off to the opera with some man. So what was her intention to-night? To goad, to tempt, to annoy? I couldn't work it out. But I was irritated by the streak of scarlet she made in the subtle colours of the kitchen. And beside Isabel she looked like a strumpet, a brazen woman of the night, with appealing eyes. Isabel fled from her side to the other end of the room, busying herself with things at the oven. I would not let my eyes follow her lest they conveyed the ache I was feeling. Then Carlotta came and put her arm through mine and demanded to know what I'd been up to, spurning the real world alone on a marsh? I pulled myself together, made some attempt to answer her.

DAN

I was glad I was alone opening the door to Carlotta. She stood for a moment on the step, backlit, in the scarlet of a matador's cape, looking terrific. She stepped in. I fear I blushed. We embraced. There was the memory of a sensation rather than a present sensation, and I was grateful. I don't think there was the slightest stir within Carlotta's desirable body: as I'd told myself so often, our nefarious clinch had meant nothing at all to her, and nothing but a flash of lust to me. So I was finally free, relieved. Perhaps that's how Act Three should end.

Carlotta then ran into the kitchen. In the moment of re-union between the three of them I registered shock, perhaps bemusement, on Bert and Isabel's faces. Bert also looked faintly annoyed. – Carlotta can never make a quiet entrance. She always stirs some kind of response: not to do so would be a failure in her eyes.

I left them to it. Gave Carlotta a glass of champagne then, by way of help to Isabel, and to expunge guilt felt by my lack of domestic effort earlier in the evening, I put the plates of smoked salmon on the table. The problem of when to break my small piece of news I still hadn't resolved. Before or after the crème brulée? With the cheese? Or should I wait till the coffee? By then we'd have had enough to drink to temper the news, which I don't anticipate will cause much of a stir in any case: I will just feel a certain relief when I've broken it.

I lit the four tall candles, Isabel's favourite Prussian blue. I was still uncertain, still undecided. Nothing for it but to wait and see how the evening turned out.

CARLOTTA

I was late, of course. Naturally I'd no intention of being on time, no matter how much Isabel would disapprove. – She's so old, in some ways. Pernickety about time. It would have been difficult to have been punctual even if I'd wanted to. A meeting at the office went on and on. I wasn't in charge. It meant I could sit back and think. I won't have to be at many more meetings like that, thank God. Not for a while, anyway. Then they'll be in New York, and rather more crisply chaired..

I dashed home, decided against a shower, saw my last night's red dress flung over the chair. Rather than hang about making dreary decisions about what to wear, I put it on again. I don't usually wear the same thing two nights running for fear of traces of one night spilling over into another. But I couldn't be bothered to re-think. Dashed it on, found some matching lipstick and zoomed over to Is and Dan.

Dan, as I hoped he would, opened the door to me. Why did I hope that? – Don't know, really, except it would mean a few seconds to take in his attitude when no one else was there. We hugged for a moment and I thought, as I so often do, God I wish Dan was my husband. Though what with all the gallivanting last night with the agile Rory, and lack of sleep, and all the hurry -what I actually felt was a kind of innocent pleasure, and a warmth, that nefarious secrets endow. Not a trace of lust on my part. Though I could swear that Dan, for all his love of Is, was pretty unnerved just having me in his arms for two seconds in the hall.

In the kitchen Is and Bert were sitting at that low table in the window looking faintly bored. Or cross, perhaps. Possibly Is was put out by my arriving forty five minutes after the appointed time. I apologised and she assured me she didn't care a damn, there was nothing that would spoil. Then I sat down with her and Bert, who looked handsomely suntanned, and began asking automatic questions about his time in Norfolk. Isabel, it seemed, hadn't had time -or bothered – to make much effort with her appearance. She was in her usual blue, no make-up. Have to admit she was looking rather beautiful. Made me feel rather over-aware of my thick mascara and scarlet lips.

Dan was at the other end of the room putting out the first course. At one moment he caught my eye. I think the look said, if only. But perhaps I misinterpreted it.

All the time I was wondering at what point I should deliver my bombshell. What kind of a sensation would it cause, I wondered? Would they all be horrified at my prospective absence, try to persuade me against it? Or would they all profess understanding, urge me to go for it? I just didn't know. Having quickly finished my first glass of champagne, Bert sweetly realised I needed another and picked up the bottle. Faint sadness at never having managed to win him over. I would have liked life in his Chelsea house. As he smiled at me in a kindly way, filling the glass to the very brim, I thought, yes, odd, but I could have grown to love him.

SYLVIE

I finished my essay just before ten. I don't think I've ever worked so hard! I read it over several times and thought it was rather good. I might get an A−, or even an A. Then I thought, to celebrate, I'd go down to the kitchen and see if I could get a bit of the crème brulée. I knew Bert'd be pleased to see me. Carlotta probably wouldn't even notice me.

I went downstairs. There was a lot of noise coming from the kitchen. I peeped round the door. They were all laughing but I couldn't make out what at. There were three or four empty wine bottles on the table and as far as I could see they were still eating their main course. – Actually, they weren't all laughing. Mama looked forlorn (I love that word, forlorn). She didn't seem to be enjoying it all as much as the others. They were all locked into an odd, far away grown up world that made no sense to me. I couldn't help feeling that it wouldn't be a good time to go in and anyway I suddenly didn't want to. I didn't want to have anything to do with any of them, though I didn't know why. It was a left-out sort of feeling that I wouldn't normally mind. But I suppose having finished my essay I wanted to tell them…Pity it wasn't the right moment for my news. I went back up to my room and got in to bed. I thought I might cry, but actually I was too sleepy and I suppose I went to sleep right away, thinking of the morning. Bert and Carlotta would be gone and I could tell Mama and Papa how I'd approached the War of the Roses, and I know they'd be interested. They always like reading my essays. Not like poor Elli. She says neither of her parents have never, ever looked at a single one of her exercise books, and she's given up asking if they'd like to because she knows they absolutely wouldn't.

GWEN

I said to myself: if you don't take the bull by the horns, Gwen Bishop, and go, there's a good chance you'll never do it.

It was quarter past six. I'd just watched the news. There'd been some dreadful murder, an axe man had run amok in Suffolk. Quite a distance from Shepherd's Bush, I thought. I'll take the risk.

So I turned off the telly, put my new coat on again. I took the brooch off the lapel. No point in provoking an attack from a jewellery snatcher. Then I left the flat, walked down the flight of stone steps, clatter clatter, ever so perky. Just as I reached the bottom, Edie Mills downstairs opened her front door to put out the milk bottles. She remarked she'd never seen me so smart, and how unlike me it was to go out of an evening. She managed to sound accusing, as if going out in a new coat was a sin, or an impertinence or some such. I said thank you for your interest, Mrs. Mills. We've always been frosty but I've better things to do than try to repair relations with a busybody like her.

I headed for the Witch and Broomstick, knowing it to be the pub with the best reputation in the neighbourhood. The hooligans and druggies favoured the Bat and Ball further down the Goldhawk Road.

I was there in five minutes, and hesitated only for a moment before pushing my way through the doors of the Lounge Bar.

The Lord knows how many years I've not been into a public house, but it all came back to me: I used to go with Bill, sometimes, when we visited his mother in the north and we wanted to get out of her stifling little house of an evening. This was a posher place, of course. But the smell of smoke, the orange lighting, the brass mugs hanging in a row over the bar – yes, yes: I wasn't unfamiliar with pubs.

It was far from full, but then it was early yet. They seemed to be nice sort of people, those that were there, sitting in twos and threes at small round tables Nothing to alarm, but no other single people, either.

I looked down at the carpet. It was a very patterned affair, the kind that makes your eyes dizzy, of deep gloomy colours. There was a big expanse – an ocean, it seemed – of this carpet to be crossed to get to the bar. I could hear my heart beating very hard, and for a moment I thought I'd turn and go. But I plucked up my courage, told myself not to be so silly. Who was going to take any notice of a middle-aged woman walking up to the bar?

The answer was, no one. Not a head turned. I reached

the bar unobserved and was greeted with a big grin by the man behind it polishing glasses. What was I after, he asked, with a twinkle?

Well, there he caught me out. In all the commotion of deciding to come at all, I hadn't planned on what kind of drink I should order. Names flashed through my head. Bill used to buy me port and lemon without ever asking if I wanted it. I didn't like that. Nor did I like beer or whisky. Then it came to me – gin and orange. And plenty of ice, I told the barman: I've a very light head. Haven't we all, darling, he said, and asked for a huge sum of money, but I didn't mind. Someone had turned on the juke box. An old Beatles number. It encouraged me, somehow. I remember dancing to that.

I took the glass and made my way back over the dizzy carpet, this time with a small jump in my step. It was all I could do not to bounce a little in time to the music. But I walked smoothly, holding the expensive drink out in front of me as if, somehow, it would lead me to the right place. Which turned out to be a table in the corner. The leather seat was gashed. Filling stuff was coming out like entrails from a wound, I thought, full of fancy. But it was a good place because it was darker than some: I could sit watching and no one would see me.

In the half hour that I took to get through half the

gin and orange I entertained myself by having a good look round, guessing about the other drinkers. The place was beginning to fill up. I thought I should hurry along – though I was nervous that drinking too quickly the gin would go to my head. It felt like time to go home. So I decided to leave the rest. I'd enjoyed myself, I'd proved to myself that I could go out alone, but I'd had enough.

I was about to get up when a bunch of five men all came through the door together. Noisy, laughing, nudging. They all made for the bar together, ordered tall glasses of beer. Then four of them went off into the far end of the room. The remaining one – a superior sort from his companions, I could see, strange how quickly you can make judgments in a pub – looked around and came towards me.

What he had seen, I realised, was that there was a free table beside me, also very small. Probably designed, like mine, for the single person. He sat down, pushed the table away a little, loosened his tie. There was something about him. I took quite a gulp of my gin and turned just far enough to take in his face: and it clicked in my mind. It was the very same man who'd struck me in the line-up this afternoon. I could swear it was him, despite the spinning the gin was causing in my head. I could swear it was him because the goodness shone out of him, just as I had seen it then.

He looked worn, tired, perhaps a touch sad. My heart went out to him, but that could have been on account of the gin. For by now it was making stars in my head and running like warm soup through my limbs. There was no hope, for a while, of getting up and leaving. I'd not have been able to walk to the door. I'd forgotten this was the nature of gin: no affect for half a glass, then it suddenly springs.

But it also made me bold. More than anything in the world I wanted to converse with this good stranger beside me. My cheeks felt so hot I was sure they'd turned red, which he would see if I turned to him. – Which I did. Gave him the slightest, neighbourly nod. In return he smiled – well, not so much as a real smile, but his lips moved in a pleasing way. I picked up my glass again, finished the drink for courage. I was about to speak when he asked a question. Yes, *he asked a question.*

Are you a regular here?

Not very regular, no.

He turned back to his drink and I couldn't bear it. – I couldn't bear it to end there, just as we had broken the ice. God give me courage. I prayed. And He did. Were you, I asked the man, by any chance taking part in an identity parade this afternoon? The words rolled like marbles in my mouth.

The man looked at me with an interest that brought his whole face alive. I was indeed, he said. Seemed he was a mate of one of the police officers, and sometimes obliged when they were getting a parade together. Had I been one of the victims behind the one-way glass?

I admitted I had, and that was how I recognised him. There'd been a mugging, I said, but I was over it now.

You poor lady, he said, very gently. I'd like to buy you a drink. I'm Henry, by the way. He stood up, took my empty glass. What'll it be?

Mind whirling, I said another gin and orange would be very acceptable, and my name was Gwen.

It's hard for me now, sitting with a cup of tea in the kitchen at home after eleven at night, to remember exactly how we got going when he brought back the gin and orange. Everything was a little unclear in my head, but the thing that shone through, and still shines all through me now, is that Henry is one of the world's gentlemen, a *good* man. He owns a small building firm – the men he came in with worked for him – a good bunch of lads, he said. They sometimes had a drink together, but usually they went off to play darts in the next room.

Very slowly, cautiously, we offered up little bits of information about each other. I can't remember in what order, but I learnt that Henry was a widower, had been for ten years, so we had that in common. He'd a married daughter in Canada, and a mongrel dog called Arthur who was a good companion. I guessed we were about the same age. He liked going to films, he said, especially James Bond, and he took his holidays every year in the Lake District, where he enjoyed the walking. For my part I told him a little about my job, and my children. We didn't speak of the mugging, but discovered we lived only two streets apart.

I eked out the drink he had brought me even more slowly than the first one, terrified of the effect it might have. But, strangely, my head began to clear. I heard myself speaking firmly and fast, his kind eyes upon me, friendly crinkles all round them. Almost two hours must have passed in what I felt was lively conversation. Unable to believe this was happening to me, I was: and how my heart was beating. Eventually I said I must be getting back if I was to get to work on time in the morning. He said he was up at five every morning, and what a pleasure it had been meeting such a brave lady.

I pushed back the table and stood up, feeling fine. But

the gin had tricked me. Although my head was clear, my legs were awash with the alcohol. I took a step, stumbled. At once Henry's strong arm was under mine, and we both laughed. He came to the door with me – there I was, part of a couple in a public place, such a strange and wonderful feeling – and offered to walk me home. But I insisted I'd be all right on my own. The last thing I wanted was for him to think me forward. If you're sure, he said. We shook hands, and he said let's have another drink some time. How about Friday?

How about Friday, Gwen Bishop? I asked myself as I walked home, swaying as if a wind was pushing me. I know he was watching me till I turned the corner, but I didn't look back.

Home – and I have to say I had a little trouble opening the front door – I caught sight of myself in the hall mirror. *Flushed.* But eyes all a-sparkle, I'd say. Funny how such a simple thing, talking to a nice man, can do that to you. Once I'd got my cup of tea, I took paper and pencil and began to work out how many hours there were till Friday evening. Gwen Bishop, I said to myself, don't get too excited. You're a mature woman in a late decade of life, not a young girl. But who knows? Maybe this gentle Henry will become a friend.

ISABEL

I sat there watching the three of them. I had the strange feeling I was looking at a play, and yet I was also one of the actors. I was taking part, and yet I was at a distance. Every now and then, in a silent flash, I pictured the next morning up in my studio trying to finish rather a wild and I think rather extraordinary mask of purple ostrich feathers. I looked forward to that. – Apart from the food, I made little contribution, though I joined in the laughter. Bert was being very funny about his 'affair' with the old lady in Norfolk: self-depreciation is one of his many *fortes*, not least because he always knows exactly when to stop.

Conversation turned – I don't know why, or how – to whether parents should encourage children in their obsession with pop music. It was Carlotta who brought it up, which was strange considering she has no children and isn't much interested in them. At some point she turned on me and said, with a sneer that was possibly meant to be funny, that she supposed I encouraged Sylvie to listen to the Beatles, and old has-beens like Cole Porter and Ruth Etting. – Dan and Bert turned to look at me. I hesitated only for a moment. Then I admitted that's exactly what I did, and Sylvie loved them.

I can imagine, Carlotta said quietly.

Well I'd never profess to be a middle-aged pop expert
like you, I said, furious. As someone who doesn't know
the difference between Brahms and Mozart, I went on, I
don't think you've any reason to be superior about your
musical opinions –

Dan interrupted by saying he was going to get the
cheese. He got up noisily. I rose too, began to gather the
pudding plates. Carlotta was scarlet in the face which
matched her dress. I think she'd had a good deal to
drink. I don't know how she'd managed to ruffle me so,
and I was annoyed by my response to her sniping. But
also I didn't care. There's an old tie of deep affection
between us, but also a top coat of irritation, some kind
of indefinable competition. What was she trying to do?
Score off me in front of Bert? Whatever her motive,
she'd brilliantly succeeded in spoiling the evening for
me. Stacking plates in the machine, my back to the table,
I felt strangely tearful. Although Bert had reverted to
more ease-making Norfolk stories, I sensed the tension
in the room had risen to high tide, as if something was
going to break or explode. I wished Carlotta would go
away forever.

DAN

What on earth was Carlotta up to? She'd been rather sweet for a couple of hours, unusually quiet listening to Bert's stories and laughing. Then suddenly she launched into all this stuff about children and pop music – not a subject of the remotest interest to her, I wouldn't have thought – and took a lunge at Isabel. It wasn't so much what she said, but the sneering way she said it. Her message, I suppose, was that she, Carlotta, was an ultra-contemporary woman in tune with whatever's going on in ephemeral worlds, while Isabel's bogged down in nostalgia for the past. I was furious.

Even as she sneered, her scarlet mouth twisting, I remembered how wildly that mouth had kissed me, how sinuous her breasts and hips beneath my hands.

Quickly I got up to try to defuse an almost tangible awkwardness that had sprung among us. Noisily, like a town crier in a pantomime, I announced I was going to get the cheese. The thought occurred that some sort of similar scene in Act Two would be good: motives in disguise.

God how I longed to get going: tomorrow morning. I longed equally for Carlotta to disappear, preferably for years.

CARLOTTA

Suddenly I couldn't bear it any longer – Isabel sitting there, so smug in her kitchen, looking from Dan to Bert with that irritating intense concentration that she sometimes rains down on people. She laughed so much at Bert, whose stories weren't *that* funny – putting one hand on her throat and tossing back her head, in the way that she does. It was as if she was on some superior kind of cloud – happily married woman, quite talented at making masks, lovely house, enough money, blah blah blah: friendly, but so self-contained she doesn't really need friends. And above all so sure of Dan, so bloody sure.

I suppose I'd had too much to drink – amazing claret with the beef. But suddenly fired up with a huge desire to attack my friend, I launched into some rubbish about pop music, knowing this would annoy Isabel: she doesn't discourage Sylvie in her tastes, but I know she also bangs on about that dreary old music of years ago that she loves. I'm not sure what I was saying, but I hit a target. It all became extremely nasty. Isabel looked at me, white with anger, and Dan tried to diffuse the whole thing by roaring on about cheese in an idiotic manner that I suppose was meant to be funny.

As he stood moving wedges of Camembert and Dolce Latte about the board, I considered whether I should take my chance, go further: I wanted to shout out loud that Isabel should stop being so bloody smug – would she like to know, I wanted to scream, that Dan and I had stood in that doorway *kissing*, and, had not Sylvie come down, we'd willingly have gone further?

But I didn't. Something about Isabel, bent over the dishwasher, trusting, vulnerable, constant…I couldn't. But I might one day. – Bert leant towards me with a look I couldn't quite read. He held a new bottle of wine over my glass. I nodded. He filled it. I drank.

BERT

What the hell got into Carlotta? I'd no idea. Until her outburst everything had gone swimmingly. Everyone happy. Delicious dinner and wine. Then her attack on Isabel. Simply a case of too much to drink? I don't think so.

Dan stepped in fast, brilliantly, risking his own dignity with some charade about the cheese. Isabel stood up, all the colour vanished from her cheeks, eyes splintered with anger, hurt, various things. I could see a hip bone protruding through her blue silk skirt, the same one she'd been wearing when I followed her upstairs to the studio. She was wearing a white tee-shirt, her small breasts sitting on shadows the shape of two new moons. I wanted to carry her off, take her away from the disagreeable scene – somewhere, anywhere, where I could hold her and kiss her eyes. I loved her so much I had to bend over to ease the physical pain, which I hoped to disguise by pouring more wine for Carlotta who was certainly unwise to accept it.

When Dan and Isabel had returned to the table I knew that the only effective deflection from the trouble Carlotta had caused would be the breaking of my news. So I spread a slice of cheese over an organic oatcake, and said I had plans I wanted the three of them to be the first to hear. I sensed a perking of interest, a slight relaxing of the wires. – I had decided on my new life, I said: it was to be in Norfolk. – Yes, Norfolk. My affection for London had vanished very quickly and I'd no desire ever to work in a city again. I'd bought Rosie's lovely house on the marsh, and although I would come to London from time to time, that was going to be where I lived. I felt Isabel's eyes hard upon me in the silence that followed.

On the marsh – have you thought about winters? She spoke quietly, brilliantly conveying this was all news to her.

But what about your London house? Carlotta asked before I could answer Isabel. (I knew that would be her concern) All that effort …

But not for nothing, I assured her. Her wonderful work on it ensured that I'd get an even better price when I sold it, as soon as possible, and she would certainly be due for a percentage.

Carlotta sniffed. I don't know what she was thinking. She seemed put out, deflated, a touch sad – or maybe she was suffering an attack of post-attack remorse. I repeated several times how grateful to her I was for all her efforts, and how lovely the house was, but she took no comfort from these assurances. She shrugged. Blinked very slowly looking down at her plate. For a moment I thought she might cry.

But her melancholy fled as quickly as it came. She looked up, jaunty, her old teasing self.

I'll take a bet you don't last more than a month on some dreary old marsh, she said.

Oh, I think he might, said Isabel. I knew she didn't want to appear too knowing in her understanding. But of course she understood.

Dan was the practical one. What do you think you're going to *do*, stuck out there, old thing? he wanted to know. I began to explain my plans – still a little vague

– about putting money and expertise into local causes which would be of benefit to the community. Carlotta briefly raised her eyes to the ceiling. Dan looked equally incredulous. Only Isabel gave me a small nod of approval.

Feeling I was being hopelessly bad at describing my new ambitions, I fell silent. Perhaps I'd left my announcement too late in the evening. I'd made a real cock-up, I thought: hadn't done it well. And what did they think, Dan, Isabel, Carlotta? What did they care? I couldn't be sure, but I don't think their reaction was as strong as I'd thought it might have been. Isabel was turned from me, busy making coffee. Dan gave an audible sigh. Carlotta, shoulders hunched, head cupped in her hands, appeared to be in deep thought. But whether it concerned my future, or matters of more interest to her, I had no idea.

ISABEL

Christ, what an evening. Different kind of tears threatened. I hurried over to the kettle. – Bert really going. I thought he might have changed his mind. Can't quite believe it. Does he know what he's doing?

The room moved. I could feel a sea-swell beneath us: invisible waves rising and falling. A sense of danger.

I couldn't speak for the constriction in my throat. And there was Dan, eyes down, hands on the edge of the table, fingers playing scales. It's his warning signal. I knew without doubt he was gearing himself up for some announcement, too. – Perhaps to meliorate Bert's news. Perhaps to relieve himself of something that that been lurking for a long time. Bert passed me the cheese board, kindly eyes. I paid acute attention to slicing a piece of Camembert, trying to deflect a feeling of faintness.

From a long way off I heard Dan's voice.

Well, I have a small piece of news, too, he said. And everyone turned to him.

DAN

My overriding feeling was that nobody would be much interested in what I had to say. I had to put it to them in a quiet and modest fashion and hope, at least, it would deflect further speculation about Bert's future in Norfolk. I was sure he'd had enough of gloomy prognostications.

My very small piece of news, I said, is that I've ditched the play I've been struggling with for so long, and I begin a new one tomorrow morning.

There was an intake of breath from Isabel, but she said nothing. Carlotta turned to me, blinking slowly like an owl in headlights. She, too, said nothing. Bert stirred. I knew I could count on him, at least, for real interest. Tell us more, he said.

I began to explain. It was to be a play about betrayal. Carlotta quickly laughed. Called *Betrayal*, suppose? she said. You've been rather beaten to it there, haven't you?

I turned on her, irritated by her interruption. Not that sort of betrayal, I snapped. Not the full blown kind. – No: what I'm going to try to explore is something far less explicit than full blown adultery – something that scarcely exists. But does exist.

Christ, I thought. I'd only just begun and already I was struggling for words to make myself clear. So foolish of me to have thought I could find them. But it was too late to stop, now

Like what? asked Carlotta. Sarcastic, sneering, challenging, she was. I'd often seen her in this mood after too much to drink. I decided to be patient. And considering the general reaction to my news was hardly elated, I wouldn't tell them much more. I pushed my chair away from the table, leant one arm over its back. With my free hand I slowly turned the stem of my wine glass

Just suppose, I said, there was a very happily married couple: loving, trusting, been together a good many years, no apparent threats. Then along came – let's say, a man, and he and the woman recognise a kind of... well, you know, a kind of lightness of being, whatever, between them. They never do much about it. Oh no. They're not potential adulterers, you see. But they feel something mutually unnerving. – They don't talk about it, either. Don't need to. And nothing much happens: a single kiss, perhaps. A touching of hands.

The listening silence had spread thick as fur, stifling. Bert went to put his glass gently on the table. The noise it made switched everybody's look.

Now what I'm going to ask, I went on, and try to answer, is this: does this mutual recognition of *something* count as betrayal? Does it cause permanent guilt, slightly spoiling things for ever? Most important of all, does it impair the solidity of a good marriage? Is it corrosive? And are the two people who share the secret for ever in fear of it being discovered?

I stopped. In putting to them a fictional idea, had I given a clue to its inspiration? I glanced quickly at Carlotta who was hunting for something in her bag. I could feel the unease of the silence. Carlotta broke it. She waved a lipstick.

Gosh, what a lot of questions, Dan, she said. Are you sure the answers are up to making a fascinating play?

– I mean, honestly, we're in the twenty-first century, aren't we? Could anyone on earth think that a *mere recognition,* or whatever you called it, is going to upset a solid marriage? – She looked from me to Isabel. – Pretty far-fetched, I'd call that. You can't expect anyone to feel no temptation whatsoever outside a marriage, or a strong bond. Bet you anything God didn't design us to be attractive only to one person in the world. But if the people concerned don't do anything about it beyond a sort of…mistletoe kiss, of course they're not going to suffer guilt, feel they've done some harm.

I just wondered, I said.

I'm not sure it's worth wondering about, Carlotta snapped back. Having finished the scarlet re-shine of her lips, she was quieter, now. – Everywhere you look, she said, there's real adultery, real betrayal. A passing kiss, or fancy, or moment of lust, is hardly going to upset things in this modern world, is it?

…just wondered, I said again.

Carlotta was blinking very slowly. I could see she was thinking as clearly as she was able. I still didn't look at Isabel but was aware her eyes were on my twirling glass. It was time for me to bow out, stop making a fool of myself.

Pretty difficult subject you've got yourself there, said

Bert, coming to my rescue as he so often does. Interesting, of course. – Be interesting to see what you do with it. But are you sure you're doing the right thing, giving up on a play? You've never done that before.

I knew he was trying to change the subject, relieve me from further incoherent stumbling. I knew he was aware of my sense of mortification as I'd tried to put over an idea that seemed to be of little interest to any of them. It was always foolish to try to talk about something you intend to write: I'd learnt that lesson long ago. So why had I tried? Self-aggrandisement? The longing to share with the people you love the excitement of a new beginning? Whatever the reason, I now cursed myself. All I wanted to do was to dismiss the whole thing as quickly as possible. I filled everyone's glasses.

I think, said Carlotta, eyes suddenly shooting at me, that despite my reservations, on reflection it's a perfectly *fascinating* idea – don't you Isabel?

Isabel, turned upon, surprised by Carlotta's question, laughed to give herself time. She said she wasn't really sure what I was hunting down. But, she agreed with Carlotta, she thought I might be exaggerating the significance of something very small. – Here she glanced at Bert before, at last, meeting my eyes. She went on to say she agreed with more of what Carlotta had said –

that it would be humanly impossible not to entertain a fleeting recognition of attraction to someone beyond the person you loved and were committed to.. And why on earth should that upset the apple cart? Why should that be a threat to some profound bond? There was no reason, as Carlotta had said.

There was triumph in Carlotta's eyes, dejection in my heart. I was convinced Isabel would have supported me. I was so sure she would have agreed with my theory.

I floundered on, trying to explain that what concerned me was the hidden stain on a relationship, should one person secretly embark on some so-called insignificant attraction. Wasn't this a threat that was not worth risking?

It was late by now. No one, apparently, was interested in this question. None of them offered an answer. I sensed an acute feeling of failure, cutting as when, each time, a play returns unwanted. I wished more than ever that I'd never embarked on the whole amorphous subject. I heard Bert give a deep sigh. Then he brightened. Tell you what, Dan, he said. I think you're onto something. If you can sort it all out in your new play... that'll be quite something. A lot of people are faced with the dilemma you've been explaining, and would be glad of an answer. And when you've finished the play you could send it to Rosie's nephew.

– Thanks, Bert, I said. I might do that.

Then Carlotta, with the impatience of one who had had enough news for one evening, pushed back her chair and stood up.

And what are you going to call the play? was her final question.

I hadn't thought about that. I answered without thinking.

Hiding, I said.

BERT

When Dan came to the end of his monologue, he looked shattered. I had the uneasy thought that his idea for his new play might have been inspired by real life. But no, surely not: Dan would never betray Isabel in thought, word or deed. I would swear on my life to that. – Besides, as he so often tells me, he never consciously writes from real life. Making it up is so much more interesting, he claims. – But he looked full of regret for having embarked on trying to tell us about it, and he didn't get much sympathy. Altogether, it wasn't the evening for news going down well. In fact it was the most peculiar and uncomfortable dinner I could remember for a very long time. And Isabel, my Isabel: she suddenly looked terribly tired, confused. If I couldn't be the one to comfort her, I wanted to go home. Carlotta, thank God, got up, once Dan had confessed the title of the play, obviously feeling the same.

CARLOTTA

Dan's incoherent ramblings could only mean one thing: he'd had far too much to drink. What on earth had got into him? Some death wish? Some sudden whim to play with fire? Though I don't think for a moment either of the others imagined he was talking about real life – the real life of the four of us round the table. It was pathetic, the way he was trying to explain, and his explanation was hopeless. I wasn't listening that hard, being more occupied by the thought of Bert buggering off just as I'd spent all that time getting his house ready for a happy life in London. – So Dan may have been making sense, but it didn't get through to me. What I wanted to ask was: are you trying to say that because you and I had one, single kiss, your marriage – to you, though not to Isabel, is never going to be the same again?

But I didn't, of course. There was enough dangerous stuff whirling in the air. An evening of increasing horror, as far as I was concerned, though the others seemed to be enjoying it – at the beginning, at any rate. I'd had enough. All I wanted was to get home.

So I stood up, full of purpose. Then I remembered. Hang on a mo, Carlotta, something inside me shrieked – have you forgotten your own piece of news?

Have to say, in all the clamour, I had. It was now or never.

I stood holding on to the back of the chair, for the room was a little wavy, the wine glasses dancing. I smiled like hell. Took my time. The others must have known something was coming, for they remained in their seats.

I said that – actually, and I was sorry – I had to be going because tomorrow was an important day for me. I was to give in my notice. And shortly – like Bert – there was to be a big change in my life. I was going to live in New York.

I don't know what I was expecting by way of response: a modicum of surprise, dismay, interest perhaps. In fact there was a long puzzled silence. I suspected that after all the other announcements of the evening they weren't able to take in something as huge as mine. After a while – my eyes went from one to another of them, recording their various degrees of bemusement – I heard Isabel's feeble voice. Oh Carlotta, she said. Why on earth?

I was brusque, determined not to linger and ramble.

Too late for detailed explanations, I said. But there comes a time in a single woman's life when she wants to try something else. A place, a job, a life, where she will fare better. In other words I'd become increasingly aware I was in a rut and wanted a change. If it didn't work out, I'd come back. – No, I wouldn't sell my flat. England would always be home: this would just be an experiment. And, yes, I'd be off as soon as everything could be arranged.

I'd no intention of waiting for their reactions. I snatched up my coat and made for the door. Dan quickly followed me. In the two seconds we had alone in the hall he asked if I was sure I knew what I was doing. I said I was. He hugged me, dryly. Then Isabel came up and said she wished I wasn't running off so quickly – though, yes, she agreed, it was well after midnight. She, too, put her arms round me: tense and taut as violin strings. I gave her a friendly smile and said I'd not be gone for a month or so, and I'd miss her once I was in New York. Then Bert took my arm. Close, we descended the steps to the path, and went out into the road. We heard the front door shut very firmly behind us.

BERT

I took Carlotta's arm because my own head was reeling. If she was off to New York, how on earth was I to organise the transformation of my Norfolk house? That was the single, acute, utterly selfish thought that battered me as we made our way slowly and uncertainly down the steps.

We stood beside my car – Carlotta's was some way down the road. A street light made a lemony haze over her hair, and distorted her face with shadows. She leant back against the car and removed my arm. D'you think I'm doing the right thing? she asked.

After some thought as to how best I might put my answer, and the wine-muddle of my brain did not make this easy – I said I thought she probably was. But such a major decision, I suggested, should not be taken too quickly. How about postponing the whole idea for a while? And while weighing up the pros and cons, with my help, how about coming to Norfolk and exercising her talents on my new house?

She looked up at me, her eyes almost invisible in their black fists of shadow, but I saw they were incredulous. She gave the smallest laugh I've ever heard, while a twitch of her mouth indicated she was attempting to smile. She said she was cold.

I opened the car door. With no fuss she got into the passenger seat and huddled her arms beneath her breasts. I sat in the driving seat and put on the heating.

I began to explain things. I would put her up in a very comfortable local hotel, I said, on her visits to Norfolk to make arrangements. I'd come up myself frequently while work was in progress, and make sure we had a good time: I'd like to show her the places of my childhood. I was sure the magic of Norfolk would win her...I said all these things without thinking, listening with some amazement to my own voice. How could I be asking Carlotta to re-arrange all her plans, come and help me once again? – But I was. And I could see she was not dismissing the ideas completely.

At last she turned to me. She said perhaps I was right. Perhaps she had made her decision too quickly. She needed more time to make arrangements in New York, to weigh everything up more carefully. So she would still give in her notice in the morning, and work for the necessary month or so. She would then spend three months, just three months, seeing to my house before she left. This she said so threateningly I laughed. But I promised: I would not persuade her to stay for more than that, even if the house wasn't finished.

Then I'll be off, she said. For a very long time.

I conceded that was an excellent plan. I meant it.

She sighed. What an extraordinarily awful, uneasy evening it had been, she observed. She regretted getting at Isabel in the way she had, although she found Isabel's smug complacency almost more than she could bear, sometimes. But then you'd never utter a word against her, she added.

I admitted that would be unlikely. I didn't know Isabel that well, I explained, but it seemed to me she was a marvellous wife and –

beautiful, added Carlotta.

That was not what I was going to say. Even in an inebriated state I was capable of exercising caution. But now Carlotta had mentioned Isabel's beauty there was no need for me to add any carefully chosen praises. I thought for the second time that perhaps she had an inkling of my feelings for Isabel. Perceptive women can usually see behind a man's most carefully constructed front. I ventured, to put her off the scent, that I thought Isabel's so-called smugness indicated her feeling of the safety of the marriage, her absolute certainty in Dan. Carlotta sniffed. Absolute certainty? she asked. Absolute certainty's a dangerous and a foolish thing.

Carlotta then sighed and said she must go. She claimed she wanted to think about my new life, which she was finding very hard to imagine. I offered to drive her home. She said no, she'd prefer to take her car. In which case, I'd walk home, clear my head. But thanks, she said, and she was sorry if she'd appeared to have run out of steam.

Simultaneously we leaned towards each other for a polite kiss on the cheek. Somehow our heads moved further than intended, and our lips met. I remembered her mouth. She allowed me to put a hand on her breast. I remembered, again. But I held back from any sign of wanting to go further. I didn't want to alarm her. One day, perhaps...but this was not the right moment.

While we were enclosed in the blurred visions of an embrace, I thought of Dan and Isabel behind the drawn curtains of the kitchen: Dan pottering about in guise of helping to clear – Isabel? What would she be doing? Watching him? I could see her so clearly, the woman I loved, filtering about in her swishing blue, climbing the stairs to get into bed beside her husband. So near, and yet so unreachable. And all the time, loving her, I was kissing Carlotta and wondering why.

ISABEL

In unspoken agreement, we left everything. For once, it could wait till the morning. We were both exhausted. I was shaken. I think Dan was too.

He put on our favourite Schubert quartet. We sat at the low table by the window. Sipped glasses of water. The thought that had been thrashing about since Dan had broken his news, and which had stopped me from fully taking in Carlotta's decision to leave, was that his new play was to be about the very thing I'd been wondering about this morning. It was uncanny, alarming. Was it pure coincidence, or something more sinister? Could Dan have any inkling? – Had some instinct made him think that Bert and I had acknowledged some innocent, but existing flare of recognition? Surely, surely not. There was not the slightest evidence. In fact, during his week here, Bert had gone out of his way never to be alone with me – apart from the accidental moment on the stairs – and never to give any hint of his feelings (which perhaps I will never know) for me. So I should have been able to feel Dan's idea had sprung from out of the blue, as did all his ideas, he always claimed. All the same I felt sick, chilled by apprehension.

Dan was still agitated. He wanted to know what I thought of his new idea, and also of his plan to give up the old one. Impossible question to answer truthfully. I simply said it was good, but it might be difficult. Dan shrugged. Plainly he wanted more from me, but I was incapable of giving it at that moment. So he asked what I felt about Bert's plan to leave. Again, I was in no position to answer. I hadn't had time to think, and I didn't much want to think. So I said I was impressed that he was so convinced it was the right decision, and he might surprise us all by taking enthusiastically to solitude. After a pause, he then asked what was it about Bert – what was it that warmed and attracted people so often? I think it's his *talent to convey*, I said. He can make everyone see things just as he sees them, amusingly, seriously, whatever – but always scintillatingly. – Always one of your priorities, said Dan. But I think it's more than that. He didn't mention what else he had in mind, and I was too tired to ask. As for Carlotta? he asked then. How do you feel about her going? I shrugged, and said I felt nothing very much. We had grown further apart, of late, though I wasn't sure why. Dan was annoyed she'd been so rude to me. I said that was no matter. I suppose I'll miss her sometimes, I said.

We went on sitting there, drinking fizzy water, till the quartet came to an end. After a spell of silence I said what a pity we'd failed – with Bert and Carlotta, I meant. But then match-making hardly ever works.

We didn't try very hard, said Dan, and thank God it didn't, I can't think of two people so unsuited. They'd drive each other barmy. Unless they happened to meet under our roof, he doubted they'd ever see each other again. Bert'd be ruminating on the marsh while Carlotta was living it up in New York. Worlds apart, no inclination to meet.

I daresay you're right, I murmured. By now it was very late. We went up to bed.

DAN

After they'd gone Isabel and I sat, as we so often do at the end of the evening, at the table in the window. Protected by the music we both love, we made little attempt to talk. I don't know what Isabel was thinking – she had on her pre-occupied look – and certainly wasn't that excited by the thought of my new play. Warned me it'd be difficult. – But then it wasn't the right time to probe for her real opinion, and considering how badly the whole thing went down at dinner I don't think I'll be seeking any more opinions at all. Just get down and write it.

The re-assuring thing, though, was that plainly she had absolutely no idea it was anything to do with real life. Unless Carlotta spilt the beans, in some angry moment, Isabel would never discover the single incident that set me thinking of my new idea. The fact that Carlotta was off to America was a very great relief: double-sure safety. My own guilt I could continue to hide. Regret, combined with a persistent edge of desire unfulfilled, would fade one day, and the skeletons facts could then be buried.

I followed Isabel upstairs, longing for the morning, the cleared desk, the beginning. Ahead of me, her blue skirt moved from side to side in the way that I knew and loved so well. But tonight, mimicking her fatigue, the silk was swaying more languidly than usual, and the slowness of our progress up the stairs filled me with longing.

In our room, with a hand devoid of energy, she undid the skirt and let it fall to the ground. She stepped from it as if from a pool of water drained of sunlight. Then she turned to me: such innocence. She had no reason not to trust me, and it must always remain like that. I knew she would never ask, so the innocence, with Carlotta far away, could be preserved.

We moved to the bed. She made no protest at hurry

I could not disguise. In the darkness we were able to discard the strangeness of the evening, and suddenly the sky paled through the windows. There were only a few hours left till morning, and the new beginning.

Chapter Twelve

SYLVIE

I can hardly believe it – it's a really weird thought but Elli's been here almost a year now.

I remember so well how it all happened, the morning after the rentals had had Bert and horrible Carlotta to supper. I came down early wanting to show them my history essay, which I'd tried very hard with, and for once I was down first and the kitchen was an absolute tip. They hadn't cleared away anything. I'd just pushed aside some pudding plates to make enough room for my cereal, when the phone rang and rang, and in the end I answered it.

I'm glad I did because it was Elli, sobbing and sobbing. It was quite difficult to understand what she was saying, but apparently her mother had gone off with her revolting young boyfriend, leaving a note saying she was finally off for good. Her father had thought she was away on some sort of business trip, but when he read her letter he had sort of hysterics, and rushed off in his car to find her, leaving Elli alone. It was Saturday morning, no school. She was desperate.

Luckily Mama came down at that moment and I quickly explained everything. Mama said we'll go and fetch her *now*. So we did.

Poor Elli. I'd never seen anyone so miserable in all my life. She was crying so much she could hardly pack. Mama was incredibly efficient about everything, and so kind and comforting that soon after we got back home Elli stopped crying. In fact we had rather a nice day. We went to a film, and then Mama took us out to lunch because she said Papa needed a long uninterrupted day to begin some new play.

Elli does go home some weekends, to her father, who's very happy for her to be living here as he's away so much he can't really look after her. But really it's like having a sister, and it's lovely. We do have some arguments, but when we disagree she goes to her room above mine and we keep to ourselves till whatever the disagreement is peters out.

She really loves the rentals. I think she wishes hers were like mine. She often says how lucky I am, and I know that's true. Her mother occasionally sends a post card from some foreign country, with no address so Elli can't write back. How can any mother be so mean? I think Elli's beginning to get over it a bit and it doesn't seem to have affected her work. In fact she works terribly hard, much harder than me, and comes top in lots of things, which Mama and Papa praise her for and I get quite jealous but I know I'll do just as well once I put my mind to it. Her parents are apparently getting divorced and I don't know what will happen in the end. But Mama says she can stay here as long as she likes, she's one of the family. Sort of unofficially adopted.

Since she's been here time seems to have gone awfully quickly. Next term I really am going to start working as hard as Elli, as I want to do well. Papa's been working at his new play most evenings and a lot of the weekends. Luckily he doesn't ever try to tell us what it's about, though I know it's called *Hiding*. Elli and I thought that was, like, a pretty boring title. I mean, who'd ever buy tickets to see something called *Hiding*? Papa didn't ask my opinion of the title, but very tactfully I suggested he shouldn't be too set on it, and maybe an even better idea would come to him. But whatever it's called I hope it works this time. He never minds about all his failures, but he's so brave, never whinges on.

Once, a few weeks ago, I was in his study. His desk cupboard was open and I saw these *stacks* of manuscripts. I said what are all those? And he just said: rejections. But he smiled, and said no matter, he wasn't going to give up. He said that in a funny way being rejected goads you into trying even harder, and he was convinced that one day he would succeed. I suppose Papa's a good example.

Mama's been having her own sort of success: masses of orders for masks which are really, really beautiful. I asked her if she could make me one for a birthday present to put up in my room. She said if she has time, but she'd an order for six for some famous carnival in Rio, and a film company wanted some, too. So she's been terribly busy and sometimes looks tired, but happy. They're certainly mega-hard workers, my parents. I'm not sure I'll ever be like that unless I find something, like them, I really want to work at because I love it.

This time last year I thought it might be history or archaeology – I rather like the idea of going on digs and discovering bits of the past. But recently I've gone off all that and I'm into designing furniture. I did a drawing of a futuristic kind of chair that Mama promised me she thought was very elegant. Elli wants to be a model. She's so thin and pretty I suppose that wouldn't be difficult, but in a gentle way Mama told her it wouldn't be a very rewarding life apart from the money. I don't know. Wondering what I'll be and do haunts me a lot, but I suppose there's lots of time to decide.

Bert sometimes comes to see us. I think we all miss him a bit. Apparently he loves Norfolk and says he'll never come back to London. The other day he took us all out to dinner, and then when he came home he gave both Elli and me £10 each! So I suppose he's still rich. I like Bert a lot. He's so sort of, like, warm, and easy to talk to. I said to Elli the other day – well, night, we stay up talking quite late sometimes – that if Papa ever had some terrible accident and died, then I'd like Bert to marry Mama and be my stepfather. She agreed that would be good. But of course he'd never, ever be able to replace Papa. No one could. And I don't even like to imagine, not for a single moment, my parents being dead. Elli said it was as if her parents were dead already.

Poor her: I'm so glad she's with us. It's like having the sister I've always wanted.

GWEN

My goodness, as I always say, the good Lord does come up with his surprises. Who would ever of thought, this time last year, that my meeting with Henry in the pub would have turned to this? This wonderful friendship. I thank my lucky stars. I thank God every night in my prayers.

Of course, I always knew he was an especially good man. When I was asked to take a second look at the identification parade, I spotted that. I can spot goodness a mile off. Seeing his face in my mind's eye on the way home – I remembered that. And then the extraordinary coincidence of meeting him in the pub, and to think I'd been in two minds whether to go. If I hadn't dared, to this day I might still be in my old life: no good friend, no outings and conversation and care and understanding. Sometimes I still can't believe what's happened, and I say to Henry is this really happening? And he laughs, doesn't think me silly, and tells me it really is.

Henry and I took things very slowly, just to my liking, just to his. I was so pleased a few days after our first meeting, when he phoned to remind me of the Friday drink. I hadn't had such a nice invitation for years, and what a good time we had. He told me a little of his wife, Mary, and made no bones about missing her. Apparently she was a lovely woman, wife and mother, a dab hand in the kitchen and spent every spare moment with her head in a book.

But he learned to live on his own, he said: it was different, but possible. He didn't feel the need to mourn. 'You can miss without mourning,' he said. And he kept himself very busy, was comfortably off, the building trade being in good shape. He helped his children a bit, but otherwise was saving for his retirement. He rather fancied a little place down on the south coast. I told him I used to know Frinton, but gave no hint I thought that was a lovely dream which I wouldn't mind sharing.

After that second drink he insisted on walking me home – said he didn't want me mugged again. I didn't ask him in for a cup of tea. I didn't want to put him off by appearing to be a woman with designs. And it must have worked because after that we met quite regularly, at least once a week. And then we began to branch out. We went to the cinema sometimes, and out for a meal. He said he was going to educate me in foods of the world. I was a bit nervous about this, of course, having something of a temperamental stomach. But he persuaded me I'd be all right, and over the next few months there was hardly a restaurant in the Shepherds Bush area we didn't visit: Indian, Chinese, Italian … the lot. Sometimes the food gave me indigestion, but I didn't tell Henry. I've always believed you should keep some things to yourself. I don't suppose I'll ever be keen on garlic, so I just make sure I avoid it. But I think Henry's pleased I enjoy trying things out, and he likes teasing me when I'm faced with a big plate of something mysterious, all spicy smells and bright Eastern colours, and I don't know where to begin, while he snatches up the chopsticks like an old pro.

Sometimes he takes me up to the West End. We went to a musical on my birthday, and I don't think I can ever remember such a lovely evening. My feet were tapping all the way back on the tube. I wouldn't have minded being a tap dancer in another life, I told him on the way home – something I've never confessed to anyone. He said he thought I'd have been a very good tap dancer, I was so nimble on my feet.

It wasn't for six months or so I invited him round to my place. He'd paid for so many meals I really felt I should do something in return, though he said that wasn't necessary at all. Anyhow, it all worked very nicely. It was a Thursday, a non-working day, so I was able to spend the whole afternoon cooking – some French stew out of a book Mrs. G lent me. I didn't want him to think I was just a cottage-pie woman. I wanted to show versatility. And amazingly he loved it, praised me to the skies. He hurried off after we'd watched the news, saying it was time I visited his place.

I went one Saturday for the midday meal. His house was nice enough, though in need of a little tender loving care of the sort men aren't up to. It was all I could do not to ask for a duster, but I restrained myself. When we'd cleared away we watched the football together on the couch, and he brought me a cup of tea at half time. Such luxury. I could hardly believe it was happening.

At some point I did tell Mrs. G about Henry: well, she kept on pointing out how cheerful I looked and I was only too happy to explain. I was careful to emphasise the nature of our friendship. I didn't want her to go thinking I was about to fly off with him. No, I assured her: Henry and I are at the age when a close friendship is better than a love affair. We rely on each other, have good times together, take care of each other. What more could anyone want at my age? She looked a bit quizzical when I said that – well, I suppose someone as beautiful as her would want a love affair for the rest of her life. But she said how pleased for me she was, and often at our coffee breaks, nowadays, we talk about Henry. It's lovely having someone to talk about.

At Christmas, I did have a little set back. I had this card from Yarmouth: Gary. He said he was well settled but thinking of coming back to London one day. He said he'd look me up, and he hoped all my scars had healed. For a while – I was alone in my flat – I felt knocked off my rocker, sick. I wondered if he would haunt me, taunt me, for the rest of my life. Would I ever be rid of him?

I told Henry, of course. He said 'Don't you worry, Gwen, I'll look after you. I'll protect you from anyone or anything that ever threatens you: you'll be all right with me.' I believed him, of course. That was very comforting, knowing there's someone to protect me. But all the same, deep in my heart there's this small, persistent fear. It was when I told him about Gary's card – we were in our usual corner of the Witch and Broomstick – that he took my hand for the very first time. He ran his fingers over mine. They were so huge, strong. His nails, I suppose from the building work, were never quite clean, but not unpleasantly black. He gave my hand a reassuring squeeze. Then he patted my knee and said he was going to order more drinks. Being the festive time of year, we were going to celebrate – not just Christmas, but the good luck of having met me in the first place.

Dear Henry. He gave me a bag for Christmas, which we spent together in my flat. The most beautiful bag I've ever seen, black leather, with my initials engraved on a small golden plaque. I'd knitted him a jumper. He said he'd wear it till it fell apart.

And so we carry on with our lovely, gentle friendship, sure of each other. Needing each other but not imposing on each other. There's never been any talk of moving in together or making it all official in some way, and

I don't suppose there ever will be. We like it as it is. It suits us very well. Each of us having our own little bit of life, and then the regular meetings that we can count on. We're not hampered by those youthful desires of the flesh – and I did once explain to Henry they'd never bothered me very much – but there's a warmth and an understanding between us that, after Barry in Blackpool, I never thought I'd find again. Only this time I won't be let down. I'm positive of that.

Only last week Henry came up with a lovely idea. He said he'd take me dancing. 'Not tap,' he said. But he knew a very exclusive place where we could glide around a ballroom with a lot of others of our own age. 'Oh my,' I said, 'I've nothing to wear.'

'You go and buy yourself a nice dress,' he said, slipping a bundle of notes into my hand, 'and what with that and your green coat and your new bag, you'll be the smartest woman there. I'll be very proud of you.'

No, it's not a dream. We're set to go dancing on Wednesday night. I was so excited at work this morning that I dropped the hoover and had quite a business putting it back together. I told Mrs. G what had happened, and why, and she laughed and laughed as if she shared my excitement.

I bought a lovely dress, the sort of blue Mrs. G likes,

and Henry is to wear his Sunday suit. He said we'd sit at a small round table lit with low peach-coloured lights, and the waiter would bring us drinks on a tray. Then the band would strike up, all the lovely old tunes – *Dancing on the Ceiling*, perhaps – that my mother used to play on her gramophone. Then we'd get up, and have a go, and I'd pray to God my feet would remember. Only twenty four hours till Wednesday.

'You're a lucky woman, Gwen Bishop,' as I say to myself so often.

BERT

The swivel chairs arrived this morning, signifying the end at last. It's finally done now. Finished. The office, built onto one end of the house with a huge picture window over the marsh, is ready to go. At opposite ends of the room we have our desks and our computers. Business, after a slow start conducted on the kitchen table, now seems to be taking off.

The house, too, is more or less finished: just a few more of Rosie's pictures to hang. She came back and saw it the other day, and unlike most people who are appalled at what others do to their houses, was enchanted. 'You'll never want to leave,' she said, and she's right.

'She's absolutely right,' Carlotta said this morning at breakfast, grumbling because it was her once-a-month day to go to London. Her firm was so shocked when she gave in her notice she was persuaded to stay on a very ad-hoc basis, working from home, attending just a monthly meeting. There's a dreamlike quality to how it all happened, still pretty hard to believe.

I brought Carlotta to see the house on the worst possible day – gusts of rain across the marsh, sea invisible, mud, cold… We sat round Rosie's fire drinking red wine and I was positive she wouldn't agree to do the house even before the promised departure to New York.

But over dinner in the hotel that evening she said she loved it, she could envisage the whole thing. And when, next morning, we went back to the house and there was a sheen of sun over the marsh, and a thread of silver tinsel sea on the horizon, she seemed lost for words. I had an inkling she just might want to prolong the time she took to transform it.

I can never be quite sure how it came about, but there was little talk of New York after that. When the three assigned months were up, and the builders were still in the house, she continued to be in charge of it all. When I moved in, six months ago now, and the place was still pretty chaotic, she asked if I would mind if she stayed till it was quite finished. She slept in a tiny room at the back while I was installed in the large bedroom overlooking the wide view.

By now she was a Carlotta new to me, very different from the frantic London woman who had both attracted me and irritated me when I returned from America. Here, she cast aside all her previous material interests, scarcely bothered with her appearance and looked a damn sight prettier for it: her striking face needed no embellishment. Also, a kind of sweetness of nature, previously hidden, seemed to appear.

My well-being seemed her prime concern, and she obviously loved the place, whatever the weather. Long before me she had established friends in the neighbourhood, and discovered just where to find the best fish and samphire, and the retired folk who sold redcurrants from their gardens. Often I would ask her if she was not lonely, missing London.

Absolutely not, she said: this was the place — although she had never known it — that felt like home to her. I didn't like to question her further, but I couldn't help wondering how she saw us. Never once did she give any hint that she expected anything more than our increasingly easy and lively companionship: we didn't go in for discussing ourselves. I came to assume that, having not found the right man in her life, she was happy to settle for living with someone with whom she got on well, with whom she enjoyed a quiet daily life, working together and just being together.

Looking back, it's hard to understand how blind I was. All the time she was working so hard, so brilliantly putting my house in order, I was convinced she required nothing more. Then one June morning I came down to the kitchen to find her not there. Unease struck me, but quickly melted away when she came through the door, hair wet and tangled. She'd been for an early morning swim. The look she gave me was ... well, I don't quite know what it was. Appealing, perhaps. Yearning. Longing. I reacted without thought. I stood up, quickly took her in my arms, muttered something about what an ungrateful cad I'd been, and breakfast was abandoned. We spent the morning watching the sun fill the bedroom: it was a very happy lost day.

So that was the turning point. In a funny way, it didn't make any great difference, becoming lovers. Our days still chuntered along in their quiet way, the excitement being establishing the business. I found Carlotta to be an extraordinarily good business woman – no wonder her old firm didn't want to part with her. I would never have guessed, in our previous life in London, how sharp was her business acumen, how persuasive her suggestions, how acute her judgments.

Together we researched the east coast for projects in need of funding, and were overwhelmed with requests. As Carlotta observed one evening, my own considerable stash would soon be gone. What we must do now is to find money elsewhere, something she sees as a challenge and, judging by the results, is another of her talents.

I go to London very rarely, and sometimes stay a night in Carlotta's old flat. I usually find time for lunch with Dan, who seems to have real hope for his new play, but then I've seen that so many times before. Once or twice I've had supper with him and Isabel, and I suppose at some time we'll have them to stay here. I've never had a moment alone with Isabel since that terrible last dinner.

But sometimes, when Carlotta's away, I ring her. I tell her what's going on, she tells me about Sylvie and Elli, all the work she now has, Dan's progress. We never mention anything dangerous. But because I still love her, will always love her, these talks are, I concede, a form of infidelity. If she was no more to me than a friend, Dan's wife, they would be innocent. As it is, it's a form of infidelity I'm not prepared to give up.

From time to time I desperately need to talk to Isabel,

to hear her voice, just to remind ... Sometimes she asks if I'm happy. I say I am and she says she's glad. She never asks about Carlotta, and I've never told her we've become lovers. She probably knows. When we speak (and I know it's at times Dan's out of the house) there's a kind of silent acknowledgement – I think, I can't be sure – that once, for a moment or so, there was a flash of light between us. All I need is to be reminded of that every now and then. It was my misfortune to fall in love at a late age, with my friend's wife – but better than never having loved at all, I suppose. I'm reminded of the truth of that on the occasions when I talk to Isabel.

I've never said to Carlotta 'I love you', and doubt I ever will. I feel other things for her in abundance: respect, affection, admiration, warmth. But not quite love. She makes no demands about my feelings and is, I believe, quieter, happier, as contented as I can make her in her new life. I don't suppose we'll ever have children. There's no talk of that. It would mean a very different life which I don't think either of us would want. We're happy, positively happy, as we are.

She swings round on her new chair, laughing. I swing round on mine which squeaks. She has the best chair. She deserves it. Her hair is windblown into a thousand curls, her feet are bare. My old, ambivalent fancy for her thrives. I don't love her, but she's wonderful. I'm a lucky man.

This afternoon, she reminds me, looking at her watch, we're to go and see again one of Norfolk's small, fine churches that's in a state of poor repair. Years of jumble sales and fetes and raffle tickets have not yet raised an eighth of what is needed to replace the roof, and official help has not been forthcoming. We are to have tea with the vicar in his beautiful crumbling rectory, and hand over a cheque. He will apprise us of other, equally indigent churches. We will come back, and sit in our swivel chairs, and do our sums – Carlotta's much better at that than me.

I love Isabel, I think, as I look at Carlotta's feet. But when impossible dreams are replaced by such pleasure as I feel in this new life, a man has to be grateful.

'Come on,' urges Carlotta, 'there's time for a smoked mackerel sandwich before we have to go.'

CARLOTTA

It's always a curious thing, as I said to Bert the other night, when you surprise yourself. If anyone had said to me, this time last year, your life is going to be facing a marsh, raising money for old churches and small local industries, I would have said they were completely barmy. But that's how it is, and looking back I'm still not quite sure how it all happened.

I was enchanted by the location of Bert's house, even though the first day I went there the rain was tipping down so heavily it was hard to see anything. I had immediate ideas about what should be done, how it could be, where an extension for the office could be added. So I agreed to Bert's cheeky idea of putting off New York for three months, and the next day the rain had cleared and a vast sky was visible.

I suppose I'd never thought much about sky before. I mean, who would? In my childhood it was unremarkable patches of blue or grey between trees, and in London it scarcely exists. For so many years I'd been looking out of windows and seeing other buildings and the tops of trees, but although sun and rain determined the day, I was never consciously aware of sky. But here: well, it knocked me out. It was a vast dome I'd been missing all my life, awe inspiring, magnificent. You could stand on the dunes, fling out your arms and become part of the blue, float away from yourself among the spumy clouds. I remember, my second evening here, a fly-past of duck in strict formation crossing the expanse of opal, knowing where they were heading, their voices making small creaks in the silence.

I'd never seen a flight of duck before. I was hooked. I was a gonner. I knew, that evening, there was no question of going to New York, or returning to London and another high-paying, high-powered job. All I wanted was to stay with Bert in Norfolk, explore the quiet life.

He was quite different here, too. Less edgy. He stopped wearing waistcoats and was no longer sarcastic. He did go on making me laugh, but he kept a polite distance.

I couldn't fathom what was going on in his mind about *me*, *us*. Perhaps nothing. I didn't ask. I couldn't bring myself to ask. He'd think it very untoward if I questioned what was plainly a good friendship. I think he imagined I was happy with things as they were, and we'd continue with the platonic arrangement maybe for years. It was certainly a very happy arrangement – we got on very well, like brother and sister. He showed me Norfolk, I taught him about computers and various tricks of business which intrigued him. But just occasionally I would look at him, reading by the fire in the evening, and think why the hell doesn't he just walk over and seduce me? What's the matter with me?

On reflection, I don't think he thought there was anything much the matter with me, but it just didn't occur to him to change the nature of our relationship. He'd had his chance, the foolish evening of the bared breasts, and he hadn't taken it. Probably thought it was too late, now. But how did he imagine the future? Perhaps he thought some woman far more perfect than I could ever be would come walking along the marsh path one day, and he'd exchange her for me. Or perhaps he imagined I'd find the equivalent man, and leave him. He must have seen I didn't give myself many chances for this: I scarcely ever went to London – he went more often than I did – and it was hardly likely I was going to fall for one of the brash summer visitors in the local pub. But actually I don't think Bert did much envisaging of the future: he wasn't a man of great imagination. One of the things I loved him for was his intense, enthusiastic concentration on present involvements.

Yes, I love him. I do. I remember once thinking I could fall for him – never in the same extreme, uncomfortable way I could fall for Dan if he was available – but I grew to love Bert. And despite hesitations, doubts about his feelings for me, I did. Gently at first. Then one morning I'd been for an early swim, and found myself hurrying back. I realised – surprising myself – I was eager to return to the house, see the picture in my mind – Bert at breakfast – turned into reality. I ran into the kitchen, hair dripping, and he looked up. I could have sworn he was as keen for me to be back as I was. I could have sworn there were some sudden sea-change in his eyes – a realization that his business partner, his interior decorator and friendly companion, was suddenly more than that. We swooped together. We went to his bed. Big sky out of the window. Scraps of it I saw when I opened my eyes for a moment. For so long Bert had pent up his love ...

By lunch-time we were spent, exhausted, elated, deliquescent. By the time I stumbled downstairs to arrange a cold lobster – we were both ravenous – I was definitely in love, and I knew that in his funny, understated way, Bert was in love with me.

We didn't talk about this of course. I would have been wary of translating anything that I now felt into clichéd and inadequate words. It was one of those times there is absolutely no need for declarations. Everything was obvious. Everything was understood.

Now I'm firmly established in his bed and we're known to be a couple. We carry on with this extraordinarily different life which I love to bits. I go off and come back with vegetables from cottage gardens, and faded plates from markets – the sort of minor triumphs that give me the kind of pleasure I'm sure I would have scoffed at a year ago. Bert loves it when I return with my bargains: he loves it when he sees me inventing new ways with fish and samphire. The other day he suggested we buy a small boat and did some sailing. I'm terrified of the sea and I'm a rotten sailor. But yes, why not, I said, and he was so pleased.

My only secret from Bert is that I have this odd yearning for a child. I haven't put the idea to him yet, but I'm sure that he'd agree. Should he be against the idea, I'm not sure how I'd feel. Sad, I suppose. But I won't think about that. I'm sure he could be persuaded.

As for Dan and Isabel – the funny thing is, I hardly give them a thought. Very occasionally a flash of their life comes to me, and the memory of that sizzling kiss with Dan.

But Isabel, my friend Isabel, has retreated. Perhaps we never had very much in common in the first place, just used each other for mutual comfort and encouragement. We did laugh quite a lot and I sometimes miss a friend whose sense of humour so exactly coincides with my own. But there was always an unspoken rivalry between us, a kind of amorphous jealousy. Though what we were rivals over, or jealous of, I can never fathom.

I would have hated her tranquil life, she would have hated mine. Sometimes I think I'd like to try to explain to her about the huge change I've taken, and why I love it. But I don't think she'd be much interested, so I don't bother. Bert apparently told her how I was enjoying it: her answer was to bet my new found enthusiasm wouldn't last long. She's wrong, there. Bert visits her and Dan sometimes when he goes to London: I've seen them only once, briefly, since I left. I don't miss them. I don't miss anything.

All I want is to make Bert happy, make our little business work, slow down time, and wonder at the sky.

DAN

Since Bert and Carlotta left, it's been an extraordinarily busy and exhilarating time. *Hiding* – still not sure about the title – was finished six weeks ago. Never have I worked on a play so long and so eagerly.

I had it typed beautifully, then six bound copies made. It was a good morning, that, coming back from the stationer with a heavy bag of manuscripts. Home, I immediately wrote a short note to Sam Fielding, and went out again to post it special delivery. Isabel asked why I kept going in and out. Why I was so restless, she wanted to know. I didn't tell her.

And now I wait. Well, I'm used to waiting. There's something quite agreeable about it because it means that there's till reason to hope, to anticipate a rewarding reply.

The morning I dread is when I see on the doormat the fat envelope addressed in my own hand. The perfunctory, scarcely courteous note informing me some minion was very interested to read the play, but it wasn't quite what the theatre was looking for.

I have more than usual hope this time, though: a, because I know it's my best play since Oxford, and b, because I have faith in Sam Fielding. He is the nephew of Bert's Norfolk old lady, Rosie. Bert arranged for all of us to have lunch at the Garrick. I imagine Sam, a very busy man, only agreed to this out of kindness to his aged aunt, but it went very well. Very jolly. We didn't speak much about the actual play, of course. I gave the briefest outline and he agreed it was a good subject, pertinent to a lot of people. I made him laugh once or twice – on other matters – so I hope he thought my sense of humour might be apparent in the play. When we parted he said would I be sure to send the finished script to him marked personal. He gave me his absolute assurance that he himself would read it first, and then pass it on to other readers.

I was cheered by all this. It meant the script was less likely to sail off into the nowhere for months and months, like so many of the others. I've been waiting for a response now for six weeks – five weeks and four days to be precise. I had a brief acknowledgement – a good sign, unusual these days – from Sam. A picture postcard of Shakespeare. Sam said thanks for the script, he'd read it ASAP and be in touch. This cheered me up, too. So good to be treated politely for once.

Since then I've been trying hard to be patient. I haven't, funnily enough, had an idea for another play. So, not writing anything, I feel rather at a loose end in the evenings. Isabel and I go to the theatre and to see films more frequently as a result. Every morning I'm down early, both dreading and longing for the post. When once again there's no news I try very hard to turn my mind to other things, but it's difficult.

And being hopelessly weak when it comes to expectation, I find myself fantasising a little. The first night, for instance – in Colchester, perhaps, or Southampton or Guildford. I don't care where, really. Sam explained the tour is the most important thing these days: success in the West End is virtually impossible for a straight play. 'Don't worry about the West End,' he said – and I don't. 'A good tour is what you want to aim for: you can make a lot of money,' he assured me.

I don't give a damn about the money. I just want the thing to be put on. I want it to work. I want all the excitement – once briefly experienced – of seeing actors saying my words. I want all the years of effort to end in just a scrap of fulfilment.

Because if *Hiding* is rejected, I'm not sure I've the will, the energy, the strength, to try again.

I have a particularly shaming, secret fantasy about the first night. I imagine Isabel and me, Bert and Carlotta, driving off to wherever in the provinces – for after that evening of my clumsy announcement, B and C are the obvious people to invite to come with us. I imagine them sitting there in the dark, watching this story about a married couple, so happy, so secure, and their two unmarried friends, Roddy and Liza. Married man, Paul, succumbs to a moment of lust with Liza, which rocks his equilibrium, although his wife Mary is innocent of his secret. She has no idea of the fear he suffers wondering if Liza will ever betray him. Mary is a hundred percent faithful wife, Paul believes … knows. Roddy is an honourable bachelor. So guilt only accosts two of the cast. What trauma will it cause? You don't learn till Act 2. In the interval the audience will wonder, speculate.

What will Isabel, Carlotta and Bert make of this? Will they recognize it's inspired by real life? Will Carlotta cast a meaningful look at me over her glass of wine? Will Isabel, much later at home, jokingly ask where the idea of the play came from?

I wonder, I wonder. With some dread, I wonder.

As my work diminishes, Isabel's increases. It seems to be a new phrase for her. She's working terribly hard, has become quite famous for her masks. Commissions from all over the place. And they're wonderful, extravagant, original things – even I can see that, and I'm proud of her. With time on my hands in the evenings, I've taken to making the supper sometimes, to give her a break. This gives her inordinate pleasure. Sometimes I'm helped by Sylvie and Elli.

It's good having Elli here, lovely for Sylvie. They get on well, do things together, rarely squabble. God knows how long Elli's going to stay, but for as long as she wants as far as I'm concerned. Her grandmother has offered to have her, but the last thing she wants is to go and live in Surrey with some dotty old lady, poor child. She's had a rough time and I like to think she's happier now.

I miss Bert just as I missed him all those years he was in New York. His return was a great bonus, especially that week he stayed here. His going away again so soon was a disappointment, but I do understand about his new life. He plainly loves it. Whether or not he loves Carlotta, despite all she organizes for him, is another matter. It might be a case of companionship and gratitude rather than pure love, but obviously we don't discuss the subtleties of their arrangement when he comes to London. But he did, after one particularly long lunch, admit he'd finally got his leg over.

'Rather a coarse way of putting it,' I said, 'very unlike you.'

He laughed, ashamed of the crude nature of his confession. But I think it explained things: if he loved Carlotta he would never have used such language. Anyhow, I'm pleased he's so contented in Norfolk, and we're going up for the weekend soon. At least he comes to London from time to time – engaged, now, in collecting antique art books, his new passion – so we see him.

Carlotta, surprisingly, has only appeared once, briefly. Apparently she's done a complete volte face. From loathing the idea of the country, she now loathes the thought of London. Well, she always was pretty extreme.

Can't say she ever looms in my thoughts. That one moment, those few nefarious seconds, have become dreamlike (not a good dream), and like a dream they've faded, leaving behind nothing but a faint unease. Yes, there's still a fear of her breaking her promise.

The funny thing is I've written so much about Carlotta, in the character of Liza, that the two have become slightly confused. Reality and fiction have become so tangled it would take much thought to re-divide them. And then am I Paul? Is he me? The only absolute certainty is that we share a guilt, a shame, that won't quite go away. What I sometimes think is that Mary and Roddy, the two absolutely innocent characters – muddles with Isabel and Bert – are the duller notes in the play. Maybe I should pep them up a bit. I'll see what Sam thinks, what the director thinks ...

Waiting, I've discovered, has its own strange tides, its own rhythms. One moment I'm fiercely patient, other times there's the rage, the fury at my own helplessness. Sometimes I wake despairing, sometimes full of hope. On a bad day the hours clunk through my fingers like the beads of a rosary. On a good day I feel feet off the ground. I've been through all the sensations. How much longer must I wait? I tell Isabel none of this, for it's so boring hearing about someone's constant disappointment. So my biggest fantasy is about the morning the letter arrives saying ... Yes: a few changes here and there (God, I'm willing to do a thousand changes) but, yes, we'd like to take on your play.

Then I'd scream into the kitchen waving the letter, tell Isabel that I'd made it at last, and we'd hug each other in mutual delight till we could scarcely breathe.

That's what I imagine, all the time.

ISABEL

I was having trouble threading a needle with invisible thread – dreaded thought, are my eyes really going now? Had I better see an oculist? – when Dr. Johnson's thought, that friendship should be kept in constant repair, came to me. Perhaps, a half submerged thought, I'd been thinking of Carlotta. Once Johnson's sensible observation struck me, I realized with some guilt I'd done absolutely nothing about keeping our friendship in repair since she'd left London – amazingly, almost a year ago.

We hardly ever speak on the phone, and when we do our conversations are no more than snippets of exchanged facts, hers more copious than mine. As always, I've little news. Nothing much changes here, except that I'm incredibly busy with the masks, which are suddenly going astonishingly well. But there's nothing much to say about my work that would interest Carlotta. So I listen to her fragments of information: office almost finished, going to buy a boat (*sail*? Carlotta?). I don't express surprise. I know about the retired postman from whom she excitingly buys home-grown carrots, and the amazing bargains she's found in Fakenham market. Carlotta: whoever would have thought she'd enthuse about such things?

She assures me she loves it all, and she's never been so happy. She doesn't actually mention Bert, but I presume they're lovers by now. They must be. I never quite like that thought, I don't know why. But I know I have a minuscule part of Bert to myself that she will never know about, and doesn't have. He and I talk every few weeks, and that's a comfort – which is odd considering I don't need a comfort.

Perhaps I just like the slight – very slight – wickedness of secret conversations with someone who, so briefly the moments could hardly be registered in time, recognized in each other – well, something. I'm not sure what.

I'm determined, of course, never to ask Bert exactly how it is with Carlotta. I wouldn't like to put him in the position of having to answer a question he wouldn't want to be asked. I'm sure it's an agreeable arrangement: he says she's changed so much, relaxed, living for the moment instead of her old way of always making plans, etc, etc.

But he never says he loves her. That's quite cheering.

And, really, all is well. The year – I've been so inundated with orders – has flown. Sylvie's so happy that Elli's here. It's like having the sister she's always wanted, she says. Elli's a sad, enchanting child. I dread the day some change is decided, and she has to return to one or other of her parents. She likes it here, and Dan and I agree she's been a wonderful influence on Sylvie who has, I think, realized how lucky she is having a stable home and constant parents. She's become much less moody and difficult.

Gwen! She recovered very fast – partly, I think, due to her friend Henry who she told me about at once. He's given her a new life: encourages her, takes her out, makes her laugh, listens to her. She looks ten years younger, despite almost white hair now. So suddenly her rather bleak days appear to be over. She tries to explain it sometimes. It's not pure love and all the complications *that* entails, she says, like it was with some boy when she was young. It's more, loving friendship. She says neither of them would much fancy moving in with the other, for fear of discovering areas of the other's life that might annoy, or cause disillusion. Once you're used to being on your own, she says, it's not easy to adapt to another's ways.

So they're going to remain as they are for the time being, under their own roofs, but secure in the knowledge that they'll meet several times a week and enjoy themselves. They're going dancing soon. Gwen's over the moon at the thought. She said she once had fantasies about being a tap dancer but her mother could never afford the lessons. But evidently she's a good ballroom dancer. 'I don't like to boast,' she said yesterday, 'but I'm a natural.'

Gwen, as I've always known, is one of those people to whom humility is an instinctive commodity, whose goodness is tangible. God knows she deserves this new found happiness. I love hearing about the things she and Henry do, where they go. Her stories have replaced her readings from the newspaper – not only a blessing, but much more entertaining.

Dan is the jumpy one, and you can't blame him. His play was finished some time ago, and although he doesn't keep me up to date with what's happening, I know that once again he's in a terrible state of waiting. He gets downstairs every morning first to see if there's anything in the post – I think he hasn't a clue that I know what he's up to. He wears a sort of sad, resigned expression that's sometimes blasted by what I suppose is a flash of hope. And meantime the postman never brings word.

I pray that this time he will succeed. I pray so hard for that. Dan deserves a measure of success. He's the best example I know of learning from rejection, of fighting off failure. But it's time he succeeds, now. If this play fails, I've an odd feeling he might not be able to summon, yet again, the energy to start anew.

The morning has sped. I do my small round of mental pictures, as I often do late morning before laying a mask aside. I think of Sylvie and Elli at school – history at this time on a Tuesday, I seem to think. So they'll be concentrating, they both love history. When the bell goes Sylvie will give her surprised smile, free now of the wires on her teeth, rather pretty. Gwen will be in a shop looking for a dress to go dancing in. She said she was uncertain of her own taste, and would bring it to show me tomorrow, and exchange it if I thought she could find something better ...

As for Carlotta. What would she be doing just now? Gazing at the computer she knows so well? How she used to scoff at me for being a luddite, no interest in modern technology. Or perhaps – heavens, it's ten to one – she's in her smart new kitchen getting something for Bert's lunch. She's probably in jeans and a top that constantly alerts people to her amazing (yes, amazing, I know) breasts. Perhaps she swarms over to Bert when he comes in, and kisses him. Shit. I hate that idea.

I think of Carlotta sometimes, but I've come to realize I don't actually *like* her anymore. I don't miss her. Our friendship is past repairing and I really don't care.

Bert: just Bert.

Can't think what he's doing. I might ring him this afternoon.

Dan's in his office, wearing his blank office face, I daresay. I don't know why he doesn't leave it, except we need the money. I hate to see him struggling so valiantly for patience. I hate the huge hope which he can't disguise, because if this play is rejected, the disappointment is going to be greater than any other. And seeing his unhappiness will be almost unbearable. How will I be able to console him? On the other hand, should ... but I mustn't think of that, tempting fate.

I must carry on struggling with this damn needle, straining my eyes. The mask is so near finished – a splurge of scarlet feathers in which pearls and beads of different colours run amok, and from whose corners stream satin ribbons of flamingo pink, each one ending with the curl of a small feather. I have to admit I'm rather pleased with it.

I jab the invisible thread again at the hole in the needle, which is no more than a splinter of light flicked through the window from the sun, and I think how much, to all of us, remains invisible.